Flowers For Lilian

by

Anna Gilbert

Dales Large Print Books
Long Preston, North Yorkshire,
BD23 4ND, England.

British Library Cataloguing in Publication Data.

Gilbert, Anna
    Flowers for Lilian

A catalogue record of this book is
available from the British Library

ISBN   978-1-84262-728-0 pbk

First published in Great Britain in 1980
by Hodder & Stoughton Ltd.

Copyright © 1980 by Anna Gilbert

Cover illustration © Nigel Chamberlain by arrangement with
Alison Eldred

The moral right of the author has been asserted

Published in Large Print 2010 by arrangement with
Anna Gilbert, care of Watson, Little Ltd.

Dales Large Print is an imprint of Library Magna Books Ltd.

Printed and bound in Great Britain by
T.J. (International) Ltd., Cornwall, PL28 8RW

FLOWERS FOR LILIAN

1

Lilian was not giving her mind to the game, I could tell. She laid down her knave of spades with scarcely a glance at the card and looked away towards the corner where her mother and Captain Hart sat together, deep in conversation. Her eyes, summer-blue in the leaf-shaded room, were watchful.

For once, then, I stood some chance of winning, more than a chance, for the card I carefully laid alongside Lilian's was also, unbelievably, a knave: the knave of hearts. She had not seen.

'Snap!' I promptly said.

She had not heard. Her face, enclosed in fair, upward-springing hair, had the fixed look of a picture in a heavy gilt frame. But I was not deceived. We were so close and already I knew her so well that my own body seemed to vibrate with the throb of energy that animated Lilian's. Anyone might have felt the peculiar insistence of her pulse-beat, threatening explosion.

But no one else was attending. Mother, dressed in her hat and cape for the journey home, was showing her holiday sketches to old Mr Iredale. Lilian's cousin Francis, all ready in breeches and boots to ride with us as far as the Toll House, had gone back to his book; was safe – yes, that was the word – with Gulliver; whereas I, not for the first time in that deceptively quiet room, felt fully exposed to a lurking threat, invisible but capable of a sudden keen thrust from Lilian's direction: an indescribable menace all the more prostrating for being, surely, imaginary.

Yet my flesh quivered in response to the first familiar disturbance of the air above the green-baized table where Lilian and I sat opposite each other, wearing, rather too warmly for comfort, our outdoor things so as to be ready when the carriage came, for Lilian too would come with us as far as the Toll House. Our jackets and tippets were identical.

'They're such close friends,' Mrs Belfleur often said. 'Almost like sisters.'

Mother would nod and smile, and they would agree on the same colour and pattern.

'It doesn't matter,' she said, when father protested. 'They don't look in the least alike, and it pleases poor Cynthia.'

For that matter the two knaves were not much alike either. Mine, for all his warm redness, was smaller, more restrained, unassertive beside Lilian's bolder, darker, gloomier knave. She *must* have seen.

'Snap!' I said again just to make sure.

10

It was in every sense a confrontation, yet Lilian and I were not exactly face to face. Hers remained in half profile. Her cheek was pale. It seemed in the last few minutes to have lost its childish curve and become angular. Into her sky-blue eyes a cloud had come. She took one of her quick shallow breaths. They always startled me, sounding as they did like gasps. In this particular intake of air there seemed more than the usual touch of urgency.

Following her gaze, I saw that Mrs Belfleur and Captain Hart were not, like the rest of us, on the point of saying goodbye; rather the opposite. Mrs Belfleur had laid down her tapestry work, put out her hand, slim and pale like Lilian's, and placed it in the captain's in a gesture that united them. They smiled at each other.

'Snap!' Lilian said, taking me unawares. She grabbed the two piles of cards and patted them into one firm rectangle to add to the dishearteningly thick one she already held.

'I said it first. You didn't hear.'

'How could I not hear?' Lilian gave another of her frightening gasps. Her upper lip was beaded with perspiration. 'In a quiet parlour like this, how could I not hear? *If* you really said it. You're supposed to say it aloud.'

'With four grown-ups in the room,' I said

in a quavering imitation of mother's reasonable manner, 'I couldn't very well raise my voice.'

Lilian's grip on the cards tightened. With her shoulders raised, her neck rigid, her face isolated from her body by the brown tippet, she looked less like a gilt-framed picture than one of the uptilted angel heads on a tombstone; only the effect was not angelic.

'I said snap twice as a matter of fact.' I bit my quivering lip. 'You weren't looking.'

Lilian jumped to her feet, struggling with the strings of her tippet. 'I can't breathe. I can't breathe.'

'Let me...'

'Don't touch me.'

Her hand, lightly pressed, was cold, her breathing wheezy and laboured. Her eyes had paled to the dim blue of fading forget-me-nots.

'You can keep the cards,' I said, intimidated. 'You were winning, anyway.'

But the gasps had taken possession of her. They seemed to set the whole room in motion, as if a storm had blown up and displaced the peaceful air. Only the trees were unmoved, I noticed, glancing out of the window for reassurance.

It was Francis who declared the situation to be one of emergency.

'Lilian is having one of her attacks.'

He crossed the room, rang the bell and

threw open the window, letting in the moist scent of leaves and earth, the murmur of the stream. Mr Iredale struggled to his feet.

'The little couch, Francis, here by the window, and plenty of cushions. What can have upset her, I wonder?' The quick, searching look under his craggy brows held the suspicion of a glare. It lighted on Mrs Belfleur. 'Cynthia! See to the child.'

It was Francis and his grandfather, I afterwards recollected, though it did not strike me at the time, who rose most promptly to the occasion. The ladies were slower in moving. I remember how calm, how compassionate Francis was, how he knew exactly what to do, how Lilian depended on him, without noticing or wanting him.

'Mother!' Breathed as if with the last exhalation of weary breath, Lilian's cry seemed to be heart-rending. I understood. It was what I would have said myself on the brink of dying, as Lilian seemed to be, from some mysterious suffocation. Indeed, I had gravitated unconsciously across the room to my own mother, who like everyone else had stood up. Only she was looking, not at Lilian, but at Lilian's mother. Infected by mother's rapt interest in her friend, I realized that Mrs Belfleur was a distinct person, fair, pretty and not old. Just then in fact she looked prettier and younger than Lilian, whose terrible spasms had robbed her of every characteristic save breathlessness.

'Cynthia!' In his agitation Mr Iredale had advanced to the sofa, retreated and advanced again as if engaged in an untimely country dance. 'Your daughter needs you.'

A quiet sigh escaped Mrs Belfleur. She made no hurried movement from Captain Hart's side but somehow contrived a deliberate, gentle widening of the distance between them. With an almost perceptible resignation she seemed to *shed* him and went over to the couch.

'Stay with me.' Lilian's pale fingers – surprisingly long, they always seemed – closed upon her mother's. 'Don't leave me – ever.'

Captain Hart picked up the fallen tapestry and without any loss of dignity secured the dangling needle into the canvas. He was a tall man, his face yellowish-brown from the years he had spent in India: almost the same colour as his golden-brown moustache. The skin was finely wrinkled about his eyes and the eyes were keenly alert as if he were looking across the torrid Indian plains for the first dust-cloud heralding the enemy's approach; or he might have been assessing the nearness and force of the attack. Only it was across Mr Iredale's parlour that he was looking – and at Lilian.

'Can nothing be done to relieve the poor child's suffering?' Mr Iredale burst out, though the maids had already brought hot water, a towel and a jug of agrimony tea. 'It's intolerable that she should have to suffer like this at her age. She's too sensitive, that's what it is.' Under their deep brows his eyes glared in my direction. 'What can have upset her?'

'I really did say it, mother,' I said desperately, weighed down as I was with guilt and remorse.

'What, dear?'

'Snap. But I would never have insisted if I'd known this would happen. What shall I do if she dies? It will be my fault. We shall have to tell father. She wasn't attending, you see, and didn't know. It seemed quite fair to tell her that I had already said snap. Twice. But I never thought...'

'She won't die,' mother said.

'But the cough...'

It was not so much a cough as a high-pitched whooping and crowing. Her hands and lips, I saw with horror, had turned blue.

'She'll feel better in a minute,' mother said; and almost at once, with a final inward convulsion, Lilian retched, Mrs Belfleur clapped a handkerchief over her mouth and her breathing became less painful.

At the same moment came the sound of carriage wheels on the gravel. Mother put her sketch book into her travelling bag and began the round of goodbyes.

'...Such an unlooked-for ending to our

holiday, Mr Iredale, but she will outgrow these attacks ... I have known other cases. So very happy that our visit coincided with your leave, Captain Hart...'

Lilian was lying quiet, so limp that I dared not speak to her; but as I approached the couch on tiptoe, her eyes opened, blue again as cornflowers or the untroubled sky above them.

'You'll come back, Maggie darling? You'll come again next summer?'

'Oh yes, Lilian, I'll come back.' Gratitude and relief like a refreshing shower revived me. 'I'll come back.'

'And you won't call at the Toll House without me? Promise.'

I had almost blurted out the willing promise when mother's warning squeeze of the hand restrained me.

'I'm glad you're better, Lilian,' she said, and drew Mrs Belfleur aside. 'Be patient, dear ... in a year or two ... she's growing up...'

'It's no use, Elinor.' Tears welled in Mrs Belfleur's eyes. 'She would never survive it if ... if Captain Hart and I... These dreadful attacks!'

'Francis.' How feeble Lilian's voice was! 'You won't go to the Toll House now that I can't go?'

In the brief hesitation before Francis replied, she seemed to move again towards the verge of distress. Her breathing quickened.

'Francis,' Mr Iredale said sternly. 'Pay attention to your cousin.'

'Very well. I'll stay until you're better.'

But he went to the table, picked up Lilian's cards and looked through them one by one until he had found first the black knave, then the red, and made some careful calculation.

'There! Those are Maggie's cards.' He added them to my meager pile. 'You have three more than Lilian. You were winning, Maggie, for once.'

'I didn't know … I didn't mean to upset her,' I whispered.

'It wasn't your fault. It wasn't just the cards.'

He smiled, stooped and kissed me; and I loved him, not just then in gratitude for his kindness; not just for a time, with a child's caprice; but from the depths of my heart; incurably, it seemed; for always.

Even mother was ruffled by what had happened though her recollection of it differed from mine as if we had witnessed the scene not only from different angles but from different altitudes. Whereas I in the valley had been overwhelmed by the looming mountain of Lilian's distress, mother, from above, had been aware of peaks and rifts invisible to me. She was vexed, too, at the unceremonious way in which we had left.

'There now!' she exclaimed as we settled ourselves in the carriage. 'I haven't had time to call and say goodbye to old Mrs Rigg.'

But as we turned from the drive of Sacristy House into the road, there at the gate of Well Cottage, in a clean shirt with his hair sleeked down, stood Johnny Rigg. In his usual cocksure manner he signalled the coachman to stop, ducked his head in a bow and handed in, with his grandmother's respects, her invariable parting gift, a bag of dried lavender.

'How kind of you, Johnny! You'll thank Mrs Rigg? I did want to see her but we were delayed…'

'Miss Lilian had one of her spasms?' Johnny Rigg was a know-all, we had long since decided. It was a source of dissatisfaction at Sacristy House that the Riggs were such very near neighbours. Well Cottage was not only attached to the bigger house; it had once been part of it; so that the Iredales never felt quite safe. Whatever happened in the house seeped mysteriously through the walls like rising damp and became known in the cottage. 'Terrible things these spasms, Mrs Ossian.' The sage words might have been his grandmother's but they came from Johnny's lips with a sprightly upward inflection like a question mark. 'We shall hope to

18

see you and Miss Maggie next summer,' he permitted himself to say, 'all being well.'

One would think he owned the village though where, as mother said, he had learned his easy manners – really a little too easy – one could not guess. We waved to what little we could see of Mrs Rigg behind the geraniums and maidenhair fern on her window sill. She had already cut down her famous lavender hedge. The dried flowers filled the carriage with the sad scent of dying summer.

The handshakes, kisses and regrets were always depressing. Rarely on those homeward journeys had I seen the church, the sign-post or the beck winding between the cottages except through a mist of tears even when Lilian came with us in the carriage and Francis rode ahead or walked through the wood and reached the Toll House before us. From summer to summer my love of Asherby Cross had grown until now as we drove away under arching trees in the soft stillness of the September day, I seemed to have left my heart there; and without Lilian, who would have talked all the way, those last glimpses were sadder than ever, more fraught with apprehension lest by some unforeseen change in circumstances, I should never experience them again. In any case, a year was the longest span of time my youthful imagination could grasp.

And this time, imposed upon the green branches, filling the sunlit vacancies beneath, haunting the long lift of moorland which presently appeared as the valley opened and the trees grew sparse – there, all the time was the vision of Lilian, unfamiliar, blue-lipped, deflated of the tempestuous energy I had learned to admire and fear.

Mother's thoughts – I turned to look at her – must have been running on similar lines. Her expression was regretful, troubled even. As often happened, we burst into speech at the same moment; but whereas my heartfelt exclamation was 'Poor Lilian!', hers, equally heartfelt, was 'Poor Cynthia!'

'Mrs Belfleur?' I must have looked surprised.

'It would have been a perfect match for her. If only... Here we are at the bottom of the hill already,' mother said quickly as the hamlet of Groat's Gate came into sight.

Since there was a good deal of luggage, we got out to save the horses and climbed the path up the bracken-clad hillside, a steeper but much shorter way than the long road winding up Asherby Bank.

'You mean to call at the Toll House then, after all? Lilian didn't want us to, not without her.'

'I wouldn't dream of passing without having a word with Agnes. She'll be expecting us.'

The low house of grey stone stood at the top of the hill with a splendid chestnut over-topping its roof tiles. When the road was made free, it had ceased to be a toll house, had weathered the change as country dwellings do and taken up the threads of life again as the Toll House Inn though the tokens of its trade were slight: a cask or two of beer and a keg of rum supplied the needs of its handful of rustic patrons and rare passers-by.

Here our holidays began and ended. Daniel Hebworthy, the inn-keeper, always made us welcome though he would perhaps have been more at ease with a gun at his shoulder or in cultivating his strip of land or tending his two cows and small herd of goats than in chatting to customers. Nor was Agnes a typical inn-keeper's wife. She had learned her immaculate housekeeping from her parents who had been upper servants and had herself been a stillroom maid before she married, so that she was most in her element when carriage folk got down at her door though they were few and far between. Sometimes we walked there from Asherby Cross for strawberries and cream, or milk warm from the cow, or a glass of the delicious fizzy drink known as Boston Cream; and we always stopped there on the day of our arrival and always called to say goodbye. Since these calls were usually brief, one never left without the feeling that it would have been pleasant to stay. The Toll House had many delightful features but its dearest charm lay in Agnes herself. It was Agnes we all loved.

She was watching from the doorstep when we came breathlessly up on to the wide grass verge.

'You're on your own today, Mrs Ossian – and Miss Maggie.'

She was a quiet young woman and only nodded in understanding when we explained. But when we stepped inside – how well I remember the clean-scrubbed flags and the cool darkness on that warm day – Daniel came forward, stooping under the low beams, and without any other greeting asked: 'Isn't Miss Lilian with you?'

He was a dark-haired, grey-eyed man in his late twenties. He wore a green corduroy jacket like a gamekeeper's, strong shooting boots and leather leggings; and there was something about him – his height, his long-ranging movements – that made him seem out of place in the small room, as if he were caged in and restless and needed a wider scope.

It was common knowledge – though I was not aware of it then – that Daniel's family were different from other folk. You didn't always know, it was felt, where you were with the Hebworthys. There was an odd streak in them, people said, and could give proof of it from more than one tragic chapter in the family history.

I had my own reasons for feeling slightly uncomfortable in Daniel's company, especially when he asked about Lilian. My embarrassment stemmed from an incident – ages ago, it seemed, perhaps last year or the year before – when Lilian and I were riding on the bough of a tree in Asherby Wood. It was rather high for us: a scramble to get up and quite dangerous to get down again. As the Lady from Banbury Cross, I sat side saddle and was able to slip to the ground with only a short though sickening flight through the air and a bump. But Lilian as Dick Turpin sat boldly astride, caught her dress on a stout twig and on reaching York, was unable to dismount.

From this dilemma we were rescued by Daniel Hebworthy who happened to be walking home that way. I had just time to pull Lilian's skirt over her drawers before he reached up, unhooked her and lifted her down. But he held her, her face close to his own, and would not let her go.

'You'll have to give me a kiss first,' he said.

Lilian shook her head again and again. When she gave in, the kiss surprised me. It was not just the peck I had expected between a grown-up and a little girl. Their lips met and did not instantly part. Watching them kiss, I involuntarily wiped my own mouth with the back of my hand to wipe the kiss away. He set her down, glanced at me and walked off.

'Wait,' Lilian called, for we had thought of going to the Toll House. 'Wait for me.'

He turned.

'Yes,' he said. 'I'll wait for you.'

But he didn't. That puzzled me.

'He's a funny man,' I said when he had gone. 'He said he'd wait.'

Lilian saucily put out her tongue at his retreating figure, we found some hazel nuts and forgot him…

'So she won't be coming,' Daniel said when we told him that Lilian was not well. It didn't at all surprise me that he seemed disappointed. Without Lilian everything was flatter and less interesting. But I was aware of a certain intentness in the way Agnes looked at her husband. There was just time to catch in her face a peculiar expression instantly fading or repressed. A quickness of apprehension, almost of anxiety, had troubled her smooth fair brow; and when Daniel excused himself and went out, she watched him bend his head under the lintel, watched with a tenderness of love so open, so crystal clear, that it made me turn to mother and catch her eye to see if she too had noticed it. It was beautiful, as I remarked to her afterwards in the privacy of the carriage, to see how Agnes loved her husband.

'Some wives don't show it, do they?' I observed.

It was too late in the year for bilberry pie, too soon for bramble jelly. Agnes cut me a slice of bread and butter, spread it liberally with honey and put it on a plate wreathed with painted poppies.

'Eat it in the garden, Maggie,' mother said.

I ate in voluptuous solitude, measuring my bites against the slow tread of the horses, visible from time to time as they negotiated the bends of Asherby Bank. Up here in a garden brimming over with the murmur of bees, the scent of flowers and orchard trees, I was alone except for a black-faced sheep looking wistfully in through a gap in the low wall. Above it, on the opposite side of the valley rose the moor. The heather was not quite faded but its high purple bloom had gone. I was not too young nor too ignorant to feel the poignancy that affects everything in late summer, or to be impressed by a latent sadness in the scene. The apples would drop, the swallows fly, the late roses would be replaced by the last. It occurred to me that when summer ended, things did not come to a halt. When I left, the life of Asherby would go on, a life in which outsiders had no part. At the thought I felt shut out and at the same time anxiously observant as if by remembering every sight and sound, I could keep the day for ever unchanged. More than ever before I hated to go. The Toll House, the garden, the sweeping hills, had never exerted so ravishing a spell even though Lilian was not with me. Because Lilian was not with me?

At once her personality invaded the scene as if she had clambered headlong over the wall or floated, airborne by her dandelion locks, to my side. I sat forward, alert. The buzzing of bees round the straw skeps had moved into a different key, a new mood, self-absorbed and with a kind of menace in it. Bees could be dangerous. And tiger-lilies, I discovered, didn't fit in among Agnes's white roses and pink hollyhocks. They brought, I suppose, an unexpected hint of passion, sultry and over-sweet.

I started. Without my having heard her come, little Jael Hebworthy had appeared: a silent child, normal in that she was neither deaf nor dumb but from the time I had first seen her when I myself was quite a small girl, I had never heard her speak. The good looks of her parents had passed her by. She was a dim, thin little thing, dangling by the arm a faded cloth doll. With inscrutable detachment she watched my steady demolition of the bread and honey.

'There you are, my dear,' I said, patronizingly, if indistinctly, in what I felt to be my mother's manner.

Her unflinching grey eyes did not leave me. They annihilated my confidence. A slow trail of honey disfigured my chin. Conscious of the loss of face, I was obliged to feel for my handkerchief. With something less than interest but unyieldingly, Jael watched. A disconcerting child. I rose and retreated to the house.

And after all Francis was there to see us off. He came riding up through the bracken just as the carriage was about to leave.

'Lilian's asleep,' he explained, as he dismounted. 'She won't know I've come.'

There was only time to say goodbye again before we drove away. I hung out of the window. He stood in the road, waving his hat. It was unusual to see him alone like that, without Lilian.'

'Isn't Francis *kind?*' I breathed.

'One can be too kind,' mother said incomprehensibly.

How was that possible – to be too kind? I pondered the question anxiously as we rolled along the turnpike, leaving him behind in the hazy sunshine with the lost summer.

2

In the years that followed, our visits to Asherby Cross became less regular. My parents had been in the habit of taking rooms with attendance at Jasmine Lodge, a comfortable little house on the green where Miss Abbot, my mother's former governess, lived in retirement. Mother and I spent most of the summer months there, joined occasionally by father when he could be free for a few days from the cares of business.

For mother it was always a homecoming. Indeed Jasmine Lodge had been her home when she was a girl. It was in recognition of Miss Abbot's years of devoted service to the family that my grandfather had left her a life tenancy in the house.

Mother had shared her lessons with Cynthia Iredale. Both girls married young; and when Mr Belfleur died, Cynthia, with Lilian still a baby, went back to Sacristy House to live with her father and her nephew Francis, who was already orphaned of both his parents. We were all only children, Lilian, Francis and I and the close companionship of those early days at Asherby was our nearest approach to the family life we would otherwise have missed.

But as the years went by, my father's business in Martlebury began to expand. In his father's time, the firm of Edward Ossian and Son had been regimental swordmakers. The foundations of their prosperity had been laid during the Crimean War and the Indian Mutiny. But in the more peaceful days of the late sixties, they set up an even more profitable line in domestic cutlery. The new venture brought new responsibilities to my father and consequently to mother, who began to find difficulty in leaving home for more than two or three weeks at a time. Few summers passed, as I recall, without a visit to Asherby, however short, when the sooty atmosphere of Martlebury became stifling and the drains more than usually unwholesome; but it was to be some years before we could contrive one long enough to restore the old feeling of belonging for a whole enchanted summer to the place which was for mother and me our second home and first love; and I remember little of those shorter visits, few details, that is, beyond the pleasure of re-union with Lilian and Francis.

It was more than pleasure: a happiness sometimes dimmed but never extinguished by the frets and worries of growing up. When Francis was sixteen, he entered the family firm of solicitors in which his grandfather was still a partner and thereafter divided his time between Asherby and the market town of Whingate, where the brass-plated, ivy-clad establishment of Iredale and Merton in the cobbled square had impressed three generations of townsfolk with its air of discreet probity. It was strange at first to see him in a frock coat and tall hat: a relief when he shed them and came down to the parlour wearing a velvet jacket and flowing neck-tie. He took to sporting a gold watch-chain with seals, carried leather volumes of poetry in his pockets and eventually a pipe. He had grown into a fine-looking man, certainly I thought so, with a tall and powerful frame like his grandfather's.

My recollections of Lilian during those early years are more involved. In memory she fascinates me still as when she faced me, blue-eyed and solemn on the seesaw, or soared golden-haired above me on the swing as I lay on the grass under the apple boughs waiting my turn. Francis grew weary of our squabbling and decreed that two minutes each on the swing in strict alternation was reasonable and fair.

On wet days we wrote our journals in the attic. My entries were long and led me, the helpless victim of my own fluency, into disclosures requiring a passionate secrecy. Not that Lilian was interested. Having completed her own short reports, she always read them aloud and with such conviction that I felt at once the drabness of my own ideas.

'Listen!' Her voice was flutelike and imperious. 'Maggie Ossian is my dearest friend. She knows I threw Francis's dictionary in the kitchen fire but she will never betray me.'

I glowed with pride in my own undying loyalty and felt myself to be a friend worth having.

When we outgrew the seesaw and stopped quarrelling over the swing and no longer dressed as sisters, we spent a good deal of time in trying on each other's clothes and sighing over the blemishes in our complexions as we flounced and brooded before Lilian's toilet glass in egotistical doubt and gloom.

In spite of mother's soothing predictions, Lilian did not outgrow her attacks. We often shared a room either at Jasmine Lodge or Sacristy House for the fun of talking while we undressed and brushed our hair. Sometimes I woke in the night to find her sitting stiffly upright or standing at the open window in a stream of cold air. 'It hurts here,' she would gasp, pointing to her chest, but she could not bear to touch her body or be touched. On no account, Dr Slater said, must she be encouraged to lie down when an attack was coming on, and I would sit up with her, yawning and shivering until her breathing grew so painful that Mrs Belfleur had to be called.

I became expert in applying remedies. 'A born little nurse', everyone said, even in the days when I was still young enough to make playthings of the nitre-soaked triangles of blotting paper we burned to relieve her breathing: little tents to be arranged on a plate like a military encampment. I took a pride in my skill and gossamer-light touch as I undid the collar of Lilian's nightdress, or bodice buttons and stays if she was dressed, or bathed her hands and feet with hot water and mustard; and I might often have overlooked my patient's distress in the thrill of ministering to it, had not the physical signs been there to remind me: the blue lips and shuddering limbs, the damp matted hair.

The spasms were unpredictable. I had not yet learned to recognise their nature or what it was that brought them on. Gradually, I accustomed myself to the idea that Lilian was not going to die. The disorder was mysterious and alarming but with more than a touch of drama. Her recovery was usually rapid. After the commotion we drank leisurely cups of coffee and made them an excuse to put our books and needlework aside. Other doctors were consulted from time to time besides old Dr Slater, the family practitioner. They prescribed sedative draughts, anti-spasmodics, removal to a house built on fine gravel, steam kettles... None of which appeared to have much more effect than Granny Rigg's tallow candle melted on brown paper and applied to the chest, or nettle juice, or fried onions and brown sugar. For years Lilian carried a hare's foot in her pocket given to her by a gypsy who swore that she would never be well without it, and may have been right. But the general opinion was that the condition would abate.

What did not abate but grew more unreasonable, more dangerously intense, was the effect of Lilian's ill-health on her grandfather. In her he saw the very replica of his beloved sister Elsie, a bright, vivid creature who had died young. He suffered from Lilian's attacks as severely, I believe, as she did; watched over her recovery with doting fondness; tried with some success to banish from her life any discomfort, any trial. She was to be kept happy. Lilian was so sensitive. Trifling things could upset her deeply. People blundered and were often needlessly, heartlessly inconsiderate.

When he spoke in this way, his brows came down; his blue eyes shone balefully; he too became breathless with anger that fate should be so hard on Lilian. Because I was afraid of him, I learned to tread carefully, to avoid crossing Lilian in any way, to keep her happy. In this, alas, I was not alone. It would be difficult to exaggerate the effect of Lilian's disorder on the rest of the household. Mrs Belfleur, so unassertive when her own interests were involved, devoted herself to Lilian's. In a mother such unselfishness is natural enough; but Francis had been exposed from his earliest years to the ordeal of seeing a lively companion, close as a sister, suddenly and cruelly transformed into a creature apparently so helpless that every personal inclination must be set aside, every effort directed towards her recovery. Caring for Lilian became second nature to him.

In time I was to form my own painful impressions of the situation at Sacristy House but the first intimations of its problems reached me like so much else, through my parents. It was one foggy morning at the breakfast table at home in Martlebury that the conversation turned upon the Iredales.

'How nice! A letter from Cynthia.'

It was long and closely written. Mother became absorbed. Father peered ostentatiously into his empty coffee cup. I filled it. Mother read on.

'Any news from Asherby?' father asked.

'No. Nothing has changed. Captain Hart has his majority as one might expect. You must remember, Maggie, to address him as Major Hart if ever we meet again. He writes regularly from Rawul Pindee but ... no, there is no news.'

'Cynthia has gone to some lengths to pass

on so little information.'

'She tells me of her feelings. So much more interesting than facts, especially when there is no possibility of change at Sacristy House.'

'I can think of several possibilities,' father said. 'Some day Mr Iredale at least will die. The others may be immortal, as you imply, but the old gentleman has already lived his allotted span.'

'I wasn't thinking of deaths. Of course we must all die. But Cynthia knows very well that Lilian will never accept...' Mother glanced in my direction and veered to another point. 'You've never seen one of her attacks, Edward. Oh, I know you think they're hysterical; but the symptoms are grave, I assure you. There can be no doubt of the harm they do to her, physically, I mean. Each one, according to Dr Slater, increases the risk of damage to the heart.'

'The property, I imagine' – Father pursued his own train of thought – 'will go to Francis. In that case what would Cynthia's position be, and Lilian's.'

'That troubles me, I confess. Francis is so very dutiful, poor boy.'

'Why should his sense of duty trouble you? Isn't it an excellent quality?'

'You're teasing me, Edward. Francis once told me, years ago, when he was quite a child, how unfair he thought it that the property should go to him. "Lilian has just as much right," he said, "except that she's a girl. But I shall always be here to look after her." I'm sure he gave up the idea of going to Cambridge because Lilian begged him not to leave her.'

'It's strange, if the old man idolises Lilian as you say, that he hasn't made good provision for her.'

'I've always felt that Mr Iredale has plans for the young people. That's what I dislike. It doesn't do to arrange a young man's life for him, especially a person of such delicate conscience as Francis. Oh dear, this dreadful fog...'

I went to the window and pressed my forehead against the pane. 'It will never be summer again,' I thought, peering into the yellow gloom. Even the houses opposite had lost their shape and definition; but it was not the houses I strained my eyes to see; rather some infinitely distant place, some time already out of reach. Somewhere beyond that thickening pall there must be sunlight as there had once been – and Francis. But try as I would, I could only recapture a diffused brightness and in the heart of it a solitary figure waving goodbye.

When in the spring of 1873 mother and I triumphantly escaped from Martlebury for the whole month of May, we had not been to Asherby for two years, the longest interval ever to elapse between our visits. At seventeen I felt obliged to conceal the excitement amounting almost to sickness that kept me on the edge of my seat as we drove along the level road to the top of Asherby Bank and saw the Toll House chimneys through an avenue of trees shimmering into leaf.

'I wonder if she'll have come to meet us. Lilian.'

But it was only Agnes who stood at the open door, smiling and holding up her new baby to be admired. The day was so fine that we went into the garden where Jael – thin-faced and tall for her age – silently brought us a tray of tea.

'He's a handsome child,' mother said. 'Does he thrive?'

'He's well enough.' Agnes put back his bonnet with a little frown and we all looked at him anxiously. Agnes had lost other children in infancy.

'In this air surely…'

There was a sharp sweetness in it to freshen the skin and set the nerves tingling. Secure in the wicker cradle his father had made for Jael, in a garden full of singing birds, how could little Daniel fail to thrive? And yet he was not a contented baby. He struggled feebly in his imprisoning petticoats and dress and jacket and shawl as if he resented them. Or was it some loss of tranquillity in Agnes herself that made him fretful? She too was restless. More than once she glanced over her shoulder as if expecting company. Whoever it was, I felt, would not be welcome.

The horses were waiting. There was no time for confidences though mother seemed disposed to linger over her tea. As soon as politeness allowed, I escaped into the road and there of course she was, Lilian: on the other side by the gate at the edge of the wood. Her coming was like a burst of sunlight.

'Dearest Maggie! I thought you'd never come.'

She had grown even more than I had done. In her blue and grey walking dress she looked at least nineteen, I thought, being much occupied with the subject of ages at the time. There was something else about her, some new brightness that kindled the very place where she stood with her un-gloved hand on the wicket under the long drooping larch boughs.

'Is Francis here?'

'No. Your beloved Francis is not here. Good Cousin Francis is in distant Whingate at his dull desk with his dull pen and papers. Dull Cousin Francis!' I knew from her bubbling mockery that she was as excited as I was and never doubted that it was for the same reason especially when she went on: 'But *we* are on holiday for a whole month –

38

you and I – at last. What's the matter?'

'I thought – there was someone here.'

It had been no more than an impression of movement under the trees behind her: a word spoken, overheard but ignored as I crossed the road too eager to think of anything but Lilian herself and her magical appearance; for there was some special quality, not only in her being there all at once to be caught sight of, but in the glow, the radiance that sparkled in her eyes, her hair…

'You haven't changed, Maggie. You were always imagining things. Do you remember when you thought the barn was haunted?'

She hugged me, not for my own sake (how did I know that, at once and with conviction?) but in an overflow of energy. Slim as she was, one could have fancied that her dress could scarcely contain the vitality it enclosed but would crack and burst and float away. Something actually did crack.

'There! Didn't you hear?' I drew away and looked past her down the greening vista of larches.

She laughed, a laugh too high and prolonged for the occasion, stooped to pick up a twig with a cone and broke it with a snap.

'That's what you heard.' She threw the twig away and tucked the cone in my hatband. 'The woods are full of rabbits, as you well know, and squirrels. I must go and speak to dear Mrs Ossian.'

But she did just glance back into the wood before she swept me across the road and into the garden.

'Lilian! How well you look! This is splendid. And your mother – and Mr Iredale – and Francis?'

'All longing to see you, especially mother. She's at Miss Abbot's now, installed at the front window keeping watch.'

'Then we must go. You'll ride with us of course?'

'Do you mind if Maggie and I walk home? You'd like to, Maggie? You'll be more comfortable with the carriage to yourself, Mrs Ossian. You can spread your skirts and commune with nature. It's such a lovely day.'

She prattled on, taking, I observed, no notice of Agnes, who listened, her head bowed with a curious effect of submission. It could scarcely be disapproval or aversion from a creature so gloriously full of life. When Agnes raised her eyes and looked at her, it was with a kind of determined steadiness as though without listening to the spate of words that came tumbling from Lilian's lips, she was facing up to the sheer fact of Lilian herself, her fair hair springing in spears of light on either side of her forward-tilted hat, her full shapely bodice and trim, elegant waist.

I went to take a last look at the baby and

40

found Jael by the cradle, speechlessly standing guard.

'Goodness, the baby! The infant Daniel.' Lilian had followed but she did no more than glance at him before walking to the wall to look at the view with a restless air of impatience.

'Do look, Lilian. He has the most beautiful grey eyes.' They looked up, jewel-like from under the embroidered cap-band, with a hint of the luminous brilliance of his father's.

Lilian came back abruptly and gave her whole energetic attention to the baby; and immediately, rudely I thought, Jael snatched him up with thunderous brows and a lightning flash of her eyes, turned her back on us and carried him away.

'She's protecting Daniel from the lionesses, Maggie.' Lilian spoke lightly but she looked vexed.

'I suppose she likes keeping him to herself. She's always seemed a lonely little thing.'

'She's welcome to him: a peevish, sickly looking object.'

'Hush.'

She had not lowered her voice and only laughed at my embarrassment. We stood talking a little longer while mother took leave of Agnes, or rather Lilian talked, even more than usual.

'...Miss Abbot? Deafer than ever. To tell

41

you the truth I have seen very little of her since she gave up teaching me. That was almost two years ago. I simply refused to go on having lessons any longer. Mother suggested a year at some young ladies' seminary but grandfather wouldn't hear of it. He can't bear to part with his lovely grand-daughter...'

After the long dusty journey the wood smelt fresh and cool. Listening to the ceaseless flow of Lilian's light voice, I experienced an odd mixture of strangeness and familiarity. With every step of the way half-forgotten impressions were revived but now I interpreted them more clearly. Having quickly discovered that Lilian's talk was all about herself, I realised that it had always been so, only in earlier times I had taken her self-absorption for granted. For all her gushing welcome, for all her endearments, she had not yet noticed me, Maggie Ossian. Some characterless puppet capable of walking at her side would have served as well.

Not that I resented it: not exactly. Lilian was so full of life that it would have been unreasonable to expect all of it to be centred on me even after an absence of two years. Not all, but surely some? Half the time as we stooped under branches and avoided naked tree roots, she seemed to be casting remarks to right and left like coins casually dropped for inferior persons to pick up while she walked on. For that matter her manner of walking was not companionable. She was for ever glancing past me or over my head; and there was a consciousness in her movements, a luxurious physical pleasure as if – I felt ashamed of the thought – as if she were parading her body through the wood to be admired. But then even for May it was an exceptionally, an idyllically lovely day: a day on which even Lilian's exhausting exuberance should not have made me feel as dim and silent, for all my new holiday clothes, as Jael Hebworthy.

It made me unobservant too. Half dazed as I was, I started quite violently when we came upon a man leaning against the fork of a vigorously sprouting ash tree and seeming in his green jacket to be so much a part of it that at first I did not think of him as Daniel Hebworthy. But at once I knew him and smiled. My instinct was to stop and pass the time of day but Lilian showed no sign of stopping though she too was smiling, a mischievous mocking pout and curl of the lips.

Daniel stood bareheaded, hat in hand. In his fine-featured brown face his eyes burned, grey and brilliant. They blinded me – the expression is not too strong – to every other detail; so that it was his eyes I afterwards remembered, as if the whole tragic story shone bleakly out of them. There was such a look in them; it could not be hunger,

I thought: the Hebworthys were not poor; but it was as though he had turned away from the world and looked into a new one. It didn't make him happy if his expression was anything to go by. He looked like a man who had no time for either happiness or unhappiness, only for wanting, for longing...

I glanced away, embarrassed, and we passed with no more than a murmured 'Good day!'

'How strange he looked!'

'Strange?'

'As if he had forgotten where he was – and who he was. Who he is, I mean. Do you remember...?'

I broke off, regretting the words. The scent of leaf-mould, a projecting bough, a feeling of embarrassment, had combined to recreate the other time, almost forgotten, when we had met Daniel Hebworthy in this very wood. I discovered that it was the last thing I wanted to remind Lilian of and was astonished to find how much I hated to think of it: such a small thing; and yet it had been distasteful. The distaste had survived to hover with surprising persistence about this later meeting.

Lilian threw her arm around me and drew my head to her shoulder so that I could not see her face as she turned to look back; and again she laughed but not lightheartedly: the laugh was artificial and deliberate as if directed between the branches and through the airy spaces of green light to the forked tree where Daniel stood. How awful if he thought we were laughing at him!

I ran on ahead to escape the uncomfortable situation and gradually forgot it in anticipation of all that lay ahead: Mrs Belfleur: Miss Abbot: Francis. 'After all,' I reminded myself, hardly knowing why such justification was necessary, 'it is my holiday.'

For most of the time our visit fulfilled my highest expectations. For one thing both Lilian and Francis were plainly glad to have me back. From the first evening when Lilian and I walked to meet Francis as he drove home from Whingate, the old easy companionship united us again. We walked, talked (of Dr Livingstone, I remember. He had died that very month), read the same books, studied Miss Abbot's *Manual of Elegant Pastimes* and laboriously made a model in cork of the Tower of London, which we instantly threw away. 'Dreadful rubbish,' Francis said.

At the back of my mind lurked a suspicion that Lilian enjoyed my visit for some other reason than the charm of my company but I did not rate that charm very highly myself and was happy to be made welcome on any terms.

'Now that you're here,' she told me, 'I can at least go out of doors without mother setting up an inquisition on all my movements. Oh yes, she still keeps me tied to her apron strings and it won't do, Maggie. It simply won't do.'

As usual we tried on all each other's clothes but for me the pleasure of this exercise had grown a trifle stale, not only because Lilian's dresses no longer suited me and mine were too short for her but for other reasons less easy to define.

'Rather too young for me now.' Lilian pulled off my sprigged batiste with some danger to the stitches. She faced the glass in her white cambric bodice and silk petticoat and looked dreamily at her reflection. She had forgotten me. She must have. I looked uncomfortably away as with her slim hands she slowly caressed her whole body, breasts and waist and thighs, with a secret sensuous delight I would now recognise as ecstasy – already known, luxuriously recalled. She caught sight of my serious face behind her in the glass and didn't care.

'Yes, too childish for me now.' She went to the window and leaned out, not bothering to cover her shoulders, almost as if she wanted to be seen only of course there was no one there, only the garden, which had no wall and on the other side of the beck ran wild and became a wood. A casual colony of wind-sown ash and birch had matured over the years until Sacristy House in the centre of the village seemed as withdrawn as the priory which had once occupied the same site. Lilian and – less forcefully – Mrs Belfleur complained of the shade but I had always found the trees companionable when a longing for escape drove me from the house to seek a few minutes' peace.

Francis felt exactly the same. Even then, though we never spoke of it, we must both have suffered a claustrophobic need to be free of the un-named influence, wilful and dominant, that exhausted our spirits and made the rooms too small. At the end of one of the twisting woodland paths stood a stone outbuilding, a barn of sorts, of immense age. Its stout walls of weathered limestone made a shelter from the wind. An abandoned stone lintel from some even older building formed with the help of cushions a comfortable seat for two or three – or four when, as sometimes happened, Johnny Rigg joined us there. Usually, however, Johnny remained standing, not out of respect but in a commanding posture typical, we all agreed, of his boundless self-confidence.

I liked Johnny in spite of his irritating assurance. Francis once said that Johnny Rigg was his best friend and that was enough to make him my friend too. Lilian on the other hand disapproved of him. In our very early days it had not been so. She had been inclined to seek Johnny's company. He was in so many ways useful. She had, as it were, taken him up but for once the grasp of those long pale fingers was thwarted and she soon put him down again. Johnny was not to be manipulated. When the four of us walked and talked together, Johnny remained noticeably, though without a trace of hostility, beyond Lilian's orbit.

'You ought to love me,' he said to her once, sensing no doubt her patronage of him as a mere carpenter's apprentice. 'We're taught to love our neighbours and whatever I'm not, there's no denying I'm your neighbour.'

Lilian didn't like that either, feeling as she did that the existence of Well Cottage and its occupants was lowering to the pretension of Sacristy House.

'The Riggs,' she was fond of saying, 'are not the sort of people one would choose to have at close quarters.'

It was impossible to condescend to Johnny. He was in every way himself: independent of any category of class or type. With no more formal education than the village schoolmaster could give him, he was well-informed and fully conversant with the books Francis lent him. He had remarkable skill and dexterity with his hands. Once Francis had asked him to make me a miniature chest of drawers for my sewing things. The result was not mere carpentry but a cabinet-maker's piece, perfectly proportioned, Mr Iredale said. Lilian had longed for it or for one just like it but Johnny had refused point-blank to make her one. The coldness between them may have dated from that time. She had not forgiven him.

Often when I made my way to the sheltered seat in the lee of the barn, Francis would be there reading. The place had become in some special way ours since we spent so much time there together. It was there too that at the age of ten or eleven I had made my great discovery. At that time Lilian and I were enthusiastic collectors of wild flowers. Our rivalry in finding new specimens was keen and not altogether friendly. Lilian was always well ahead by the time I came to Jasmine Lodge and I expended a good deal of earnest effort in trying to catch up.

I had been scouring the fringe of the wood and the stream's edge without much luck when suddenly in a shady dell a few feet from the water, there they were: three long spikes of vividly blue flowers, so tall amid their glossy leaves that I scarcely needed to bend my head to sniff at them.

'Look, Francis.'

'What is it?' He spoke without looking up from his book.

'Come and see.'

My excitement brought him reluctantly to his feet. I had reached out, exultant, to break off a stem when he joined me.

'Don't touch it.' He seized my hand. 'Do you know what that is? It's monkshood, the most poisonous plant you could have found.'

'But I wanted... Does Lilian know about it?'

'No, I'm sure she doesn't. It's very rare. I've only seen it once before, up by the Toll House. People used to make liniments with it.'

'The monks?' I suggested.

'Perhaps. Leave it alone. No, you can't have one to press but you can draw it for your collection.'

'It will be mine? Not Lilian's.'

'Yes, of course. You found it.'

I fetched my flower book and made two careful inexpert drawings: one of the whole plant: the other of the five-sepalled flower. We did not speak for a whole hour while the soft breeze moved leaf-filtered sunlight over my paper and the pages of Francis's book: an hour distinct from all others in its mingling of security and danger: the safety of being with Francis in the drowsy summer warmth (he has saved my life, I thought romantically): and the deadly venom of the blue flowers. In my sketch the flower head became a long-jowled face under a deep hood, secretive and sinister, like one of the monks who had practised their secret arts in this green secluded place.

Lilian had to admit grudgingly that the monkshood was mine.

'If it had not been so very poisonous,' I told her, 'we could have used it for a liniment when you have one of your attacks.'

'I don't want your old monkshood,' she said with justifiable fury. No doubt she resented my smugly restrained triumph and my busybody way of showing the sketch to all our acquaintance and warning them not to touch the plant.

Sometimes Francis would read aloud, from Mr Darwin's *Origin of Species,* for instance. It surprised me that so shocking a book could be so achingly dull but my indifference to its contents was more than compensated by my close study of the reader's face, his fair hair and brows and the firm contours of his cheeks and lips. Those were times of absolute contentment and un-broken sympathy. The minutes lengthened into half hours until Lilian joined us and the mood of the place changed.

'Why do you sit here? It's dismal. Oh, you two can stay but I'm going up the hill where there's something to *see.'*

And usually since the dread of one of her attacks was never far from our minds, we went with her wherever she chose to go. It seemed to me this year, however, that Lilian would have been content to walk up the hill herself, if Mrs Belfleur had not made it clear with unusual firmness that she was not to go out alone.

'Perhaps she's thinking of your health,' I said when Lilian protested angrily. 'You know you sometimes...'

It was not easy to speak openly of her attacks for fear of upsetting her.

'Oh those! I've got over them ages ago. At least – I'm supposed to have grown out of them.'

She looked all at once thoughtful and I regretted having raised the subject particularly as I was feeling warmly disposed towards Lilan at the time, having persuaded myself that I had seen through her motive in occasionally wandering off on her own. She was trying – delightful thought – to leave Francis and me alone together. When I taxed her with this, she laughed, a genuine spontaneous laugh of real amusement.

I had proof of her thoughtfulness, as I naively imagined, on the occasion of our expedition to Hagg Barrow.

'We really must go this time,' Francis said, as we sauntered along the lane one morning.

'We say that every year.'

It was no more than a semicircular hump on the horizon, the nearest of scores of prehistoric burial mounds to be found on high points of moorland in that locality.

'Then let's go.' Francis turned to me

quickly. 'Do you know, Maggie, that's what is wrong with me. I talk of doing things and dream of them happening but I don't make them happen. Time goes by, and I achieve nothing. You see, it isn't at all what I would have planned for myself, the life of a country solicitor... Sometimes I have a horrible presentiment: a sort of vision of myself as an old man here at Asherby: the same half-hearted fellow only old like grandfather. Everything will change but I'll go on – the same.'

'I don't want you to change,' I almost said, and wish now that I had. To stay for ever at Asherby, to grow old there! What could be more natural or suitable or unimaginable on a May morning in one's eighteenth year?

'In this case,' I said instead, 'it's perfectly simple. We just set off, now.'

The tumulus seemed quite near, a mere mile away by a moorland track. Francis had told me about the Bronze Age barrows or howes: low mounds above the ancient pits where the ashes of the dead were buried with some of their possessions.

'You're right, Maggie. Only – isn't it rather near lunchtime?' He consulted his watch with what I thought of as his solicitor's expression; that is he screwed up his eyes and pursed his lips as if his exact reading of the watch-face involved the exercise of professional judgment. 'And I suppose Lilian will

53

want to go. This afternoon – or tomorrow perhaps. There, you're laughing at me and thinking, "He never does a thing *now*," and you're quite right. But the barrow has been there for three thousand years. Another day won't make much difference.'

Lilian, after a few thoughtful seconds, seemed eager to go.

'Tomorrow. No, not morning. After lunch. That will give us more time.'

In her hands the plan took such definite shape that even in advance the outing became an established fact. As surely as the sun would rise, we would walk up to Hagg Barrow the following afternoon. And after all, nothing was required in the way of pre-parations but to put on thick shoes, an old skirt and a shady hat; except that Lilian looked far more elegant in her blue and grey walking dress than was suitable – not to mention the horsehair petticoat supporting the backward thrust of her skirt.

'Wouldn't your plaid dress have been more comfortable?'

'Yes, it would. But the gathers are torn.' She spoke carelessly. 'I didn't want to keep you waiting. This will have to do.'

At first she walked quickly and soon drew ahead. It was kind of her to leave us together. I followed demurely at Francis' side along the lane between Well Cottage and the churchyard wall, thence to the stony track leading uphill past Comfrey Farm. Hawthorn was in bloom and there were primroses in plenty. Beyond the farm one felt the strong upward surge of the open moor. But I saw and felt these things imperfectly. My vision was limited to the figure of Lilian walking quickly ahead. The thrill of going at last to Hagg Barrow with Francis was subdued to no more than an undercurrent to the experience of walking behind Lilian.

'She'll tire herself,' Francis said anxiously, 'going at such a pace.'

Sure enough, though she could not have heard, her pace abruptly slackened. Francis and I paused to look back at the village and the rustle of her skirt ceased. When we caught up with her, she was holding her hand to her side and frowning.

'You're tired.'

'I'm sorry. I should have taken your advice, Maggie. This was a stupid dress to wear. It's far too tight.' She gasped and added the dreaded words, 'I'm horribly short of breath.'

'We must go back,' Francis said at once.

'No, please. Not you and Maggie. I'll go back myself. Don't let me spoil the walk for you.'

I searched her face anxiously. She looked remarkably well, her eyes bluer than the sky, her cheeks and forehead cool. With a sigh she clapped her other hand to her side. I smiled inwardly, convinced that I had seen through her ruse. She was acting a part and doing it badly. Unlike myself she had never seen her own fearful symptoms and could not know how devastatingly they changed her. This was a hopelessly unconvincing picture of a delicate young lady in need of a restorative. Dear Lilian! Her air of fatigue, even the deliberate wearing of a too tight dress, were stratagems designed to leave me alone with Francis. I looked modestly down. It was not for me to thwart her kind intention.

'I insist, Francis. You mustn't disappoint Maggie. She has only two more days. There may not be another as fine as this. If you put off the walk for my sake, I shall be really upset. You'll make me feel responsible.' Her voice rose, this time in genuine resentment at not having her own way. I knew that stiffening of the neck and shoulders. These things were not assumed. I grew anxious, half expecting the first startling gasp. Lilian must not be crossed...

'Perhaps, Francis, since it is all down-hill...'

'I shall stay here for a while, then go back and sit quietly in the garden and sew. But you two must go on. I insist.'

Francis hesitated, took out his watch and looked at the dial with his judicial frown. It was an evasion, I knew, and my heart sank. He would weigh us in the balance, Lilian and me, unable to cross her, unwilling to disappoint me.

'It doesn't matter,' I said. 'We've never been to the Barrow and I don't suppose we ever shall but it doesn't matter.'

'There now, Francis. Maggie *is* disappointed.'

Francis put away his watch with an air of decision and drew my arm through his. 'We'll go,' he said. 'We'll walk slowly so that I can keep an eye on you until you get back to the farm.'

How could he fail to see the triumph in her eyes? Wilful she might be but there was no subtlety in Lilian. She certainly couldn't deceive me. I would tell her afterwards that I knew it was all put on for my sake. Nothing remained but to enjoy the walk. It would be enjoyable, that is, when we could be sure that Lilian was safely home, or almost there. From time to time we stopped to look back: very often in fact. For a few minutes she rested on the flat-topped stone where we had left her; then she rose, shook out her skirt and went down the track, too quickly, anyone could see, for a person supposed to be suffering from shortness of breath. But Francis seemed not to notice even though, near the farm gate, Lilian began to run.

'She'll be all right, I believe. And now' – with an air of heartiness – 'for Hagg Barrow.'

Its slight curve, swelling above the smooth

ridge of the horizon, had moved a little nearer; but for one reason or another the expedition fell flat even when the track brought us to the shoulder of the hill and we felt the reviving upland wind. We talked with rather too conscious an animation. Francis liked to tell me about his work but my questions lacked warmth. They seemed forced out of me by politeness. Francis, for his part, was preoccupied; his anecdotes were dutifully amusing.

'I'll tell you what, Maggie, I don't feel it was quite the thing to let Lilian go back like that. Aunt Cynthia makes such a fuss about not letting her go off alone. Because she might be taken ill, I imagine.'

'I suppose that must be why.'

He had taken out his grandfather's ancient pocket telescope. The village was scarcely visible through the trees but he directed the glass towards Comfrey Farm and the track beyond its gate.

'There's no sign of her. She must have reached home long ago. Do you want to look? The glass isn't a ha'porth of good but grandfather likes to think that it's still being used.'

The landmarks swam towards me, blurred by some defect in the ancient glass: circular pictures surprisingly close but oddly distorted and wavering like objects in an aquarium: the kitchen window of the farmhouse; the apse of the church floundering like a grey whale; green glimpses of woodland between the village and Asherby Bank on the other side of the valley; an empty glade where trees had been felled. It did not remain empty. Into its ring of light from either side came a figure, one blue, one green. With the curious swimming motion imposed by the glass the two advanced towards each other and stopped, so close that they might have been one; so deliberately and lingeringly united that I could scarcely think of them as separate people; as Lilian and…

I put the glass to my other eye and directed it to the right, to the top of Asherby Bank where the Toll House faced the road under its towering chestnut; and I imagined rather than saw the garden where little Daniel lay in his wicker cradle and Jael kept watch; and the green where Agnes hung out her stainless washing and wished, perhaps, for company…

'May I?' Francis held out his hand.

'In a minute. I want to look at the Barrow.'

There was really nothing to see. The glass robbed the horizon of its splendid sweep, divided and conquered it so that, viewed on its own, the tumulus was just a low curve of rising earth. It shimmered indecisively, a slight incident in the drama of the hills.

'You said there was nothing there.' I spoke

at random, conscious of the two figures in the clearing and the need to fill in time until they no longer clung face to face like sea-creatures mysteriously, compulsively fused; until they swam apart. And all the time I told myself that it could not be; it was not as I thought. The thing was impossible. 'When you first told me about the barrows I thought of treasure. Bronze bracelets and such things.'

'They found arrowheads, an axe or two and bits of charcoal but they've all gone. No, it's just the place itself that's interesting. Listen! There's a curlew. Did you hear?'

'Why did the Bronze Age people choose such lonely places?'

'Because they were afraid of ghosts. They preferred to keep them up here in the wildest, emptiest places. The barrows were for their leaders, you see. A chieftain would be a strong, dominating sort of person likely to have a strong, dominating ghost.'

'One certainly wouldn't want it in the village.'

'I rather envy the ghosts. Imagine having a splendid place like this to haunt. It appeals to me, the feeling it gives of having shed all the complications and found simplicity. High – and empty – and free.'

'Free?'

An impression of his face remained as I turned and pointed the glass towards the woods again: a forewarning of something that was to weigh increasingly upon my heart. There was resignation in his manner, an acceptance of his own nature and so of his destiny. With such an expression a person might rise to his full height, then stoop to pick up a heavy burden, knowing he would carry it for the rest of his life.

The two people had moved but they had not parted. Together they were making their way towards the shelter of the trees. My hand was unsteady, the glass maddeningly – or mercifully – imperfect so that the whole scene trembled. But I could see that they were hurrying. Presently they disappeared and became part of the quivering wood. It was safe. I handed back the glass with a sudden feeling of lassitude and loss as if someone had died.

'It's further than I thought.'

'You're tired, Maggie.'

Without another word we turned our faces from the wind and went back to the village.

3

'You'll come in,' Francis said when we had failed to find Lilian sewing quietly in the garden.

I shook my head. Sacristy House had temporarily lost its appeal.

'I'm sorry, Maggie. We really must go another time.' His consoling hug, his cheek laid against mine, made me, to my annoyance, tearful. 'Do come this evening. We have only two more days.'

Visits between the two houses were continual. We used them indiscriminately, casually dropping in on each other with the ease of two families long used to living as one. Mother and I usually spent the evenings at Sacristy House. I liked to sit beside Mrs Belfleur so that I could watch the progress of her interminable tapestry. It showed signs of becoming a life's work. A series of canvas panels depicted scenes from medieval life: turrets and keeps, ladies and lapdogs, huntsmen, hawks and hounds. Year by year they took shape in endless variations of crimson and blue, green and gold. To me this leisurely unfolding of times gone by was mysteriously comforting. It soothed my constant apprehension that our days at Asherby Cross would come to an end, especially now that ominous cracks marred their hitherto perfect mould. Mrs Belfleur had only to thread her needle day after day to demonstrate that time was inexhaustible, no part of it entirely lost.

'And what have we been doing today?' Mr Iredale asked when we were settled with our needlework, books, music and chessboard. He was much confined to the house and enjoyed a daily account of our activities.

'The children have been to Hagg Barrow.' Mrs Belfleur smoothed down the tree she had worked that afternoon – Were those oranges hanging stiffly from the boughs? – and gave her attention to the two figures beneath.

'So you've been to the Barrow at last.' Mr Iredale turned to Francis with the slightly sardonic interest he sometimes showed towards him. 'And what, may I ask, did you find there?'

I knew exactly why Francis did not reply at once. He was as usual considering the feelings of everyone else in the room before he spoke. It was not so much a virtue as an affliction from which he helplessly suffered. I was aware of the way his mind worked and felt the same mastery of his thoughts as when I detected his manoeuvres to let me win at chess. I felt sure that he hesitated to

63

mention Lilian's reason for turning back because he knew from experience how any mention of her health could cloud the atmosphere.

A pause lengthened by no more than a few seconds becomes noticeable. Francis looked across at Lilian for help.

'Children!' she said belatedly. 'Really, mother!' and I guessed that she too was at a loss.

'Did you find much evidence that the track was being used? It must be sixty years or more since the Barrow was excavated,' Mr Iredale observed. 'I suppose you took the pocket glass.'

Lilian had been idly turning the pages of a book. She became suddenly still. In Lilian even a state of stillness could convey the force of passion, in this case a passionate interest. The air seemed all at once to hum and buzz with anxiety, filled with warnings of things that must not be said. In panic I realised that I alone knew what they were. I alone knew the extent of the others' ignorance, including Lilian's. I too sat still, containing my knowledge like a hard stony core; and yet it was too blurred and indistinct to be called knowledge.

'As a matter of fact, sir,' Francis said at last, 'we didn't go as far as the Barrow after all. We turned back...'

'Do be careful, dear.' Lilian had got up

abruptly, almost upsetting her mother's tray of embroidery wools and gone to the piano as if to evade this new piece of information. Was she wondering how closely we had followed her down the track and what we had seen through the glass?

'A paltry mile.' The blue glare was directed towards Francis. I flinched in sympathy. 'What is the matter with young people these days? I thought nothing of walking up there before breakfast when I was your age.'

'Francis would do it easily enough,' mother said. 'But he had the girls with him, Mr Iredale, and it's uphill all the way.'

Serenely, with her green-threaded needle poised, Mrs Belfleur scrutinised the lady's pointed hennin and her hand in it's wide sleeve extended to the troubadour in tabard and hose. So far the lovers had no substance, only shape, a single shape as he bowed his head over her hand.

'What did you do all the afternoon then?'

They all waited, including Lilian. It was absurd. Francis and I had nothing to conceal. The circumstances had been so trivial, all except one. But for that one significant glance through the telescope, I would have gone on believing that Lilian had turned back for no other reason than to leave me alone with Francis; and that was the most natural thing in the world. We had rambled together along every path in Asherby.

Nothing could have been more innocent.

The word – I had never had occasion to use it before – made me feel hot and uncomfortable, confronted as I was for the first time with its opposite; not just evasions but deception made faintly sickening by some further taint; something much worse than pretending to feel what one did not feel, be where one was not. The two people who hurried across the clearing were conspirators bound together by a shared purpose. The glass had isolated them in a closed circle palpitating with guilt.

I hastily turned over a page of the music book in my lap, pretending to study my part in the duet Lilian and I were about to play. The performance promised to be a disaster. I hadn't practised the piece. Lilian always went too fast. Her slender fingers narrowing at the tip seemed able to reach still further than their length of bone permitted. She could always astonish me by stretching one and almost two notes more than the octave. That was what she was doing now, stretching out from C to the C above and then to D, without a sound and listening, on tenterhooks. And she had never from start to finish thought of me or my feelings for Francis. It wasn't fair.

'Lilian had to come back,' I said baldly, 'because her dress was too tight. Francis and I walked on a little but I was tired and we turned back quite soon.'

'A pity.' I felt the fiery stare upon me. 'A pity, I must say.'

'Really, Maggie!' Lilian said without turning round. 'I should like to know whether we are going to play this duet or whether we are not.'

'I didn't see you, Lilian,' her mother said. 'Where were you? Elinor and I were in the garden all afternoon.'

'Oh, I strolled about. Are you ready, Maggie?'

'Where?' Mrs Belfleur had flushed with annoyance. 'I particularly dislike this habit you've developed of walking off on your own.' Her tone was sharp. 'And so does your grandfather. You know it very well. It's quite unsuitable.'

'You must not treat me as a child, mother.' Lilian struck a few loud chords with such an effect of impatience that mother raised her eyebrows and moved her chair further from the piano. I propped the music on the stand and sat down on as much of the stool as remained available.

'I really don't know it at all.'

Her tight-lipped explosive expression warned me that she would have no mercy. Wits astray, fingers beyond control, distracted to death by the consciousness of Lilian half a bar ahead, I stumbled through the piece and when it came mercifully to an end, bowed my head, shamed and stunned by the torture of it.

'Maggie must practise,' Mr Iredale said. 'She was holding Lilian back all the time. Play us something on your own, my love.'

'Yes, do,' mother said. 'A solo will suit you better, Lilian. You will be able to do exactly as you please.'

'Come, Maggie.' Francis was setting out the chessboard. 'What about a game? You can be as slow as you like. In fact the slower the better.'

He nodded encouragingly at every move I made and to the strains of Schumann my bruised spirit revived; and perhaps after all Lilian too was sorry for me. At bedtime she came and put her arms round me.

'Let me come and sleep at the Lodge tonight. We shan't have many more chances to talk. You don't mind, mother?'

'Of course not, darling.' Mrs Belfleur returned dreamily from her tapestry world, leaving the lovers under their shadeless orange tree. None of us, I have since thought, minded anything so long as Lilian was happy. Seeing her restored to good humour made us all more cheerful and affable than usual as we bade one another goodnight. It became, during that last half hour of the day, a humour so buoyant, so blissful – as if Lilian drew upon some secret source of satisfaction – that I gave way as usual to the sheer force of her vitality, as one might forget everything else in the nearness of a waterfall or a firework display. The events of the day underwent a change in perspective, an alteration in scale. They shrank and receded and my room, now that Lilian was in it, became a separate world where one made no judgments, only listened and watched.

I managed with a hand glass while Lilian sat at my dressing table. She wore an amber-coloured peignoir a shade darker than the soft fair hair which never grew into the long smooth tresses we all aspired to at that time. She took out the tortoise-shell combs and even then it sprang back actively from her face in shafts of light.

'Mother,' she said, 'is becoming intolerable. Don't look shocked, Maggie. It's no use comparing us with you and your mother. You're quite different. You lead an altogether different kind of life. Mother has nothing to do but stitch her tapestry and watch over me and interfere. Why doesn't she find another interest? She irritates me to death. That was why' – she bent her head and brushed her hair over her face so that her voice came from the centre of a light cloud – 'when I saw them in the garden this afternoon, I couldn't bear to sit with them. "Yes, Cynthia" … "No, Elinor." "Do you remember, dear?"'…

'So you went somewhere else?'

'Yes. As a matter of fact' – she took a lock of her hair and brushed it upward with slow luxurious strokes – 'I sat on that stone by the barn. All my myself.'

'But you don't like it there.'

'Nor do I. But there I was.' She waited. Her eyes, I thought, were wary, calculating; but that was probably because I expected them to be. When I did not speak, she went on, 'You don't know what it's like to be cooped up in the house and garden, day in, day out, except for a few calls and the occasional cup of tea with Miss Abbot! I must have my own life, and I'm tired of having mother always in it.'

'And yet you didn't want to go away to school. You said so.'

'Leave Asherby?' Her face in the glass had changed. It was suffused with some feeling that excluded me as if another person had come in and taken all her attention. A shiver passed through her. She threw back her head as if overpowered. 'What *are* you talking about?'

I turned back the counterpane and got into bed. Presently, she shrugged off her peignoir and lay down at my side; but she was restless all night and disturbed my sleep. Consequently towards morning I slept heavily and woke in the early dawn to find myself alone.

For some time I lay still, thinking of Lilian

– remembering the May morning years ago when we had gone out to wash our faces in dew and gather wild flowers. We had rambled about happily enough but the expedition had not been a success: neither dew was forthcoming nor flowers, other than a few trailing stems of stitchwort clawed up with handfuls of grass. There had been another morning when we had gathered mushrooms. 'It's my field. They must all go in my basket,' Lilian said, holding it out. 'You're only *helping*, Maggie, and I'm *letting* you…'

Her necklace and bracelets and her hare's foot still littered my dressing table but her peignoir had gone – and her clothes. A white snake of stocking lay by the door. She must have gathered up her things and crept out. The air from the open window was cool. When Lilian had one of her asthmatic attacks, she felt a desperate need of air. Her manner for the past few days had been excited, more heedless even than usual; but as yet she had shown no sign of the drowsiness and depression that sometimes followed such overwrought moods and led to spasms of breathlessness and choking.

It took me only a few minutes to dress. I persuaded myself as I laced my stays that I was hurrying to find Lilian and help her and even debated whether to fetch remedies from Miss Abbot's kitchen or from Sacristy House. There was not a sound in the house below or above. Only the birds were singing their hearts out. Was it the thrill of passion in their song – or the knowledge that Lilian would not have hesitated to rouse me if she needed me? For whatever reason, my search, if it could be so called, was half-hearted. I went out not exactly to find Lilian but to avoid staying in bed and wondering where she was.

Beyond Miss Abbot's garden a path followed the beck to Sacristy House, a secluded way used only by our two families. The Iredales' windows were still curtained. I dared not disturb the household. With some idea of filling in time, I took the familiar track through the trees and soon came to the stone seat.

It was a curious feeling to sit there absolutely alone. Behind me like a fortress rose the barn, its massive walls built centuries ago to keep out the fiercest weather and to hold fast in a mysterious privacy whatever lay inside. I became aware of the light insistent babble of the stream. There came a moment when it ceased to soothe. Its endless repetition held a note of agitation. It would not have been easy to express what it was that I imagined as I sat stiffly listening. It is not easy now when later events have clarified those troubled fancies to which inexperience could give no pictorial shape or form.

What *had* shape and form was the comb

on which my fingers idly closed. It lay among the leaf-mould at the end of the seat; a tortoiseshell dress comb such as Lilian wore in her hair. She must have dropped it. It was true then that she had sat here yesterday as she said. The relief was enormous. In my remorse I exonerated her completely. The whole tissue of deception had been of my own fabricating. Lilian really had suffered a slight attack of breathlessness on the way to Hagg Barrow, had been anxious not to spoil the outing for Francis and me and had spent the afternoon alone in this very spot. The blue figure in the glade had been someone else, not Lilian. Mr Iredale's silly old telescope distorted everything. Indeed, I could not believe that even Lilian would behave so recklessly. It would be madness to forget her station and good name, to stoop so low and enjoy so degrading an adventure. It would be wanton and cruel.

The tortoise-shell of the comb was hard; its teeth were sharp. Torn between loyalty and suspicion, I almost threw the thing away. And yet it seemed – it was – concrete proof that Lilian had been here, as she said. I tucked it in my hair, feeling ashamed of having doubted her. After all she was my dearest friend. And all at once I knew where she must be. Where else – in her nightdress – but in her room? She had simply slipped away to sleep more comfortably in her own bed. At that hour she would run no risk of being seen.

Like the birds I burst into song, subdued out of respect for the early hour but taking some pride in the tuneful execution of 'A Welcome to Alexandra the Fair' and remembering to breathe from the diaphragm and direct my breath towards the frontal cavities of the head as my singing master advised. I was mortally hungry. Soon the servants would be astir and I could beg a slice of bread and butter. By that time Francis might be down. Still singing, I pottered to the water's edge and leaned over the turtle-shaped boulder where Lilian liked to sit trailing her fingers in the beck.

'Look, Maggie,' she would call and enjoy my shuddering recoil as the water moved over her hands and turned them into strange white claws.

I made an ineffectual dab at a minnow or two, glanced in a proprietary way at the green leaves of my monkshood growing in the shade of the twisted willow, dried my hands on my petticoat and looked back at the barn.

It was one of several outhouses leased by Mr Iredale to Jim Atkins of Comfrey Farm and built, like Sacristy House, of stone from the old priory. For all I know part of its structure may actually have survived from the distant days before the Dissolution. It certainly had the appearance of withstanding the elements until the elements themselves should cease; and, as I said, to enclose and bury deep whatever it was required to shelter: in this case – the door creaked as I pulled it open – such bales of straw as were left from last year's harvest.

A cat picked its way among the fallen wisps, found the exact point where sunshine from the half open door met the ravaged side of the stack, curled its tail about its feet and stared – silken, smooth, yellow and brown like the straw itself – into the light. At some time in its history the barn had been given a second storey, a loft under the rafters and approached by a ladder. One could have climbed up with the help of the hemp rope hanging from an invisible hook, and crept into the dark recess. That is, a person or persons who wanted to hide could have done so. Not I. Where straw had been taken away, the bales sagged perilously. A small movement might dislodge the whole stack.

Impossible to tell whether the thought came of itself or was suggested by the sound of just such a movement, a soft settling and creaking from the farthest depths of the stack or from the loft above it where the section of a beam gave to one corner the effect of a room, withdrawn and intimate.

I was, as Lilian said, always imagining

things. It was probably a similar sound that had startled me years ago and inspired my story that the barn was haunted. Its age and size would be awesome to a child: were still as a matter of fact. I stood, all movement suspended, each nerve and sense exposed to the atmosphere of the place: to its thin light and thick darkness: to the sharp stale smell of straw; and I felt in response to my own attentiveness an answering anxiety as if the barn itself with all its crannies and spaces, even the minute cavities of air between the stalks of straw – were listening too.

The cat rose, apprehensive as an indrawn breath, and sprang past me into the day-light; and in a flash I remembered Lilian, golden too and inscrutable, as she sat at my toilet table taking the combs from her hair. She had been wearing them last night, both of them, so how could she have lost one – here – *yesterday?*

On some invisible thread a spider swung startlingly close to my face.

From behind an arm encircled me. A voice spoke. I drew back.

'I wouldn't go in there if I were you.'

4

'Oh Johnny.' I turned to look up at him. 'You startled me. I wasn't going in, not any further. But why shouldn't I?'

Johnny didn't answer at once, nor did he release my hand but somehow manoeuvred himself between me and the door which he closed behind him. He so contrived things that I found myself a few paces from the barn with my back to it and presently it seemed perfectly natural to be sauntering with him along the bank of the stream.

'You're up early, Miss Maggie.'

Hearing the normal tones of his voice, I felt that his first remark had been pitched unnecessarily loud. He had stood with his back to the daylight and spoken directly into the barn. The words had soared up to the rafters as though challenging the unseen occupants with whom I had peopled the place.

'What on earth did you think I was doing?' I pulled my hand away. 'You really frightened me.'

'You're going home tomorrow,' he said, instead of answering. He might have arranged my departure. His confident air of knowing everything had survived the years unshaken, had grown and flourished. It was as though he supervised his small world, the village of Asherby Cross, like a competent and, in the main, benevolent stage manager familiar with every detail of the production. I could not think why it was that as we chatted on this particular morning my faith in Johnny's benevolence should waver. He was, as always, kindness itself to me and yet I detected an underlying sternness as if he had less pleasant things to think about.

'Granny hopes to see you if you can find it convenient to call and bid her goodbye.'

'Of course I will. I don't suppose we shall be back until next summer.'

'By that time I'll have gone.'

'You really mean to go to sea then?'

'What else is there for a man like me? I'll never make my fortune in Asherby. There's only room for one wheelwright and carpenter's shop here, and it'll be another thirty years before Mr Ogshaw gives up. No, as soon as I can find a berth, I'll sign on as a ship's carpenter and see the world.'

He talked on with such determination that I could not interrupt. It so happened that I knew something of the dreadful conditions aboard merchant ships at that time. One of my father's friends was Mr Samuel Plimsoll, the Member of Parliament for Derby, who was working so strenuously on behalf of the unfortunate crews. Only last December his book *Our Seamen* had shocked the public with its revelations about the coffin ships as they came to be called, rotten unseaworthy vessels, grossly overloaded and over-insured by avaricious owners in the confident expectation that they would sink. I knew that each year there were hundreds of wrecks, especially of grain ships and coastal vessels carrying coal, and that five times as many men died at sea as in the mines, perilous as they were. Long extracts from Mr Plimsoll's book had appeared in the *Martlebury Gazette* and other papers. Johnny must have known the appalling conditions and chosen to disregard them.

'Nothing venture, nothing have,' he was saying. 'You think it will take a long time for a ship's carpenter to get rich? You're right. But it's only a beginning. I want to see what's going on out there.' The cheerful jerk of his head indicted an unexplored world beyond Asherby. 'I can keep an eye open, take chances, risks if need be. Funny. Two things I've always wanted – plenty of money and a beard.'

'Then you must have them, Johnny.' I tried to stifle my fears. 'I believe you could do anything if you set your mind on it. But Francis will miss you. And what will Mrs Rigg do without you?'

'That's the one thing that worries me. But

she's come round to it at last. I'll be able to provide for her all the better by spreading my wings a bit. Meantime, she's comfortably placed and safe enough with Mr Iredale to give an eye to her. He'd never let her down after all the years she's lived next door to him. So long as she has her bit of garden...'

We had come in sight of it, a sheltered plot bright with tulips and lilac coming into bloom and protected from north winds by the cottage itself which in its aspect had an advantage over the big house. Mrs Belfleur and Lilian often lamented that they had no south-facing sitting room.

Birds were feeding on Mrs Rigg's grass plat. From across the beck we watched a robin hop through her open window on to the kitchen sill.

'According to Granny that's the same robin that fed from her hand when she first came here. "Thirty years is a big age for a bird," I tell her. "Well, there's always been a robin there," she says. She'd sooner see it in the palm of her hand every morning than a gold sovereign.'

Ten minutes had passed. My clamorous appetite told me that it must soon be breakfast time at last. One could not be dull in Johnny's company. All the same I would not be sorry to leave him. I was conscious of an unusual lack of ease as if he were trying too hard to engage my attention though no such effort was necessary. We had reached the place where the stream emerged from underground to flow between the cottage and house on one side and the wild garden on the other towards the village green. The ground rose over a culvert to form an arch edged with rough stones.

Afterwards I recollected that Johnny had stood all the time facing past me in the direction of the barn whereas I had my back to it and faced the cottage. And yet for some reason I remained conscious of the barn, perhaps because Johnny had not shut the door properly. For the second or third time it creaked though there was no wind. Puzzled, I had half turned, when all my attention was captured by an incident which was to give a sombre colouring to my thoughts for a long time to come. I can never recall that morning by the beck without the sensation of peering through the bright surface of life into the darkness lurking beneath.

A flutter of wings on Mrs Rigg's window sill did no more than distract me for a second: there were birds everywhere. But presently through a gap at the bottom of the thorn hedge appeared the triangular face of the straw-coloured cat. She eased herself through and trotted steadily across the grass towards us, her smooth tread all the more sinister because of what she carried in her mouth. A few feet away she became aware of us and stopped, uncertain.

'Johnny! Look! She's got Mrs Rigg's robin.'

He swung round in one movement, swift and accurate as any cat, and seized the creature by the neck.

'It's too late.' I picked up the torn robin. Its eyes were already sightless; it's new spring plumage was ruffled and blood-spotted.

Johnny glanced at it. His lips tightened. He changed his grip and without a second's hesitation dashed the cat's head against one of the stones and threw it down, dead. Appalled, I stooped and laid the robin on the grass, instinctively putting it an inch or two beyond the reach of the cat's astonishingly dead claws. The Arcadian morning seemed littered with carcases.

It surprises me, recalling the incident, that I felt no impulse to reproach Johnny. The deed was hideous but the impression it left was not one of indifferent cruelty; rather of a passion for revenge finding expression in an alarmingly efficient execution. Rightly or wrongly, it enlarged my respect for him.

'You knew how,' I said, awestruck, when at last I could speak.

'Yes. You have to know the exact spot. Otherwise it would have suffered.'

'And it didn't?'

'No.'

He had simply extinguished it. I averted my eyes from the corpses. Indeed Johnny seemed to propel me politely away from them – and the barn – in the direction of the road.

'It was just behaving according to its nature,' I ventured. 'The cat.'

'Yes. And so was I. I've got a nature too, and it's my nature to get rid of things I don't like, particularly anything that upsets my old granny.'

'An animal, I suppose you mean.'

'In this case an animal.'

It seemed to me, shaken as I was, that if the cat had been a person and that person posed a threat to Mrs Rigg's happiness, the outcome would have been – not identical surely, not *that* – but no fear of consequences would have stopped Johnny from dealing with the matter as he thought fit; and it was this impression – unfortunately as things turned out – that was to remain with me.

Sentiment would have been strikingly out of place but some hankering after moral order in the universe made me say: 'Even a barn cat must matter, mustn't it? You know what it says in the Bible. Not even a sparrow is forgotten by God.'

'What about the robin?' Johnny asked unanswerably. 'If the cat had been drowned as a kitten, you'd have thought nothing of it. They can't all live. And if it had been spared to spend the rest of its natural life catching rats, there would still be rats in that barn till kingdom come.'

'So that was why you didn't want me to go in,' I cried triumphantly. 'Because of the rats. It was kind of you, Johnny.'

In the circumstances the word may have been unexpected but there was no doubt that he was looking down at me with a sort of protectiveness.

'Well,' he said slowly, 'I wouldn't want you to come across anything that would upset or frighten you. There are some things it's better to steer clear of – and for that matter, some people. You'll find that out, if you haven't found it out already.'

'Oh I know, although I haven't actually met any of the bad ones. I've been lucky so far.'

'Let's hope your luck will hold.'

We had wandered into the road and there on the deep bank in the shadow of the churchyard wall – the unexpected sight made me jump – sat Jael Hebworthy, clutching a bunch of flowers. We both spoke to her. She did not smile or answer. Her colourless face was curiously arresting in the blue shade; and she held her motley bunch of primroses and king-cups in such a way that the flowerheads seemed all turned towards us, a crowd of small faces quivering with the same watchful tension as Jael's own. And there came to me – from what medley of half-formed impressions I cannot tell – the conviction *that she ought not to have been there.*

Even so, I was surprised at the sharpness in Johnny's tone as he said: 'Run off home, Jael. Your mother will be wondering where you are.' With the swiftness of a wild creature she leapt to her feet, took the woodland path and vanished, leaving behind a whiff of anxiety, unspoken, unspeakable: a disturbing impression of silent suffering.

It worried me until the welcome sound of Miss Abbot's breakfast gong banished her from my mind. We turned and presently came back to the mournful scene of conflict.

'Oh dear, we can't leave them here.'

I carried the robin to the hedge and covered it with earth and leaves.

'Do you think Mrs Rigg would like a bird as a pet?' I suggested. 'It would be company for her while you're away. Please let me give her one.'

'I don't much like the idea of keeping song birds in cages.' Johnny seemed put out and answered curtly.

'They get used to it, you know, and at least they're *safe*. I'll ask Francis to see to it, and I'll choose a pretty cage in Martlebury.'

'If you think it would please the old lady.'

He picked up the cat by the tail and carried it away, its head dangling helplessly.

'Maggie.'

Lilian was at her window when I went by.

She had pushed up the sash and was leaning out, fully dressed.

'Did you wonder where I was? I couldn't sleep and came back here. Never mind about my things. I'll fetch them after breakfast.'

'You dropped one of your combs. I'm wearing it as a matter of fact.'

Her smile faded. For a second or two she hesitated – but this time didn't even bother to lie.

'You can keep it.'

She disappeared. I took the comb from my hair and when I came to the stepping stones, threw it into the water.

5

'Wonderful news!' Mother looked up, beaming, from her letter. 'It's from Cynthia. Oh, how splendid! And Major Hart has added a message.'

'You don't mean' – Father laid down the newspaper – 'that Lilian has relented?'

'We mustn't think of it like that but it's true, I suppose. At any rate they're to be married in August and sail for India at once.'

'And Lilian?'

Even in those first flabbergasted seconds I realised how momentous it would be if

Lilian went too.

'No, no. She will stay with Mr Iredale. That was always the difficulty, you know. As a child she so strongly resented the attachment. Yet Cynthia couldn't leave her.'

'Did Hart want her?' father bluntly asked and was severely ignored.

'The gratifying thing is– Wait, I'll read it to you – that Lilian actually took up the matter of her own accord. Major Hart came home on leave and wrote at once to Cynthia. Here it is. "Lilian recognised the handwriting. Can you imagine my feelings when she came and put her arms round me and said, 'Mother, why don't you marry Major Hart? I'm sure he loves you.'" There!'

'That was charming of her,' father said. 'We are to assume then that Lilian has taken to thinking of others.'

'Lilian's attitude has been all that could be wished. She was urgent that they should marry soon, no later than Cynthia's forty-second birthday. That will be on the 19th of August. Lilian is quite reconciled to staying on at Sacristy House without her mother. Cynthia thinks she is looking forward to taking on the housekeeping and from Mr Iredale's point of view nothing could be more suitable. He so dotes on Lilian' – Mother sighed – 'that he will scarcely notice when Cynthia has gone. Oh, how I shall miss her, Edward.'

87

'Lilian will be able to do just as she likes in future,' father said. 'Who would not be magnanimous in such circumstances?'

'You won't mind if Maggie and I go to Asherby for the wedding? It will be while you are in Scotland.'

'Of course you must go.'

And of course we went, together with a number of relatives and friends of the Iredales and Harts. Jasmine Lodge and Sacristy House were full to overflowing. Rooms were taken at the Fleece. Every inch of stabling in the village was bespoken. The weather in the last two weeks of August was perfect that year: hot days of settled sunshine: mornings and evenings of dew and moonlight. There can never have been a more delightful occasion. The bride and groom had loved each other for years, had waited unselfishly, and loved all the more for having waited. In temperament and age they were perfectly suited. Major Hart was able to endow his wife with an amplitude of worldly goods that freed her at last from dependence on her father.

I have learned almost to dread those times when every omen is favourable. The happiest outlook can be the prelude to events of a very different kind: or is it merely that disasters emphasise by contrast the brightness they destroy?

Wedged between Mother on one side and

the box containing our new hats on the other, with Mrs Rigg's green and gold bird-cage on my lap, I found no hint of change in the place itself as we drove between harvest fields to the top of Asherby Bank where the road plunged down and the purple moors rose towards us, lovely as a mirage. But for once Agnes was not there to welcome us. We actually had to knock at the closed door and wait. There was time to notice a faint air of neglect. A pair of unwashed milk cans lay on the green. The white dimity curtains were – unbelievably – fly-blotched and yellowing.

It was an unknown woman who opened the door, wiping her hands on an apron of coarse sacking. She seemed uncertain as to what to do with us until she learned our name and bade us go in.

'I'm afraid Agnes must be unwell,' mother said. 'Are you – you must be her sister, Effie.'

The woman nodded.

'I'm at my wits' end, Mrs Ossian. I came two weeks ago like I always do towards harvest time and have done since we were girls, for the chance of a bit of gleaning. More for old times' sake than for the need, thank God. But I found Agnes so poorly that I haven't been able to leave her.'

'And the baby?'

'Him as well.'

'Oh I do pray she keeps this one.'

'There's no telling whether it's him being sickly that frets her or t'other way round. But they're going downhill fast, the pair of them.' We listened in shocked silence as she described her sister's symptoms. '...And yet it's hard to find anything properly amiss. It's more as if she'd given up. She doesn't eat or talk or ask for anything. I'll tell her you're here.'

Presently she invited us upstairs. Agnes was sitting up in bed with the baby held tightly, too closely in her arms, as if they depended on each other for existence. Jael stood at the head of the bed facing us with her back to the wall so that the three of them had a strange desperate air of making a last stand.

'You've come for the wedding.' Agnes's voice was weak, her mouth tremulous and pale. Her eyes, I noticed with concern, had lost their soft warmth. She seemed already distant, drifting away on an ebbing tide.

'I'm very sorry, Agnes dear, to find you like this. Have you everything you need?'

The words, the old intimacy, touched some hidden spring. A look of agonised grief twisted her features. Mother went quickly and bent over her, taking her hand. 'Tell me. What is it?' Agnes shook her head as if racked by a distress so inward and deep that it cut her off from human help. 'Maggie, take Jael downstairs and show her your wedding

90

hat. A breath of air will do her good.'

The little room was closed and ugly. I longed for air myself. But mother's stratagem failed. Jael silently refused to budge and Agnes to talk. After a few minutes we were obliged to leave, helpless and unhappy.

'Does Daniel realise how ill Agnes is?' mother asked as Effie showed us out.

Her face hardened. 'You'd best talk to him yourself, Mrs Ossian, if you want to know. I might not be here for all the notice he takes of me. Our side of the family was never good enough for him. He's always had notions above hisself. And now...' She stopped. I believe she was a hard-headed, close-lipped woman not much given to talking especially about family matters. Like Agnes – and they were typical of country folk in those parts – she would keep her feelings to herself and die of them rather than confide in her neighbours. But she was sufficiently won over by mother's sympathy to blurt out, 'He's gone to the bad, if you ask me. He's like a man in a dream. Half the time he isn't here. It's beyond me where he goes all day – and night.'

'He has had the doctor to see Agnes?'

'She won't hear of a doctor. Nothing will persuade her. It's my belief she wants to go, him being as he is, and go she will before long.'

She spoke with a bitter acceptance that alarmed me.

91

'But that's wicked and wrong,' mother said. 'It isn't like Agnes. And she must have medical attention. I'm afraid if pneumonia sets in, she will have no chance. Do keep her warm and try to make her take some nourishment. I shall speak to Daniel and insist on his calling in Dr Slater.'

An opportunity of speaking to Daniel came almost at once. Half a mile from Asherby Cross we saw him walking towards us in his green velveteen jacket with a bag slung on his shoulder. He had probably been acting as beater for a shooting party: the grouse season had begun. As he came nearer mother asked the coachman to stop.

'Mr Hebworthy.' She leaned out of the window. 'I wanted to speak to you. It's about Agnes.'

With unbelievable rudeness, without so much as raising his hat, he stalked on, his face set in a dark scowl.

'Yon's a surly chap,' the coachman observed over his shoulder. 'He looks as if he's going to his own funeral.'

'Poor Agnes!' Mother sighed. 'But we mustn't be hard on him. Grief and worry have that effect sometimes. He must be very unhappy. I shall try again.'

We drove on in silence. Mother did not confide her thoughts to me. As for mine – I felt weighed down by apprehension, chiefly for Agnes but not only on her account. Daniel's appearance had alarmed me. His heavy walk, his features without light, his downcast eyes, were those of a man unresponsive to anything but his own obsession. He seemed tormented like a soul in purgatory. There was something about the Hebworthys, people said. Daniel was not like other men. More than once I had been struck by the burning seriousness of his manner, his look and – unwillingly I recalled it – that startling kiss. It was all his fault, this feverish love. He was so much older; Lilian was just a girl. But all the time I knew that Lilian was not the girl to be tempted into any course of action she did not want, seek, long for... Oh, but Daniel was not a man to be trifled with. Even I could see that. Even I could see how utterly passion could possess such a man; how quickly his smouldering intensity could blaze into violence.

Here I found myself shying away in panic from a situation beyond my scope. After all I was no more than an outsider, far too diffident to intervene in the lives of others even if I had had the wisdom to know how. The feeling of being an outsider persisted when we arrived. For the first time Lilian had not come to meet us. It was with the constraint of strangers that we greeted each other. In the few months since we had met she had taken another step forward, had outstripped me again and grown older. I felt a distance in her manner and would have put it down to the fact that she had other guests, other duties, if there had not also been a look of hardness in her face. She smiled less, talked less, listened even less than usual. She showed no warmth of interest, for example in the topic that occupied mother's mind and mine.

'I don't wish to speak of it in front of your mother, Lilian. This is a happy time for her. But I was distressed to find Agnes Hebworthy in such a state. Have you visited her?'

'Not lately.'

'I should think not,' Mr Iredale interposed. 'There is no need for Lilian to upset herself by visiting the sick. Sitting in stuffy bedrooms and listening to tales of woe can do her nothing but harm. She has her own health to consider.'

'Agnes puzzles me,' mother went on. 'One would think... Oh Maggie, did you not see? It's as if her heart is broken. That really can happen, you know.'

Lilian stood at the window with her back to us, looking out.

'Her husband,' mother said, recovering herself, 'seems quite unapproachable...' and she told of our meeting with Daniel.

'He's always been an arrogant fellow.' Mr Iredale spoke irritably. 'There's no way of helping such people. Cynthia sent up a basket of invalid food and I put in a couple of

94

claret. And what do you think?' He glared at us. 'Mrs Hebworthy sent them back. Francis found them on the doorstep. Soup, wine, everything – and that skinny girl scuttling away. Unpleasant. Such a thing has never happened before in all my time at Asherby.'

'Why should she behave so – resentfully?'

Lilian pushed open the window abruptly.

'I hate these trees,' she said violently. 'They suffocate me.'

'Trees?' Mr Iredale looked at her uneasily. 'You can't hate trees, my love. Are you tired? All this running about has been too much for you; but it will soon be over and then we shall have some peace on our own, you and I.'

'And Francis,' mother said.

In the evening I went to meet him and had got as far as the bottom of Asherby Bank when the gig came cautiously round the last bend.

'Maggie! I hoped you'd come.'

The nagging doubts and sorrows of the day left me. Nothing in the world could trouble me with Francis by my side as we drove through the warm heather-scented evening. It was possible even to resurrect a hope which had suffered more than one secret burial. If Lilian really did love someone else, she could not at the same time love Francis. With shameless selfishness I forgot Agnes in revived dreams of my own happiness.

'We were wondering, grandfather and I, if you would stay on for a while after the wedding?'

'Mr Iredale?'

'Well, it was my idea but he agreed at once. Lilian hasn't realised how much she will miss Aunt Cynthia. She hasn't thought of it at all. She doesn't, you know, think ahead.'

'Does Lilian want me to stay on? She hasn't said anything.'

'As a matter of fact we haven't mentioned it for fear of disappointing her if you couldn't – or wouldn't. I do hope you will, Maggie. It would be splendid. For me, I mean.'

'We could go to Hagg Barrow.' I looked at him severely and he laughed. 'For that matter we could go now. This very minute.'

I persuaded myself that it looked inviting; a slight upward curve, a variation of line between the blue limit of the moor and the bluer sky. Hagg Barrow did not interest me; but to go there with Francis? The prospect had already taken on the glamour of an ideal never to be realised.

'You're mocking me. But at least I haven't been there without you. When the time does come, we'll go there together.'

'Just the two of us. Without Lilian.'

He looked surprised, then serious.

'Without Lilian. Just you and me.'

We spent the evening going over the wedding arrangements which seemed to have fallen largely into Francis's hands. Despite her supposed eagerness to take on the housekeeping, Lilian appeared to have escaped all responsibility for the breakfast, the sending out of cards and her mother's packing. The family and servants had conspired as usual to keep her free from either drudgery or excitement. Her mood, I soon saw, was not sociable. For long periods she was simply not to be seen.

'Lilian has given up her room,' Mrs Belfleur told us. 'So thoughtful of the dear child. I don't at all like her sleeping in the back attic but she would have it, and we couldn't have put a visitor there.'

The attic had its own little staircase which came down into the back porch. When Lilian was not to be found, it was assumed that she was at the back of the house or with other guests. Obviously she could not be with them all at once. I alone perhaps suspected that she was with none. On the eve of the wedding she was not in the parlour to bid us good night when we all dispersed to our various lodgings.

'It's very sensible of her to have an early night,' someone said.

From my window I watched a honey-coloured moon rise over the church tower, heard the quiet bell strike the hour, eleven o'clock, and reached my great decision. The awfulness of it made my cheeks burn. I clenched my hands, willing myself not to weaken. I was the only one who could do it. There was no one else to remind her of her duty; to rescue her – yes, that was what it would be – from the ruinous situation she had involved herself in and at the same time relieve Agnes of her misery, if it was not too late.

'Lilian,' I would say. 'I know what you are doing.'

But that was not true. I knew nothing with any certainty except that she would be furiously angry. Her nostrils would dilate, her eyes grow fierce, her voice take on its most imperious note. I felt my splendid resolution slipping away, routed by the plain fact that I was afraid of Lilian and always had been even when I loved her most. Still, I must do it. In that quiet hour, in the safety of my room, the interview was far enough away to seem at least possible.

Somewhere in the trees an owl screeched: a sign of death. It set me shivering. Above the church tower the moon had turned pale. I thought of Agnes, paler still, as she sat up in bed clutching the baby with that desperate air of having been shipwrecked and abandoned; and without wasting another minute I walked out of my room, out of the house, along the moonlit path and round to the back of Sacristy House.

Only then did it occur to me that the back door would be locked. Relief made me bold. I turned the handle carelessly and pushed just to make sure before retreating. To my dismay the door opened. There was no going back now. With my foot on the first stair I suddenly realised what it would mean to Lilian to be awakened in the dark and confronted by an accusing figure bent on laying bare her most intimate secrets. It would make her ill. There was not the smallest doubt of it. I felt all the old terror of those choking breaths, the retching, the waxen hands. The wedding day would be ruined and it would be my fault.

All the same I am glad now to remember that I went slowly up to the door of the attic. There was no need to go any further. The door was open, the room full of moonlight, the bed empty.

When Major and Mrs Hart looked back on their wedding as they must often have done during the long uneventful evenings in Rawul Pindee, they would remember a morning as warm and sunny as they deserved. She must have remembered how magnificent he looked in his uniform. Did he recall her bonnet of shirred grey velvet and marabou plumes, her grey satin dress with cherry coloured ribbon loops? My own particular memory is of Francis in his blue frock coat and quilted waistcoat, throwing out half-pence for the village children as we left the church; scrupulously, with his lawyer's expression, casting them equally to right and left so that no one need be disappointed. The manes and tails of the horses plaited with white: the ribboned whips: the scattered flower petals: the gifts of silver and glass all crated and labelled for the voyage: occasionally I can summon them up, sunlit and sparkling again. Then the black cloud comes down. The flowers and dresses lose their colour. The congratulations, the breakfast, the toasts, take on the unreality of a masquerade.

But at the time every detail impressed me vividly. I had been to weddings before; but never before had I understood so clearly the meaning of the vows because never before had I understood what it meant to break them or cause them to be broken. I could not see Lilian's face as she sat in the first pew, only the back of her white straw hat, its blue-lined brim caught up at the side with a cockade of blue feathers; but I could imagine the arrogant tilt of her chin and almost feel the wilful beat of her pulse. She seemed unassailable. All the same I must speak to her. My heart sank.

We came out into the sunny morning. Mother and I waited on the church steps until the Harts and Iredales left the vestry

100

and walked down the path. A cluster of women from the village stood by the lych-gate. They had been there to watch the bride arrive and had waited to see her leave. One young woman gave Mrs Hart a posy and curtsied, her face grave.

'Why doesn't she smile?' I said and immediately discovered that none of them smiled. Their unsmiling faces were pale under the dark yews.

Mrs Hart had taken the posy and walked on, leaning on her husband's arm. We followed.

'You won't have heard, ma'am.' It was Mrs Rigg who touched mother's sleeve. Her weatherbeaten face was woeful in its linen sun-bonnet; her deep old voice trembled. 'Agnes Hebworthy is dead.'

Mother clutched my hand.

'Oh Maggie. Our dear Agnes. And the baby?'

'He went first. I've been up there. Effie sent for me for the laying-out.'

'I must talk to you, Mrs Rigg.'

We walked aside and stood by a flat-topped table tomb a little way from the path where the clamour of the bells was less deafening.

'...late on, yesterday. When Effie went upstairs, Agnes was standing at the window holding the baby. "He's dead, my little boy," she says. "Stop the clock, Effie, and turn the

101

glass to the wall. It'll do for me too." She wouldn't let go of him and nothing would drive her back to bed. "Where's Daniel?" she says. "He doesn't care. He's forgotten us. Where is he?" "Get back into bed," Effie says. "You'll catch your death." The nights are cold up there, Mrs Ossian, but she walked up and down the live-long night with the window open. That was how the chill of death came on her. And Daniel never came. He was out all night, not for the first time, it seems.'

'What has come over him? He was a good husband when they were first married. They were happy then.'

'There's been some evil going on. Some woman, Effie says. Nobody knows who – and it's better for her that they don't. There's no place for a scarlet adultress such as her in Asherby. You ask them.' She glanced towards the women at the gate. 'They'll not tolerate it. Unless it's someone from one of the farms over Whingate way…'

'Is Daniel at home now?'

'That I don't know. I was there when he came walking in, early on. I'll never forget his face, Mrs Ossian, when he saw the two of them lying there cold and forgotten. "My God," he says with the tears running and every drop of colour gone from his face. "What have I done?" Yes, he called on his Maker and went down on his knees, I will say that for him.'

'That was a sign of repentance if there was need of it.'

'"You might at least have been with her at the end," Effie says, "however you treated her before that." "Don't torture me," he says in such a tone it turned my blood to water. He went to the window as if he didn't know where to put hisself. "There's been some woman," Effie says to him. "She's driving me out of my mind," he said. Then he shut up, sudden, and flung out of the house with a face as black as a cloud. There's no knowing where he is now. Johnny's gone looking for him. He's always thought a lot of Daniel.'

We left her standing mournfully under the joyful shower of bells.

'I wonder if we could keep this from Cynthia,' mother said. 'She would be so grieved. They'll be leaving in a few hours. I'll speak to the servants.'

'And the others? I could tell Francis.'

'Yes. But no one else until Cynthia has left.'

'I'll go up there myself as soon as this is over,' Francis said when I had told him the news, 'and see what's to be done. But your mother is right. Aunt Cynthia mustn't know – nor Lilian. It will have to be broken to her gently. She loved going up to the Toll House. We can't run the risk of upsetting her, today of all days when she already has to face the parting with Aunt Cynthia. She has taken it all so well, not thinking of herself at all. But a thing like this. You know how sensitive she is...'

Was that a sensitive face? From across the room I studied it, animated now under the blue-lined brim. The lower lip was long and full. The cheeks were well rounded now that she was in health. The bright springing hair redeemed the face from its tendency to hardness though when she smiled, the mouth so wilful in repose was charming enough. How could I look at my friend, my oldest friend, with so cold and critical a detachment? Even at the thought the detachment changed to bitter revulsion.

'You're quiet, Maggie.' Francis found me on the window seat. 'Let me bring you a glass of wine.'

'I don't want anything, thank you.'

'This news has upset you – and no wonder. We used to have happy times at the Toll House.'

I envied him his uncomplicated regret. My grief for the death of gentle Agnes should have been a pure emotion unclouded by the secret knowledge which oppressed me with the guilt of others. The one consolation, if it could be so called, was that the secret had been kept. By her death Agnes had inflicted on Daniel the sharp sting of remorse and brought the affair to an end. Lilian had escaped but other things had also come to an end. The old enchantment had gone from Asherby. Nothing could bring back the untroubled bliss of earlier summers.

'You'll stay on, Maggie? Can you?'

'I don't know.'

The afternoon wore on until it seemed at last that every conceivable good wish had been spoken, every kind word said except for the final farewells. When Mrs Hart came down, quietly radiant in her going-away dress, we could congratulate ourselves that nothing had been allowed to spoil the day for her. Only the family and mother and I were there in the hall to see them off. The guests had dispersed. Some of them had already left the village. The carriage was at the door. The servants were still loading the innumerable packages. There descended upon us the awful realisation that some of us at least might never meet again. Mother dissolved into tears and so did I.

'It's been a wonderful day.' Lilian flung her arms round her mother with all her old exuberance and a new satisfaction, I fancied, at having got her way; and yet in spite of everything my heart grew lighter. She had always the power to inspire me with her zest for life. Even then I longed to believe that it was some other woman Mrs Rigg had spoken of. Lilian could have nothing to do with evil and death.

'You'll be good, Lilian darling – and well –

and happy.'

'Yes, indeed, Mother. I shall be well and happy.'

'Come, Cynthia.'

But before Major Hart led her away, Mrs Hart turned to me though we had already said goodbye.

'Take your happiness when you can, Maggie,' she whispered. 'Don't let it slip away. I almost did. One shouldn't.'

They were gone. We stood tearfully in the drive and waved until the carriage turned into the road – then went back to the hall to find, inevitably, that one package had been left behind: a great bulky bundle stitched up in hessian and oilskin.

'Aunt Cynthia has forgotten her tapestry.'

'Of all things!'

'How can she exist without it?'

'Francis, you must go after them.'

There was no shortage of vehicles. While Francis rushed round to the stable yard, Lilian and I lugged the bundle into the drive and heaved it up behind so that he hardly needed to draw up before clattering out into the road and setting off at a spanking pace in pursuit of the carriage. We followed as far as the church and watched him out of sight.

That was how we came to be alone together, Lilian and I, for the first time for three days. After the bustle it was suddenly quiet. The velvet softness of a late summer afternoon lay upon flowers and leaves and stone and on the limpid water of the stream.

'It's all over,' Lilian said.

Hatless in her white gown, she raised her golden head and seemed to grow taller, unscathed and triumphant. What future was she planning for herself now that she was free? Suppose – I faced the thought incredulously – suppose the affair was not after all at an end. Now that Daniel had no wife... But it was unthinkable. We must go up to her room, I thought, and talk.

We took the short cut back to the house by way of the barn. I went first, lifting my skirt and treading carefully for fear of spoiling my satin slippers in the grass. We had got to the point where the beck flowed out of the culvert when in the belfry tower the bell swung again. But this time it was a single tolling note, followed by another, and a third. There came a pause and then three more solemn strokes.

'Someone has died,' Lilian said. 'A woman.'

'It's Agnes. We didn't tell you and Aunt Cynthia.'

I looked away from her and up into the sky for fear of seeing in her face a look of terrible joy. We stood still. It seemed to me that there was nobody left in the world but our two frozen white-clad figures, no other sound than the melancholy tolling of the bell: one stroke now for each year that

Agnes had lived. Twenty, twenty-one…

Then we saw Johnny Rigg coming along the road from the direction of the Toll House. He was walking doggedly with his head bowed as if he had been on his feet for a long time and had not found what he was looking for. He was in his shirt sleeves. His hair was ruffled. If he saw us, he paid no attention as he left the road and crossed the grass to his own gate. But there he paused, seemed to change his mind and went instead to the barn. At the sight of his face, his hesitation, I felt a sudden darkening sense of disaster. He dragged open the door, unwillingly, I thought, and disappeared inside.

Thirty-three, thirty-four, thirty-five… Unconsciously, I had gone on counting. The last stroke of the bell left a quiet so intense that the sound from the barn seemed loud; and the sound itself was strange, a wordless cry, fearful and frightening. Then Johnny came out and leaned against the edge of the door, feeble and sick.

'What is it?' Lilian called. 'What's the matter?'

He became aware of us. An extraordinary change came over him. He stood up as though his strength had returned and came marching directly towards us across the grass and into the beck ankle-deep. It was strange and frightening to see him trampling furiously through the water as if he didn't see it, as if he saw nothing but Lilian. He came right up to her and seized her hand.

'I'll show you what's the matter,' he said. 'There's something you ought to see.'

There were purple marks on her wrist as she tried to pull it away. She had turned deathly white.

'You're hurting her...'

I might as well have protested to the wind. Back he went, splashing over the stones and dragging Lilian after him, the sky-blue ribbons in the flounces of her dress, the frilled edge of her petticoat all soaked and darkened by the brown water. I watched petrified as they stumbled out on the other side; then I ran down to the stepping stones, darted across and caught them up by the stone seat. The wall of the barn glared like a white rock in the sun; the doorway was startlingly dark.

'No,' Lilian said. Her voice was thin and terrified as if she already felt the advancing shadow. 'No, no.'

Johnny pushed me back as he thrust Lilian inside. All the same I saw in the cool light that flooded the barn – the green coat on the floor: the sagging bales: the taut rope: the noose: and dangling from it, the man.

6

'You'll come back soon, Maggie.' Lilian's voice was thin and sharp. 'Don't leave me for too long.'

'It will be no more than an hour.'

'I can't bear to be left alone.'

I folded the discarded poultice into a towel and brought cologne to bathe her temples. Her hair ribbon must be tied just firmly enough to hold back the short ends of hair but not too tightly. I propped her up with a fourth pillow and opened the sash window three inches at the top and three at the bottom, letting in a sharp whiff of sea air.

'Miss Abbot will sit with you until I come back.' Lilian turned up her nose. A ghost of the old mischievous sauciness haunted her drawn features. 'She'll tell you all about the other boarders. You only need to listen.'

'You'll be meeting your friends the Barn-ards, I suppose.'

The note of envy in her voice made me turn back to smooth the top sheet again and move the glass on her side table an inch or two nearer to the bed. As recently as a week ago I would have stayed with her but the doctor had insisted on my taking regular exercise; and there were times when the confinement of the sick room, the smell of saltpetre and liniments and Lilian's unceasing demands were more than I could endure.

At first her need of me had been flattering. My response to it had changed. There was no doubt that she preferred my company to Miss Abbot's but I had learned that when she begged me not to leave her, it was from dread of solitude. Any companion would do, I told myself sternly, provided she was not left alone.

All the same I couldn't bear to leave her for long. Once free of the house where we had taken first floor apartments, I would walk briskly or even run across the grass to the cliff's edge, exhilarated by the screech of gulls and the sheen and shadow of their wings against a sky of autumnal blue; but it was never long before thoughts of Lilian pricked my mood. Remembering her weakened frame and thin face, I felt guilty.

'You're back, Maggie.' Her eyes would brighten; would promise for an instant a re-blossoming of their cornflower blue; and I would read her all the letters again: from Mr Iredale, Francis and mother, and one from her own mother written on the voyage. Those paragraphs in my own letters from home which would do her no good, I suppressed.

The letters, so different in every other way,

had one theme in common.

'I would never have thought,' mother wrote, 'that Lilian would have missed Cynthia so much, not in quite this way. Naturally, deeply attached as they were, one might have expected some revival of the old trouble but not such a complete collapse as this…'

'You must not grieve for Aunt Cynthia, my dearest Lilian,' Francis wrote. 'Remember how happy she is and how happy you will be once your health is restored. Let's plan some alterations to the house. You always wanted to furnish a sitting room to your own taste. I'll have some catalogues sent down from Harrods. Meanwhile we cannot be sufficiently thankful that you have Maggie with you. Where could you find a better nurse or a more devoted friend?'

These last words may have comforted Lilian. To me they had a staid, middle-aged sound, infinitely dreary.

'Are they doing everything possible to make you comfortable, my love?' In his ferocity Mr Iredale had scored the paper with his steel-nibbed pen. His old-fashioned copper-plate shook with anger and anxiety. 'I have told Miss Abbot and Maggie Ossian to see that you have all you need. No effort is to be spared, or expense. The sooner you are back in Dr Slater's hands the better I shall be pleased. It was wrong of your mother… I never wanted it…'

His sentences were not always complete. An occasional incoherence made me wonder if the old gentleman was failing.

'Yes,' Miss Abbot said, having heard such extracts from the letters as had penetrated her deafness while she pottered about the sick room, 'the distress of being parted from her mother has been too much for Lilian. She bore up so well until the wedding was over. Then, you know, Maggie,' Miss Abbot lowered her voice to impart so striking a discovery, 'there was that very unpleasant affair of the man Hebworthy. To think that Lilian actually saw him – dead! I believe that may have been the last straw when her feelings were already overwrought. It was enough to upset anyone.'

I could agree with deep sincerity. No one knew better than I how upsetting it had been. The last glimpse of Daniel Hebworthy had been of a kind to shatter not only Lilian's health and sanity but my own peace of mind – and for a long time to come.

This morning the seat on the cliff path was empty. The Barnards had not yet arrived. I watched the long waves break on the chalk cliffs, changeless in their disregard of human concerns. Alone with the gulls on this high point I could review the events of Mrs Hart's wedding day as if they had withdrawn into the middle distance like the sailing vessel now moving across the boundless blue;

though my mind was still inclined to slide away from the memory of Daniel Hebworthy, just as I did in fact turn away from him, my hands clapped over my eyes, and cower silently by the door of the barn; so that I didn't actually see Lilian, nor her face. But I was aware of her white figure arrested in a total suspension of life. Then the shuddering began. It shook her from head to foot. I heard the flailing sound her feet made on the straw-strewn floor as if the paroxysms actually lifted and set her down again. Then she came stumbling out into the daylight, bending forward like an old woman.

Johnny closed the door.

'You'd better go home,' he said grimly. 'I'll fetch the constable.'

But instead he turned his back, knelt down and was violently sick.

For my part it was not until later that I felt the full horror of it, by which time the reality had been garishly touched up and made still more frightful by imagination. Even if I had not known Lilian's predicament; even if Daniel had meant no more to her than he did to me, my instinct would have been to help her, to take her hand and lead her away. I was so well used to looking after her, so thoroughly drilled in the family habit learned from Francis and the rest, of putting Lilian first, and now there was special need. I guessed how she suffered. Again and again I had thought her guilty only to feel ashamed of my suspicions. Now my doubts were ended. With scarcely a word, with another of his devastating acts of retribution, Johnny had made it quite clear. He knew everything. Why else should he decide that Lilian before all must see the end of Daniel Hebworthy unless he knew that she had, in a manner of speaking, established a claim to be his chief mourner? How long had he known?

I put my arm round her and felt her lean on me with her full weight.

'How could Johnny be so cruel?' I said. 'It was a cruel thing to do.'

She still could not speak. Caught up as I was in my now certain knowledge of her guilt, I forgot that she too had made a startling discovery; that she had suffered not only from the sudden sight of her lover dangling hideously from the rope but also from the knowledge that Johnny knew her secret and might betray it. Astonishingly, when every other faculty ceased to function, her instinct for self preservation survived and proved stronger than grief.

'Don't tell Francis,' her teeth chattered so that I could just make out the words, 'that Johnny Rigg made me look.' She moistened her colourless lips. 'I don't want Francis to know how much he hates me. He always has. I mean, he must hate me' – her voice rose hysterically – 'he must hate me to drag me there and show me – that.'

'Could he have had some other reason, I wonder?'

Reason plainly had no part in the affair but perhaps she would confide in me. Perhaps I ought to make her tell me. What in such circumstances did people do? But there never had been circumstances quite of this sort.

'He always hated me, always. What has such a thing to do with me? I can't help it. It isn't my fault.' Even in the growing hysteria, cunning persisted. 'Don't tell Francis about Johnny Rigg. He'll think – Francis will think we found it by accident. I mean – we could easily – just have gone in – and seen.'

She broke into a passion of weeping.

'I won't tell Francis. Come, we'll go home.'

My own response to Johnny's behaviour was so far from reasonable that it verged on the superstitious. Once again I saw him as both judge and avenger. His treatment of Lilian was a purgation she had been forced to undergo – and justly. After all was she not responsible, even if indirectly and unintentionally, for the deaths of all three Hebworthys? Mrs Rigg's dark hints as to what would happen to the evil woman who had bewitched Daniel, if her identity should ever be known, convinced me that the whole incident must be hushed up, wiped out and forgotten.

If only Johnny Rigg held his tongue. I looked round. He had vanished.

I wondered unhappily if it would be wise to go after him at once and appeal to him to have mercy. But to speak of it would serve to resurrect the horrible affair and make it still more inescapable. Besides, old loyalties – and snobberies – die hard. I shrank from discussing Lilian's indiscretions with such as Johnny Rigg and so wavered and did nothing. As for Johnny, he kept away. When he interfered no more, my hopes rose. It would have been heartening to think that he kept quiet out of chivalry or compassion. Only gradually did it dawn on me how peculiarly active his silence was. It must have kept Lilian in constant terror lest he should speak. Her good name was in his keeping. How very uncomfortable that must be!

I have never known what her feelings for Daniel actually were. Did she really love him, a common man of uncultivated tastes and habits? How was it possible? I could not understand an emotion so insistent that it made one scheme and cheat and forget all pride and decency. Love, now that I thought of it, seemed to me a gentle lasting thing. It sustained the spirit and filled one's life with an inexhaustible awareness of the other person; just as every wave breaking quietly into foam down there on the sand might say, 'Francis … Francis…'

Lilian, I think, was incapable of loving in such a way. She had probably felt for Daniel a passion as near to love as she could ever reach. Certainly she never loved again. The sight of his tortured unseeing eyes, the obscenity of his contorted lips and mouth must have stunned her capacity for love – for ever – and desecrated every memory of it.

It was not so much because I understood and sympathised that I stayed on at Asherby when Mother left as because it was impossible to leave Lilian. For several days she existed in a state of shock and could not sleep or eat. When eventually her frozen state had melted into constant restlessness and so progressed to choking and wheezing, we knew that she would be ill: very ill. For some weeks her condition was serious. The repeated attacks took a fearful toll on her strength, and Dr Slater admitted at last that her heart was affected. There had always been the possibility. It was assumed that the excitement of the wedding and the absence of her mother had been too much for her highly strung nerves; and the Hebworthy incident – Mr Iredale could not contain his wrath at the man's presumption in having chosen that particular place to make away with himself – had been the last straw.

Meanwhile, a wave of sympathy for Agnes and her baby brought a crowd of local people from farms and hamlets as well as from Asherby itself to her funeral. Daniel's fate was more bizarre. A jury was hastily convened, an inquest held in a room at the village inn and a verdict of suicide returned. In those days the barbarous practices associated with suicide had mercifully died out though coroners were still empowered to direct that the corpse should be buried on a public highway. It was not until some years later that this became illegal. However, Coroner Grayson was humane enough to order burial in the churchyard though it would be unsanctified by the rites of the Church.

Things turned out differently. When Mr Ogshaw went to the back room of the Fleece to nail down the coffin, the trestle table was bare, the body gone. Enquiries were set on foot but they proved fruitless and were probably half-hearted. There hung about the whole affair an unnatural silence. Asherby had been minding its own business for a long time, since long before the foundations of the Norman church were laid, as the burial mounds on the moor could testify. Remote from highways, unknown to railways, shut away in their wooded valley, the folk of Asherby had learned to take charge of their own affairs.

Being fully occupied indoors at the time, I knew nothing beyond the bare facts. But if there was little to know, there was much to feel. The Hebworthy tragedy was in the true meaning of the word a sensation. One sensed the shock of it in the air itself. Without setting foot in the village I was aware of the surge of outrage. It reached me through servants' gossip and the talk of women at their doors, particularly Mrs Ogshaw, the carpenter's wife, who had a reputation for plain speaking and an unpleasantly loud voice. The mood of the village was one of anger towards the woman who had seduced Daniel Hebworthy and broken his wife's heart. Daniel – such a handsome man – was forgiven. His death redeemed him. She, the unknown woman, had been the evil-doer. On every doorstep and at every hearth she was invested with every kind of iniquity. The complete mystery surrounding her identity robbed her of all humanity. As the legend grew, she became diabolical. Every dog in the village would be let loose if she so much as set foot in the place.

It so happened that the Ogshaws' dog was a particularly evil-tempered bull terrier to be avoided even in the happiest circumstances. It became for me a constant menace, a kind of embodiment of the danger threatening Lilian. My secret knowledge weighed on me as if the burden of guilt were mine. I grew almost afraid to open my lips for fear of betraying Lilian.

Not until long afterwards did I realise the

damaging effect on my own nerves of that final glimpse of Daniel Hebworthy. Small wonder that it distorted my view of events both before and after.

One afternoon I went out to post a letter and was tempted into walking a little further than the pillar-box. Needless to say Mrs Rigg caught sight of me and coming to her gate, begged me to step inside. To tell the truth I had been avoiding the Riggs and was on the point of refusing when she said: 'I feel so doleful, Miss Maggie. The sight of a fresh face'll do me a bit of good.'

She ushered me into the living room. A folded blanket, a pile of clean under-garments, a half-filled kitbag – explained her low spirits.

'Johnny is going away?'

'Directly. He's upstairs now, putting on his things.'

It was such a relief that I felt ashamed and exerted myself to comfort her. Presently he came down. I had not seen him since the day of the wedding. Our meeting might have been awkward especially as his behaviour then was uppermost in my mind. But it was clearly not the time to speak of delicate matters. Johnny's thoughts were concen-trated on preparations for leaving. With his usual ruthless efficiency he had probably put the unpleasant business from his mind.

'You've found a ship?'

'The *Emma Gray*,' he told me. He had been to the nearest port two weeks ago to sign articles at the agent's office without seeing the ship herself. She was a screw-steamer refitting at Newcastle after a battering on her homeward voyage. The *Emma Gray* was no longer in her first youth, it seemed. She would sail as soon as possible with a cargo of coal for Malaga. Meanwhile Johnny was to join her at once to work on repairs. I could only pray that she was not one of the rotten old vessels Mr Plimsoll had denounced, sold cheap to greedy speculators and patched up when they should have been scrapped. But my confidence in Johnny's ability to look after himself was as boundless as his own.

I listened wide-eyed while he gave me a colourful account of some other ship he had seen limping into port. She had been damaged when pirates boarded her as she lay becalmed off the African coast with a cargo of cotton seed. The master and crew had given a good account of themselves and sent the barbarians about their business but naturally things had been knocked about a good deal…

'Pirates in 1873! It's like a story. I do think you're brave, Johnny.'

'Come, Miss Maggie, it doesn't need much courage to talk about other people's adventures.'

'But to chose a life with so many risks. It

will just suit you, won't it?'

My admiration was perfectly sincere but I had spoken lightly. To my surprise the compliment roused no answering smile. Johnny put the last of his things into the kitbag and drew up the strings with a gravity which made me wonder if I had offended him.

But presently he said, quite without his usual swashbuckling manner: 'I used to think I was a brave sort of fellow and in the heat of the moment with my blood up I could enjoy a fight as much as any man. But that isn't courage. It's no more than instinct – like an animal.' He had rolled up the blanket and was securing it with a strap. 'Steeling your nerves to act in cold blood, to do what you don't want to do because you think the thing is right – I'm not good at that.'

'There can't be many people who are.'

'Francis is.'

The terse reply came promptly as if from the forefront of his mind. It surprised me. The notion that Francis might have to 'steel' himself to do what was right suggested a resistance to it that I would not have expected. I wondered if the two of them had been involved in some recent test of courage and longed to ask.

But Johnny seemed to regret having given such a very particular example for he went on briskly: 'Well, Miss Maggie, it'll likely be a long while before we meet again.'

'By that time you'll have achieved one of your ambitions.'

'The beard?' He stroked his chin in anticipation. 'Yes. The other may take longer.'

I wished him well in both enterprises and took my leave. How was it that every time I saw Johnny he impressed me with – was it his wisdom? We had mocked the shrewdness he had shown as a boy and dismissed it as cocksure and boastful; but it had developed into a quality more profound. I respected his judgment because it was always based on a lively awareness of what was going on. Inevitably I thought of Lilian. With a shiver, I thought how helpless she would be if he should ever think it right to speak.

'Johnny has gone away,' I lost no time in telling her – with a casualness I did not feel. She made no sign but as I bathed her hands and face, 'How long?' she asked feebly.

'Six months, I believe – or more.' She closed her eyes and presently slept – more soundly than she had done for a long time.

There had been times during those anxious and difficult weeks when Francis had puzzled me. Not that his kindness ever wavered. He alone understood that I too was under strain.

'It was a terrible business your finding Hebworthy, you and Lilian. You've been splendid, Maggie. You haven't let it upset you. You're stronger than Lilian.'

'Not so sensitive, you mean.' I spoke

quickly to forestall the usual remark. He may have detected the resentment I could not repress.

'I didn't mean that. I meant that your character is stronger. There, you're surprised but it's true.'

'But Lilian is so...'

'Forceful, yes. But that isn't a sign of strength. She can't manage without help. You can. I'm deeply grateful to you, Maggie, for staying to help us out like this. No one else could have taken charge as you have done. You know us all so well.'

I knew him well enough to understand that where help was most needed he would supply it, and I found no comfort in the knowledge. He and Lilian grew closer than ever. The peculiar nature of their relationship intensified; she wilful, ailing, demanding; he sympathetic, dutiful, protective. He had known her so long: it astonished me that he should so often misinterpret her character. I did not know then how especially liable to error good people can be: how they bestow their own virtues on others as Francis endowed Lilian, for instance, with his own delicacy of feeling.

'If only I'd been there,' he said, reverting to the incident of the barn, 'I might have helped you both through such an ordeal.'

'Yes, it certainly would have made a difference.' With my mind on the difference it would have made if Francis had been there to see Johnny hauling Lilian through the beck and thrusting her into the barn, I spoke too emphatically and went on quickly, 'Especially as you had to bring the tapestry back after all.'

'That was a wild goose chase. There wasn't a hope of catching up with them.'

He had taken the opportunity of calling at the Toll House to offer condolences and help and had stayed talking to Effie. He told me no details. During those first days he was unusually quiet and withdrawn and occasionally absent on unexplained business. One morning I went into the kitchen and heard one of the maids grumbling over a pair of his long boots.

'Every morning this week,' she was saying as she scraped off the wet clay, 'he's put them out like this. And he wasn't home till nearly cock-crow.'

It was unlike Francis to stay out late. I concluded that he too was finding it difficult to sleep.

That was the first rumble of discontent to reach me from the servants' quarters. Mrs Hart's departure had unsettled them though I went in each morning to give orders and took charge of the sick room. Fortunately I was not needed at home. Nevertheless my parents disliked the situation.

'Your father insists that the Iredales

should engaged a nurse,' mother wrote. 'I have told him how difficult it would be to find a suitable person who would be willing to stay in Asherby; and servants always dislike having a nurse in the house. Still I shall make enquiries...'

A few days later I found Bella waiting for me in the hall. Her solemn face gave me some inkling of what was to come. Sure enough she wished to give notice.

'Oh Bella! At such a time! But why? Are you not happy here? You've been at Sacristy House for years.'

To my surprise her eyes filled with tears. I had always taken her wooden composure for granted.

'I never thought of leaving until Mrs Belfleur went away. Mrs Hart, I mean. It's different without her. I can't get used to it. She was always considerate – no temper or tantrums. Not like some.' She looked significantly towards the stairs.

I begged her to think it over. But a day or two later cook announced that she was tired to death of cooking for an invalid; it was as much as she could do to satisfy Mr Iredale never mind Miss Belfleur whom there was no satisfying and never had been. The gruel pan was never off the hob; the kitchen was cluttered with infusions of this and that; all those cordials and tisanes. She was a cook, not an apothecary.

Finally the kitchen-maid, a girl from one of the poorer farms, packed her things and went home, declaring that she daren't go past that barn at night or even in daylight when there was nobody about.

She was soon replaced by Hetty, a rather slow-witted girl from the village. The others hovered on the brink of departure.

'Talk to them, Maggie,' Francis urged.

I went to the kitchen and pointed out the predicament they would place the family in if they left, and they promised to stay a little longer.

'So long as you're here, miss, to take charge,' Bella said.

'But Miss Belfleur is another matter,' cook added.

Towards the end of September Dr Slater suggested that Lilian should have a complete change of air. He thought the mild climate of the Isle of Wight might suit her condition.

'I'll go,' she said when the plan was put to her, 'if Maggie comes too.'

My parents approved on the understanding that I would return home by the end of October whether Lilian stayed or not. Miss Abbot was pleased to come with us as chaperon.

On the day we left, Francis carried Lilian out to the carriage though I believe she could have walked.

'You'll come and fetch me, Francis?' Her long fingers entwined his and held them tightly. He disengaged them gently.

'Whenever you say. You must think of nothing but getting well. I think, Maggie' – as I installed myself at her side – 'if you let Lilian sit there, she would be more comfortable out of the sun.'

I got out and walked round to the other side; and turned my head away as we drove off, not wanting to see the look of tender concern he directed towards Lilian. For the first time in my life I was willing to leave him...

The barque I had been watching had dwindled to a black spot in the wide sea – was gone out of sight. Perhaps that was why I felt sad. A departing ship is always sad to see.

'Miss Ossian.'

The Barnards were coming along the path: Mrs Barnard in her wheelchair pushed by a man-servant: young Mr Barnard walking quickly ahead of them as he always did. As usual he took off his hat too soon. His strides grew longer than ever.

'You have beaten us this morning, Miss Ossian. We were delayed. A slight mishap. Mother mislaid her spectacles.'

We had first met on this very seat; had spoken of the weather; Mrs Barnard had chanced to see the name on the flyleaf of my book and felt sure I must be the Miss Ossian from Broomwood Place in Martlebury in which case I would know her friend Mrs Blower of Cotsdean. Mrs Blower had often spoken of the Ossians... We became friends. Mrs Barnard had been ill, was well on the way to recovery and impatient to be rid of the wretched chair.

'I shall go on to Ventnor to change my library book,' she said, 'while you young people have a walk. Why don't you take Miss Ossian to look at the old church, James? You're looking tired, my dear. I don't approve of this nursing.' She made the same remarks every day and had done her best to see that I enjoyed such quiet amusements as Bonchurch and Ventnor offered at that time of year. I had visited them in the house they rented on the undercliff and had drunk tea in the sheltered garden amid the palms and myrtles; had gone with them to concerts and musical evenings and been taken to call on their friends.

We took her advice and strolled up the hill to the little church of St Boniface, rose-clad and elm-sheltered and so tiny as to be no bigger than a sitting room. Even so late in the year its churchyard was overgrown with flowers. We stood amid golden rod and redhot pokers, looking down at the sea. After the staleness and stress of the sick room I succumbed to the charm of the place: the fragrance, the colour, the ancient tumbling contours of church and cliff.

Already perhaps I was growing weary of the conflict that was to divide my heart between the pangs and unsatisfied longings of life in my beloved Asherby and the contrasting monotony – as it seemed – of life at home. In Martlebury I pined to be with Francis and Lilian; in Asherby I was happy with neither of them. Here was neutral ground, a spell of pleasurable escape into an impersonal, passionless mood: not alone but with a companion who didn't matter.

'I should like to stay here,' I burst out unguardedly. 'How delightful it would be!'

Mr Barnard's pleasant features flushed. He turned to me with the eagerness which often made him seem no more than a boy though he was several years older than I.

'You feel that too? It gives me great pleasure to think that you enjoy – that you are as happy here – I mean to say, that you enjoy our – Bonchurch, that is, as much – no, not as much as I do. That would be impossible. But to tell you the truth, Miss Ossian, I have very much wanted to say how happy your company has made me. Meeting you was such an extraordinary stroke of luck.'

It was impossible not to like him. His pleasure in my company was whole-hearted, uncomplicated by any over-anxious loyalty to another person. The simplicity of it made

131

me feel safe. With Mr Barnard I could be at ease. He did not belong to my real life. Our acquaintance was already coming to an end. I would be leaving in a few days.

'It was lucky,' I said warmly. 'Mrs Barnard has been so very kind. I should have had a dull time of it if we had not met.'

'You give me courage' – he had taken off his hat and laid it on the wall where we sat. One of his abrupt gestures sent it rolling into the dust at my feet. I picked it up and flicked it with my handkerchief. 'Thank you. I'm a clumsy oaf. When you leave Bonchurch' – he looked suddenly downcast– 'Mother is making a good recovery but it may be some time– Heavens, how tedious it will be! The only thing is' – he brightened – 'when we go back to Stone Barnard – I'm often in Martlebury. Would it be possible, do you think – Would Mr Ossian allow me to call? To enquire...? If you have no objection.'

He beamed in relief at having taken the tremendous step.

'I'm sure father will be pleased. He will want to thank you and Mrs Barnard...'

I handed him his hat and we sauntered back, talking amiably, through lanes hoary with faded flowers of old man's beard, with sudden glimpses of silver where the hedgerows dipped, the murmur of the sea so constant that I did not know how soothing it had been until I could hear it no more.

'Thank goodness, you're back.' Lilian threw down her book. 'I'm dying for some reasonable person to talk to. I simply haven't enough breath to talk to Miss Abbot. One has to shout. How sedate and calm and fresh you look! Come to think of it, you always do. Nothing *ruffles* you, does it Maggie? But then you've no cause to be ruffled. Can you imagine what it's like to be propped up here like a stuffed owl without strength enough to reach out for a glass of agrimony tea?'

'I never saw anyone less like a stuffed owl.' I unpinned my hat and took off my jacket. 'But there are only six more days, Lilian dear, until the end of the month.'

Her lips trembled. Her peevishness melted into real distress. I handed her the glass and sat down on the bed, my heart wrung with pity.

'It's no use. I can't stay here without you. Write to Francis – at once – now – and tell him to fetch me home.'

'But the air. Dr Slater said…'

'What air? Steam kettles and that awful stuff you burn! I might as well be a smoked herring for all the sea air I breathe. In any case what use is air if I die of loneliness? It's different for you. You've had a very pleasant holiday with your Barnards and your music and walks. Think of me for a change.'

'You're getting better. You couldn't have

harangued me like that a fortnight ago.'

'Do it now. Write to Francis this moment and go out and post it – or send somebody. You must.'

It was not her overbearing manner that influenced me, though that had increased unreasonably almost insanely, I sometimes felt, in proportion to her helplessness, so much as Miss Abbot's attitude.

'You'd better do it,' she said when I sought her advice. 'I shan't be able to manage her on my own. There will be difficulties as it is at Sacristy House even if Bella and cook stay on. The only hope is that dear Lilian will make a sudden recovery. You know that has usually happened. But her illnesses have never lasted as long as this and now that her heart is affected, I feel the responsibility, Maggie. Really I do.'

Instead of replying to my letter Francis came at once and took charge of all the arrangements for the journey.

'You did right to send for me,' he said. 'It would do her no good to be left here on her own and in such a state of agitation. It's a pity to take her away before the change of air has had time to take effect. But since you can't stay longer...'

'Father did say...'

'Oh, I'm not reproaching you. We've trespassed on your generosity too long as it is. Now, I should like us to leave the day

134

after tomorrow. Grandfather has not been well. He mustn't be left too long. It'll do him good to have Lilian home again.'

The packing occupied me for the whole of the next day. I had dealt quickly with my own possessions and was considering how most strategically to deal with all the paraphernalia of the sick room: herbal pillows, bed-rests, bottles, dressings for poultices – when Mr Barnard called. I found him standing at attention amid all the plants and ornaments of the little sitting room as if aware of his faculty for displacing them.

'Mother thanks you for your note.' Relaxing a little, he gingerly laid his stick against a side table crowded with china souvenirs. 'It was a blow, naturally. Two days earlier than I – than we both expected.'

I laughed at his seriousness.

'It could scarcely be a *blow*, I think.'

'Indeed, yes. I had hoped – Mother will be sorry not to see you before you leave. But' – he grew cheerful – 'she will write to you. And now, if I can be of any help.'

There was nothing left to be done except to return two or three books and convey my regrets to the few acquaintances we had in common. He was too considerate to keep me from my packing. I rescued a Coalport replica of Osborne House just in time as he grasped his stick. At the front door we met Francis returning from the livery stable.

There was time for no more than a brief exchange of conventional remarks.

'I'm glad to have met your friend,' Francis said when Mr Barnard had made a rather ungainly departure sideways down the steps, looking back all the time. 'He seems a very good fellow.' He looked down at me as affectionately as ever. Had it always been the remote kindliness of a benevolent uncle? It seemed now to set me at a distance more impossible to bridge than any rift that coldness could have created between us. 'Lilian told me he had been attentive and that you've had a happy time of it here in Bonchurch. Stone Barnard is a beautiful old place in a very pleasant little park. I drove past it once on the way to Cotsdean. Your time here hasn't been wasted, my little Maggie.'

At least he did not feel obliged to pat me on the head.

As I had left some of my things at Jasmine Lodge, it seemed sensible to travel back to Asherby and stay there overnight although this would involve me in an extra journey from there to Martlebury. Half unconsciously, I had come to a decision and was young enough to want to dramatise it a little. For a variety of reasons – and for one sad secret reason above all – my days at Asherby had come to an end. I must leave, taking with me every trace of the happy times I had spent there: my sewing things, my album of pressed flowers, my collection of quartz and feathers, my sketch book. Nothing of Maggie Ossian would remain.

Little Maggie! Tears of self-pity had obligingly welled. The memory of that infuriating diminutive banished them.

7

Jasmine Lodge,
3rd November, 1873

Dearest Mother,
By this time you will have received my hasty letter. I was obliged to be brief as the postman was waiting. You and Father will be displeased, I know, until you learn the circumstances which have made it necessary for me to stay a little longer.

Imagine our feelings when we arrived after a long and tiring journey to find that Bella and cook had gone. Would you ever have thought they would behave in such a way? To leave like that with an invalid expected and an old man no better than an invalid, was not that unkind?

Mr Iredale was sitting all alone in the parlour. He had had no luncheon or tea and seemed thoroughly confused. He could not remember where we had all been and was angry with Francis and me (especially me, I recalled) for having taken Lilian away. Miss Abbot at once sent Ada to lend a hand. So far she and I have prepared the meals but I fear this cannot last. Ada dislikes being taken from her own work and Miss Abbot is afraid of losing her.

I promised Francis that I would stay until he had time to advertise and I do hope you and Father approve. Of course I spend my evenings here as you bade me and take all my meals here; but I go to Sacristy House first thing in the morning and I am busy there most of the day. Lilian is not yet able to stay up all day and Mr Iredale has changed a good deal. He has grown shrunken and feeble and wears himself out by always being angry. It is all so different now...

At this point my letter came temporarily to a halt. A lamp must be lit for Mr Iredale. He could not be left to sit in the dark. I tried to think when Lilian had last taken a dose of her medicine and remembered in dismay that I had not put out the little phial of stimulant for the heart which should always be on her table in case of emergencies. So far it had never been used. Suppose this should be the one time it was needed? She was still too weak to move about the room unaided.

Or so I thought. But when I scurried across to Sacristy House and up the stairs to her room she was standing at the window looking out into the early twilight.

'Do you know' – she did not turn her head – 'I think I'll have my bed taken downstairs. I've taken a dislike to this room, not to mention the misery of being shut up here all day with no one to talk to – and all night too.'

I went to her side and looked out. The air was thick. The trees in the dense little wood had not yet lost all their leaves, but through their thinning foliage could be seen the dark outline of the church and above it the belfry tower.

'I have such a feeling sometimes that the whole thing is moving this way.'

'How horrid!'

The church was unusually large for so small a place, a legacy no doubt of the long-vanished priory. From its wooded knoll it dominated the village. I saw how over-powering it might be to an invalid troubled with sick fancies; how easy it would be to be depressed by the tilted headstones and humble mounds at its feet and to feel their mute warning – or reproach.

'I could have the morning room as a bed-room. Grandfather could come and talk to me. I'll go mad, I tell you, if you keep me here.'

She had a wild distressed look. She was

139

alarmingly thin. Her white wrap hung in loose folds from her shoulders. Her jaw was fleshless. Something must be done – and quickly – if she was not to fall into a decline. But the domestic problems weighed so heavily on my mind that the minor upheaval of turning the morning room into a bedroom seemed too much to undertake.

'If only we had Bella and cook!'

'Why should you want them? They've behaved disgracefully. The selfishness of such creatures is beyond belief. Mother was far too good to them. They aren't capable of gratitude or loyalty. They don't care if I die.'

'I only meant,' I said when the tirade was ended, 'that without them it's difficult to fit everything in. Oh, how I hope there will be an answer to the advertisement in the *Courier!*'

She watched indifferently while I unpacked the phial from a travelling case and set it with the glass on her table – then made up the fire and settled her in a chair to await her dinner.

'Bring me a newspaper or a book, will you, before you become immersed in your little duties? Surely Francis should be home. You'll send him up to me at once? I want to tell him about my plan.'

'It's only for a while,' I told myself as I lit Mr Iredale's lamp and mended his fire. 'A very short while. And there simply isn't anyone else.'

From the kitchen I heard Francis already unharnessing the cob. He came in by the back door and went directly into the hall.

'Lilian!' His voice was carefully pitched between eager greeting and caution lest she should be disturbed. 'Are you awake?'

'Francis!' She had come out of her room and was leaning on the banisters. 'Look! I'm dressed. Come up quickly. I want to talk to you.'

I heard him go up two stairs at a time and their voices, absorbed, interested, intimate, as I carved slices from a leg of mutton. Then I put plates to warm, counted out knives and forks, measured blackcurrant cordial for Lilian...

'Where are you, Maggie?' Francis looked round the door. 'Lilian has told you of her idea? It's a capital notion. Let's make the change tomorrow – Saturday – while I'm at home.'

'We shall need help.'

'I'll find someone.'

'Were there any replies to the advertisement?'

'Yes, two. I forgot.' He came and laid them on the table then rushed upstairs.

They were the first of a series of applicants for the posts of cook and housemaid in 'a small country establishment of one lady and two gentlemen'. We could not be too particular. Almost any female possessed of two hands and feet would do. All the same there were limits, as Miss Abbot pointed out, to what one could tolerate. A drunken cook was one of them. She was soon sent packing. The next was a skilled cook but she was sickly, poor woman, and did not rise until late. Meals were hopelessly unpunctual. Sometimes she lacked strength to knead the dough and it was painful to see her yellow face glistening with moisture as she bent over the stove. Eventually she was forced to stir her sauces sitting down with her hand held to her forehead. We could not turn her away but the prospect of a third invalid in so ill-served a household could not be faced. After much difficulty Francis succeeded in having her admitted to a home for destitute working women in Whingate.

We became cautious and thereafter took on only women of robust health. One bright-looking housemaid vanished after a few days taking with her several pieces of jewellery and a silver tea urn. Since it was far from easy to leave Asherby in haste especially so encumbered, we concluded that she had been a professional thief with accomplices. Indeed Granny Rigg had been wakened by horses' hoofs at dead of night and had got up joyfully in the mistaken belief that Johnny had come home.

We were left with only Hetty and daily help

from Mrs Suller who came from the far side of Groat's Gate. By this time I had been away from home for five months. Mother found some consolation for my absence in the dubious state of Martlebury's drains and in persuading herself that, however indirectly, we were being of help to her dear Cynthia, 'though I very much dislike your being made use of in this way'. Father's messages, delivered at second hand, were more peremptory. Even so, I believe she toned them down.

Except that rising grew more painful as the mornings turned colder, ice formed on the water in my ewer and the path to Sacristy House was often white with rime, I scarcely noticed the passage of time. Occasionally I looked about me and found that Asherby had become unrecognisable. I had not known it in winter; had not suspected that bitter winds could strip it of every scrap of sheltering foliage and turn the sloping street into an icy tunnel. No wonder people stayed indoors. Unfortunately they included Mrs Suller, who refused point-blank to come all the way from Groat's Gate more than twice a week, and who could blame her?

Meanwhile with a good deal of trouble we had transferred Lilian to the morning room. With fresh curtains and her own pictures and books it became a cheerful apartment and brought her once more into the centre of family life. And yet for all our efforts she did not improve. It was not hard to guess what it was that gnawed at her spirit; but at least, I reflected, standing at her window one dark day in December, at least the church was out of sight and the churchyard with its tumbled memorials. From here could be seen no outward reminder of Agnes Hebworthy's broken heart. But was a reminder necessary to one who had played her part in breaking it?

Lilian sat fidgeting in her chair by the fire. Her expression was dark, the outward sign surely of inward gloom. Without the vivacity which had been her greatest charm she had become – pathetic. I acknowledged it unwillingly; acknowledged too the reason for my reluctance. It was her pathos that drew Francis to her more tenderly than ever. He could not resist it; and why should he resist it? She had done wrong, was sorry for it, had suffered. It was only right that she should be made happy again.

So I argued and knew all the time that there was something lacking from my analysis of the situation. It did not lend itself to so cosy a solution. Some element of doubt, some misgiving, made me seek safety in speech.

'You're so quiet, Lilian. How you used to talk? Do you remember?'

'There's nothing to talk about now.'

'Now? You mean, since you've been ill?'

She looked at me quickly as if I had touched lightly upon a hidden dread. 'Yes, of course that's what I mean. There's nothing to see, nowhere to go except across the passage to the parlour. Isn't it strange? I used to think this house was big. When we played hide and seek there were so many places to choose. Now it's grown so small that it smothers me, like a coffin.'

'It will be better in the spring.' Her last words had shaken me a little. I cast about to find another topic – and as things fell out – found one.

'By the way there is something to see. Whatever is amiss with Granny Rigg?' Without my consciously noticing it as we talked, a flutter of white outside had come and gone, come and gone. Now I laid my head against the left side of the window frame and could just command a sufficient view to the right to see the old woman on her garden path. 'Come and see.'

'It's too cold over there. What is she doing?'

'She's been out on the road and now she's going in again.'

'There's nothing remarkable about that, is there?'

'No, except that she's just in her dress and apron, no shawl – and there she goes again.'

Unremarkable as it should have been to see Mrs Rigg walk down her garden path to the road and up again, it became all at once disturbing. I could not see her face, only her stocky figure in its blue gown and white apron as she trotted back and forth, back and forth with a crazy persistence, as if she had lost her bearings and was trying hopelessly to find them.

'There's something wrong. Goodness me, there's Miss Abbot. She's just come out of Well Cottage in her bonnet and cape.'

Heedless of the cold air, I threw up the window and leaned out to see her bustle up the path, take Mrs Rigg by the arm and try to lead her indoors – in vain. Mrs Rigg simply turned and trotted out into the road again, looked along the valley and came back.

'I must go and help. She shouldn't be out there in the cold.' But before I could close the window, Miss Abbot had seen me and come quickly through the cottage gate and across the wet grass.

'Oh Maggie! Such sad, sad news.'

For Mrs Rigg there could be only one kind of sad news. I knew what it must be, knew what it meant to her and with a great upsurge of sorrow, shared her desolation.

'Johnny?'

'His ship. The *Emma Gray*. She has had a letter from the owners. The postman told me. He had to read it to her. The ship is lost. It foundered somewhere near Gibraltar.

146

There are no survivors, not one. She won't believe it. I'm afraid it has turned her wits. Oh dear, there she goes again, looking for him.'

She hurried back, took Mrs Rigg by the hand and coaxed her step by step into the cottage. I closed the window, feeling stricken to the heart.

'What is it?'

'Johnny. He's gone. His ship is lost.'

I burst into tears. Mingled with grief for an old and dear friend was disbelief that all his bright awareness, all his cleverness and confidence should have been cut off so soon and brought to nothing. His end, if it had to come, should have been touched with some nobility. To founder in a rotting ship was not good enough for Johnny – or indeed for any man.

'Poor, poor Mrs Rigg. He wanted to grow a beard – and get rich. There were so many things he could have done and now he'll never...'

Recovering a little, I was aware of a silence in the room and reproached myself for having blurted out the news. I should have known better. Instinctively I glanced at the table to make sure the phial of stimulant was there.

It was not to be needed.

'Is it not a terrible thing?' I propelled the remark towards the centre of the silence.

'Terrible. Too terrible to speak of.'

She was lying back in her chair. I caught a flash of blue before she closed her eyes and kept them closed, to conceal their expression perhaps: their lack of sorrow, their relief, their triumph, I thought, with a sudden burst of bitterness. Her attitude was more relaxed than it had been for months. She was at peace: safe.

Once again I had been misled. Once again I had underestimated her monstrous selfishness. It was not remorse that had laid her low, nor sorrow for her lost love. It was the nagging fear at being found out. Miraculously she had escaped, her reputation unstained. She was free to begin life again as if nothing had happened. Even Daniel Hebworthy's body had been removed as if some supernatural agency had been bent on wiping out all trace of the affair. And now the secret was safe, sunk fathoms deep with Johnny.

A memory came to me of the barque I had seen at Bonchurch as it crept across the wide sea and vanished from sight, and with the memory an awed sense of the mystery of things: of Fate's capricious power to destroy Johnny and by his destruction release Lilian.

It wasn't fair. The wrong people suffered; always other people; never Lilian. I turned my back on her, burning with resentment. It wasn't fair.

8

It must have been a week or two later that we sat in the parlour of Sacristy House, Mr Iredale, Lilian and I. For the past few days Francis had been kept in Whingate by heavy rains which made the roads impassable but that afternoon the carrier had been able to reach Asherby at last and had brought a message that he would be home by evening.

'I might have known that we'd never see the end of that tedious tapestry.'

Lilian had been turning over the pages of a recent copy of *The Gentlewoman at Home*. She spoke quietly. We were neither of us anxious to wake Mr Iredale who, as Lilian said, was better company when, as now, he was asleep. I had particular reason to dread rousing him. His dislike of me had grown no less and in his often confused state of mind he no longer bothered to hide it.

It had been an act of desperation on my part to unwrap the tapestry.

'How could I have left it?' Mrs Hart had written. 'We must find someone to bring it out. Meanwhile if one of you would like to go on with it...' There followed a paragraph of careful instructions and warnings. The

149

bulky package had stood about until it became absolutely necessary either to unpack it or stow it permanently away. I was short of needlework, not having provided myself with sufficient occupation for a whole winter; and had at last cut open the oilskin wrapping and found a new panel all ready for stitching.

'It's like old times,' Lilian said as I seated myself in her mother's chair and laid out the tray of wools in the old way. She spoke with the touch of mockery which was all the humour she knew. Now that it had lost its lightness of heart it jarred on me. I could neither respond in the same way nor agree. It seemed to me that there had been a good many changes since Mrs Belfleur sat where I was sitting now.

'It's no use planning to refurnish this room.' Lilian flicked rapidly through the remaining pages. 'One could never make it elegant. We need more space and a better aspect.' But she bit her lip thoughtfully as if she had some plan in mind. It was as Francis said a sign of improvement in her spirits that she should think of the future again; but my view of the improvement in Lilian's spirits was less innocently glad than his. Yes, since hearing the news about Johnny, she had certainly revived.

Francis had gone to Newcastle to make enquiries about the *Emma Gray* and very unsatisfactory they had been. From the agent he had learned no details of the wreck but gossip at the quayside had not spared the owners. The ship had been insured for almost £800 – twice the sum paid for her when she had last changed hands – so that the owners made a handsome profit from the disaster which left destitute the wives and children – and at least one grandmother – of the drowned men. Father had written directly to Mr Plimsoll who was still fighting to have the Merchant Shipping Act amended. Meanwhile the Board of Trade would hold an enquiry into the loss of the *Emma Gray*. It would be of little help to Mrs Rigg, who was so withered and shaken by grief that she had shrunk into a mechanical creature of one idea, for ever trotting in and out of her cottage like the old woman in a weather house.

Not without some impatience at its triviality, I gave my attention to the new panel. It would depict a knight riding away from a castle, followed by two men-at-arms. In Mrs Belfleur's serene hands the work had always looked so simple. Why, in all those hours I had watched, had I not watched more intelligently? I threaded my needle and hesitated anxiously over the horse but even then gave less attention than was needed to its practical difficulties. Instead, half enviously, I identified myself with its rider. He was going away.

A longing for spring swept over me, an impulse so strong that it brought into the room a memory of fresh turned earth and sap rising. Even in Martlebury spring was delightful. Mario the Italian would come with his barrel organ and solemn monkey and I would lean out of the window above the lilac bush. When Lent ended, there would be dances...

My dream was shortlived. Mr Iredale snorted and woke. I looked up to find his eyes upon me and braced myself for the familiar ordeal. It took a new form.

'Cynthia.' It had been a mistake to sit in Mrs Belfleur's chair by her table with her work in my hands. 'Has she gone, Cynthia? I thought Maggie Ossian was here.'

'There he goes,' Lilian said indifferently. 'That *is* Maggie, grandfather. Mother is in India.'

'Where's Francis?' He swallowed with champing movements as if his mouth was dry – and stared about him. 'I've told Francis. That girl is here too much. I've told him to send her away. She means mischief.'

'Oh really, Lilian. I shall have to go back to the Lodge. I simply can't bear it.'

'He doesn't know what he's saying. Listen, grandfather.' She began to read aloud from her magazine. '"A bronze lamp on an ornamental stand with a ruched shade is an object which few ladies who value elegance

152

and artistry in their homes would choose to be without.'"

'Send for one, my love, if you want it. But don't let Maggie Ossian know. I thought she was here a minute ago.' He felt about in his pockets. 'She's taken my spectacles.'

He would recover himself presently, realise who I was and fall silent, content to glower from eyes less bright under brows less sharply spiked than they had once been.

'You know what she does.' To my dismay his antagonism took a new turn. 'She leads Francis on. I've see it.'

One must not mind an old man's foolishness: a worn old man in frayed slippers and socks rumpled about his thin ankles. But how grateful I was that we were alone: that Francis was not there!

'You shouldn't allow it, Cynthia. It isn't fair to Lilian. Why isn't Francis here? I want to tell him about my will. He mustn't be allowed to do anything foolish. He knows his duty.'

'Yes, grandfather.'

'You must be careful, my love, or she will come between you and Francis. That's what she will do.'

'Nothing can come between me and Francis, grandfather.'

I unthreaded my needle and put it back in the case. No one – I told myself and in some obscure way told mother – no one could be expected to go on listening to such things. But it was not Mr Iredale's hostility that stung so keenly: it was the bitter truth of Lilian's reply. For years, for all my life, in our triple relationship, I had been the insignificant third, happy to be wanted sometimes, an inoffensive companion to be waved farewell to at the end of summer. Those long-anticipated arrivals and tearful departures had marked the heights and depths of my rapture and despair. For Lilian and Francis my visits had been no more than pleasant interludes in a partnership as unquestioned as the home they shared, the air they breathed. Between them existed ties of kinship, upbringing and habit neither needed to express. Confronted by a closeness so impregnable, even a friend became a stranger.

All this I had long known. Lilian's carelessly confident remark drove home the truth of it with the ruthlessness of a physical blow. The pain of it goaded me into a startling response: the thought that after all Lilian might be wrong. Suppose I were to tell – what I knew. Would not that come between them? With a few words I could estrange them from each other. The secret I had kept for Lilian's sake could be used for my own. It was a thought so vindictive, so shameful that it sickened me. Bundling away the unfortunate tapestry, I pushed back my chair and stumbled out into the hall without apology or excuse. None was required. Neither of them cared. In the half darkness I heard their voices; Mr Iredale's full of anger still: Lilian's empty of interest.

'Why is she still here? She never used to be here in winter.'

'We can't do without her, grandfather.'

The flat statement of fact untouched by any tenderness cut me to the heart. I would bear it no longer. The roads were clear. I would go home at once to those who loved and wanted me. There were other people, one person at least besides father and mother who cared for me and delighted in my company. There was nothing in the world to stop me from going; nothing to bring me back, ever. Like Bella and cook – bemused by the rapid succession of cooks I had forgotten her name – I would pack my boxes and go. They had done the right thing. Their instinct had been sound. The Iredales, I told myself crudely, could stew in their own juice.

Francis would return to find me gone. Forgetting in my spleen that there was no means of reaching Whingate that evening, no train to take me from there to Martlebury, I went purposefully to the front door, then grasping the handle, paused. He would be cold and hungry after a drive of seven miles exposed to the weather. He had been looking paler, older. The news about Johnny had deepened the frown between his brows.

He had taken Johnny's death very much to heart.

I turned back towards the kitchen and felt a sudden revulsion from its unswept floor, unscrubbed table and unpolished saucepans: its reek of stone and earth and stale food. It was growing dark. I hesitated, undecided, weary of the endless conflict: on the one hand my concern for Francis and a sense of duty to Lilian and the old man, both in need of help: on the other, the longing to disentangle myself from a situation which constantly wounded and angered me.

The kitchen door opened and Hetty appeared, grimy-faced, poor girl, from a long battle with the intractable stove.

'There's someone here, miss.'

A caller at the back door! Who could it be?

'She's come asking about a place, miss. A young woman.'

'Ask her to come here, Hetty, and bring a lamp.'

I closed the parlour door and dried my eyes. It wasn't likely I reminded myself, that a suitable person would arrive like this, at such an hour; would drop from the skies at the critical moment when I had reached the very end of my tether. Yet where – if the arrival was not supernatural – could she have come from – and how? It was too dark to see my face in the glass. I smoothed my hair and rehearsed the usual questions.

'I'll bring the lamp straight away, miss.' Hetty spoke from the kitchen. 'It needs filling.'

The figure that hesitated in the doorway and then approached me was slim and youthful and dressed from head to foot in unrelieved black. Even in the twilight the blackness was intense and perhaps for that reason her face in its oval bonnet appeared ivory pale; but her manner was perfectly composed.

'I understand, miss, that you are in need of a cook and housemaid.'

Some quality in her voice caught my interest. It was low, restrained and without being educated, the accent was refined, or at least not coarse. She stood motionless, her hands in their black gloves clasping a black reticule. The slight nervousness, the tremulous hope, were mine, not hers.

'We are indeed. I should explain that I am not the mistress here. My name is Ossian. This is Mr Iredale's house.'

'Yes, Miss Ossian. I understand.'

We faced each other in the rapidly fading light. I was aware of a kind of – what was it? – a completeness in her as if, young as she was, she had come into the fullness of whatever personality nature had designed for her. It was not boldness. Her attitude was quiet, a model for prospective servants. If she was absolutely free from any of the small signs of diffidence natural on such occasions, it was not from presumption: rather from an untroubled awareness that they were unnecessary.

'Are you offering yourself as cook or housemaid? You will realise the difficulties of either position while the other is unfilled.'

'I could do both, Miss Ossian.'

'But surely–'

'I can cook well enough and I understand the running of a household. The girl in the kitchen would stay, I believe. Between us, we could manage.'

I could scarcely believe my ears. It was as though she had already observed and summed up the situation. Did she at her age propose to take on responsibility for the whole establishment? Strange as it was to be presented with a possible solution to all my own problems – an answer almost to prayer – it was no stranger than my intuition, despite having seen no more of her than the dimness of the hall allowed, that she could do it.

'Tell me, what experience have you had? You seem very young. Where have you come from?'

She told me that for the past three months she had worked in the stillroom at Whingate Hall where her mother had once worked and before that, her grandparents.

'It was a larger household than this and I

learned the stillroom work but my mother
had already taught me housekeeping from
when I was ten years old.'

'Your mother is–' I paused, conscious of
her mourning.

'Dead. All my family are dead.'

Hetty was bringing the lamp. She set it on
the table. Its yellow glow – a dim substitute
for the golden sunshine in which I had often
seen them – lit the girl's pale features.

'You didn't recognise me, Miss Maggie, I
could tell.'

I knew her then. It was Jael Hebworthy.

9

I took the lamp and led her into the dining
room, my astonishment quickly giving way
to remorse. How was it that I had given so
little thought to Jael? Often as I had brooded
upon the sad events at the Toll House, all my
sympathy had been for the dead. To Jael,
who had survived to suffer most, I had given
scarcely a thought. Casting my mind back to
that terrible time, I remembered having
heard that she had gone away with her Aunt
Effie. The silent colourless child – for she
had seemed no more than a child – had
faded from my memory; to my shame. We

should have enquired after her, gone to see her, given help. Her thin black figure was a reproach, the embodiment of an utter loneliness.

I turned up the lamp with trembling fingers.

'Your dear mother,' my voice too was unsteady. Was this the time to express sympathy? She did not encourage me.

'Yes,' was all she said.

'And little Daniel...' An agitated review of her losses brought me inevitably to her father, and silenced me. Why had she come here of all places? But of course she had come in innocence. She knew nothing of the fatal connection between her family and – Lilian.

'...these parts where I was brought up,' she was saying. 'I belong here. There aren't many families hereabouts where a girl can find good service. When Aunt Effie saw the advertisement in the *Courier*, I remembered how kind Mrs Belfleur was, and Mrs Ossian.' Her tone was modest, her voice low. 'They were two such nice ladies.'

'You know that Mrs Belfleur is no longer here?'

How much, apart from the extinction of her entire family, I wondered grimly, did she remember of Mrs Belfleur's wedding day? Its awful memories saddened me again: the grave-faced women under the yews, the

160

empty joy of the bells, and later their solemn tolling as we listened, Lilian and I, in our white dresses, by the stream.

'Mrs Belfleur is in India, isn't she?'

I tried rapidly to put my thoughts in order. There was no doubt in my mind that she must have the position if she wanted it. It was the very least – outraged pity once more quickened my pulse – the Iredales could do. But the strange perversity of it! Could it be right to let her seek refuge in such a servitude: to wait upon, of all people in the world, the very one who had done her so grievous a wrong? I tried to shake off a superstitious foreboding that the evil which had destroyed her family might fall upon Jael too, young, defenceless, untouched as yet by an inkling of the truth. If she should find out... With no lightening of the heart I recollected that Johnny was dead; it rested with me alone to see that she never did find out. And for this very reason her coming was providential. It rescued me from the shameful temptation to betray Lilian.

And the effect upon Lilian of this constant reminder of the Hebworthys? The purity of Jael's face, the self-reliance and dignity in the carriage of her slim shoulders, her entire absence of self-pity, were deeply touching. She made no plea for sympathy. Her restraint won my respect and hardened my heart against Lilian. She, in contrast, seemed coarsened by selfishness, clinging convolvulus-like with her long fingers to any stronger growth she could use. Yet it was Lilian who had taken all our attention at the time of the tragedy, not Jael, who had most needed it.

Jael was waiting quietly like a figure of patience carved in jet. She had her mother's air of gentle submissiveness but her features were firmer and finer, her face thinner. She must be tired and cold.

'How did you come?'

'I walked from Whingate.' She caught my glance at her shoes. They were clean and bright. 'I changed them in the kitchen.'

'Seven miles! Alone?'

She made no complaint, no observation of any kind.

'And you would really like to work here?'

Her eyes were suddenly brilliant, lit by an intensity of feeling that startled me.

'I want it more than anything, Miss Maggie.'

How could one deny her even if it was the wrong thing for her to want? Still I hesitated, reluctant to let her walk unknowing, where, knowing the truth, she would not choose to go.

'I must warn you, Jael, that Miss Lilian is not an easy mistress. She is often unwell and that makes her more exacting than you might like.'

'I understand. But Mr Francis is different.

He was kind to Aunt Effie and me.'

'Yes,' I cried in relief. 'That is true. And he very much needs the comfort of an orderly home.'

Again, I had made the mistake of thinking first of Lilian. She must for once take second place to Francis. If she disliked having Daniel Hebworthy's daughter constantly before her eyes, she must put up with it. Having arrived at the word 'must', I found myself enjoying it.

The rattle of the gig forced me into action. I hurried out.

'Maggie!' Francis cried. 'What are you doing out here without a wrap. There's nothing wrong?'

'No, quite the opposite. An excellent thing. Who do you think has come? She has walked all the way from Whingate.' I explained quickly. 'I haven't engaged her or told Lilian yet. But I know you will want to do something for Jael. She's eager to come.'

Jael stood up as I bustled him into the dining room. He was affected as I had been by the sight of her frail figure, isolated in the depths of her mourning.

'If only I had known,' he said, recovering himself. 'I could have brought you from Whingate in the gig.'

'Thank you, sir.'

He asked her a few questions, his protective kindness roused by her friendless state. Unlike me he had no cause to hesitate. The irony of her coming to Sacristy House of all places and wanting more than anything in the world to come, was naturally lost on him.

'You would like to work here? Then of course you must come. Look on this as your home so long as you are alone in the world.'

'Thank you, sir.' Her grey eyes shone with a deeper gratitude than she allowed herself to express. 'You'll want to see this letter from the mistress.'

'No references are needed, Jael. We knew … your family.' Francis's voice trailed away uncomfortably. 'You've had a hard time of it.'

'Let me show you to your room, Jael.'

'Thank you, miss. But if you'll excuse me, there's a good deal to be seen to in the kitchen.'

'What a remarkable stroke of luck!' Francis exclaimed when she had left us. 'For her – and for us. Do you really think she'll stay, Maggie? You know how they've all come and gone. Let's tell Lilian.'

It was he who told her.

'What do you think? I've engaged a new servant. Guess who?'

'How can I possibly guess?' Lilian sat up on her couch, smiling and pouting.

'Jael Hebworthy.'

In his enthusiasm Francis spoke rather

loud. I believe he glanced at me to acknow-
ledge my share in the triumph; so that he
did not see Lilian's face suffuse with colour,
then grow pale. I saw it, and watched her
mercilessly, knowing that whatever objection she might raise, it could not be the real
one. The only argument for sending Jael
away could never be expressed.

She must have seen that from this predicament there could be no escape. She
moistened her lips. The smile, the pout, had
gone. Her face was wary.

'Does she really want to come here?'

'More than anything,' I said.

And Francis went on: 'She has an affection
for this district. It's natural enough when
she has lost all other connections with her
childhood.'

'We were all so fond of her mother,' I said.

'Yes, indeed.' Francis looked a little
surprised, not by the statement presumably
but by my tone. I too was surprised by the
measured, incisive way in which the words
came out. To me they sounded like a threat.
Lilian looked at me sullenly. I no longer
cared how she looked or how she felt. Oh
yes, it was time for me to go before my
indifference turned to active dislike. The
sight of Jael had revived all the revulsion
from Lilian's heartless escapade I had for so
long kept to myself.

'Francis.' I followed him into the hall.

'You'll take care of Jael? You won't let...'

'What do you mean, Maggie? You don't think I'll be unkind to her surely?'

'Oh no. Not you...'

'Then who?'

'No one. No one could be when she's so lonely and poor – and sad.'

She was a perfect, an inspired servant, devoted in her duties and for all her frail looks, tireless. From the evening of her arrival the house responded to her faultless touch. In no time at all a fire had been kindled in the dining room and Hetty, with clean hands and face, was laying the table for three under Jael's guidance. Of necessity the meal was simple; collops of beef devilled on a gridiron, the remains of an apple tart and cheese; but it was daintily served and Lilian without protest ate at the table instead of from a tray.

I thought it only fair to stay until Jael had learned the ways of the household. This she did so quickly that I could have left at the end of the week and would have done so had not Miss Abbot, to my surprise, begged me earnestly to stay. It had been such a comfort to her, such a rare treat to have a companion throughout the winter that she could not bear to part with me. If only my parents could be prevailed upon to let me stay! Indeed, I did not like to leave her for though she did not mention it, I knew that she was increasingly troubled with cataract and could no longer enjoy sewing or reading. When I promised to stay until the end of April her delight gave me a real glow of happiness. In fact, since Jael's arrival we had all improved in spirits and grown less irritable. Something of the old cheerful atmosphere returned.

The next few weeks were for me almost a holiday. I wrote letters, read to Miss Abbot, took walks as the days lengthened and the roads dried out and frequently popped into Sacristy House, to be struck dumb each time by its improved appearance. The cleanliness and regularity made it increasingly like the home it had been in Mrs Belfleur's time; and the best of Jael's many virtues was that she was completely self-effacing.

'One simply isn't aware of her,' Francis said when he called at Jasmine Lodge one evening to advise Miss Abbot about an investment. 'Everything is done by invisible hands.'

'She was always like that.' Yet even as I spoke I was aware that it was not quite true; or at least as a description of Jael it was incomplete. Some forgotten incident tantalised me: one which, if remembered, would alter the picture.

'And she's a splendid cook, like her mother.'

'Lilian likes having her?'

'How could she not? Jael has made us all so much more comfortable.'

His manner was easier and less harassed than it had been for weeks, possibly because Jael's remarkable ability as a servant was most strikingly shown in her dealings with Lilian. Even that word is too intimate. The relationship between them was as impersonal as it could be considering that in a short time Jael had added the care of the sick room to her other duties. Thanks to her efforts it was kept in spotless order, the medicines within reach at night or when Lilian was resting, the drops carefully measured out. Since Lilian never had to ask for anything, since Jael was only there when needed and was otherwise invisible, no complaints were possible. By the sheer perfection of her conduct, Jael mastered Lilian's waywardness.

As for Jael herself, she was so well fitted to her role that no loose ends of personality were left showing. All her energies were directed towards her work. If she had other impulses, other thoughts, they were certainly not expressed in words. She had changed from the speechless child she had been only to the extent of finding her tongue, but even now it was with extreme caution that she embarked on the adventure of speaking. It worried me that she should have so little to tell and no one to tell it to, that she should have so little pleasure in her life, until I made an interesting discovery. With every other avenue of opportunity closed to her, Jael had found an outlet for her starved imagination in the simplest and most natural way. Lacking people, she had turned to flowers.

They were not easy to find at that time of the year even in Asherby but in her solitary childhood Jael had roamed the fields and meadows, woods and heaths and knew where to find the earliest spring blooms. Bowls of snowdrops and aconites appeared in the hall and parlour; posies were placed at each cover on the dining table and on Lilian's tray. As spring crept on, the house was fragrant with violets, primroses and daffodils; and with these common flowers Jael mingled rarer ones such as no one else would have thought of gathering so that her arrangements had an unusual quality, like Jael herself.

I paused in the hall to admire the effect of a blue china bowl on an oak chest: a bowl brimming over with pink-tinged wood anemones, primroses and lady's smock, all silken, innocent and vulnerable. Only... I turned as Jael came downstairs.

'How pretty!' I said. 'But I should never have thought of putting in that stem of cuckoo pint.'

Now that I had noticed it, the purplish spike in its cowl-shaped bract was strangely forceful: a masculine intrusion into the modest femininity of the rest.

She coloured faintly, perhaps from pleasure at finding that we shared an interest.

'Lord-and-ladies, I was taught to call them.' She deftly restored a fallen primrose to its place. 'I like the name. It sounds like company.'

Her slim shadow fell upon the flowers as she moved. A coolness crept in at the open door. There was no sun. The flower heads, upturned or downward hung, had a curiously disturbing delicacy.

'They were always my playmates,' Jael volunteered shyly, 'ever since I can remember.' She looked at me, wondering if she dared venture further. 'They all have different faces, like different people.'

Overcome by these confidences, she went quickly into the kitchen. I was left with the impression – common enough – that it had all happened before: her swift noiseless departure; the look of the flowers, their faces all turned towards me with a candour so unanimous that it seemed significant: a kind of tension in the air that puzzled me.

Whether anyone else noticed the flowers, I cannot tell. In those first weeks they symbolised for me Jael's transforming influence. If I had left then, I would have taken with me memories of Sacristy House made sweet again. Unfortunately, I stayed just long enough to see the picture begin to change. Into that more serene sky crept another cloud. The sad affair of Well Cottage, disturbing enough in itself, was to have more far-reaching consequences than any of us could foresee.

10

The spick and span state of the house stimulated Lilian's interest in it. As she grew stronger, her half-hearted plans to provide herself with an elegant sitting room became more purposeful. I see them now as signs of an attempt to regain her self-respect. Her reckless adventure with Daniel Hebworthy had been oddly out of keeping with the social ambitions we had often teased her about. She had had time during the long hours of her illness to see it in a more sober light. Whether or not the daily sight of Jael stirred her to remorse, it probably made her ashamed of having entangled herself with the father of her servant.

I was surprised when more than once she mentioned Stone Barnard with eager interest as to how many rooms there were and how many servants. I had to protest that I knew nothing of Stone Barnard except what

Francis had told me; and suggested that she should ask him about it. I dare say she did. Whatever her motives, when she took to poring more earnestly than ever over the magazines and catalogues Francis brought her, and talked of nothing but new dresses and jackets, portières and plant-stands, embroidered footstools and plum-coloured velvet, it seemed a matter for rejoicing that she had found so harmless a pastime. And when a rumour spread through the village that Asherby Hall was to be occupied again by the young squire and his new wife who was hospitably inclined, Lilian's aspirations seemed likely to be fulfilled at last.

I had grown used to hearing her grumble about the parlour: an old-fashioned room with well worn horsehair chairs and curtains of red serge, a square of Turkey carpet, pipe racks and toppling piles of *Field and Furrow* and *Oddities of the Law:* a man's room where Mrs Belfleur's unassuming personality had drooped and wilted and left no trace.

Lilian and her grandfather were installed there as usual when I dropped in one afternoon, taking care this time to sit behind the settle where Mr Iredale could not see me and presently he seemed to forget that I was there. They resumed the conversation I had interrupted.

'If only I could have recesses on either side of the fireplace, with shelves to display

172

china.' Lilian sighed. Her voice had always lacked warmth. It was thin and light like a cool wind breathing through a keyhole.

'We can only contrive that, my love, by taking out part of the wall. Still it wouldn't be altogether out of the question. Cordwell could do it. Cordwell at Whingate. He's one of our clients...'

I had heard it all before. Darting from the Lodge by way of the beck-side path, I had felt the first cold sweet breath of spring; but here there was no contact with the world outside. With its closed windows, heavy curtains and leaping fire, the room kept its own unchanging season. The two voices, one light, the other deep and husky, made a surprisingly close harmony. They gave an impression of absorbed exclusiveness like that of children in their miniature world behind a nursery screen. My thoughts wandered until I became aware of a phrase which had cropped up more than once in the conversation. There it was again. Well Cottage.

'That was in the old days,' Mr Iredale was saying, 'in your great-grandfather's time when the house and cottage were all one. Even so it was none too big. There were three of us boys and the two girls, your great-aunts they would have been only they were dead long before your time. They were delicate girls. Always delicate. You're very like Elsie. She was a bright lively girl, fair haired too.' Over the arm of the settle I saw him looking at Lilian with a sad fondness. 'Doctors were useless in those days. But things have improved. Slater knows what he's about. And your mother was always a healthy girl.'

Lilian fidgeted, found a feather protruding from the threadbare cover of her cushion, plucked it out and banged the cushion in disgust.

'You were telling me about the house.'

'It was a bustling crowded place when I was a boy but then your great-uncle Thomas went into the army and Henry joined his father-in-law's firm and Anne died – and then Elsie. The place was too big. Your great-grandmother used to walk in and out of the empty rooms, fretting...'

There had been besides this smaller parlour a spacious drawing room, white panelled, with a fireplace in the style of Adam, gilt chairs, a spinet ... a prim, pretty, gracious room, long enough to accommodate a dozen guests in the days before ladies' skirts became unreasonably wide. When the alterations were made it was the drawing room which had to be sacrificed. A dividing wall had cut it in two, leaving on the Iredales' side only a small room which Francis now used as a study. The larger portion had become the cottage parlour. 'My father cut off too much, in my opinion. He pinched the house and made the cottage too big. He had it in mind to let it to a tenant of some taste and standing, a single lady perhaps. Asherby was a more considerable place in those days. There were several well-to-do families besides the squire's. But the cottage was never let for long until he let it at a pepper-corn rent to John Rigg as a favour to my brother Thomas. Rigg had been in his regiment and lost a leg in the Afghan affair in '41.'

'What a pity!' Lilian spoke with unusual warmth. But her mind, I discovered, was not on the Afghan affair. 'It must have been a charming room.'

With alarm I felt, in the hot-house close-ness of their mutual sympathy, the rooting of an idea, the rapid growth of a plan. His mind, troubled by ghosts of a vanished past, hers, directed with reviving energy towards the future, by opposite routes arrived mysteri-ously at the same point; and somehow the suggestion which burgeoned and burst into bloom came not from Lilian's lips but from her grandfather's as if the idea were his.

'I believe you like to think of the old days before the house was altered.' She stretched out her tapering fingers, more slender now than ever, and grasped his hand. 'Am I really like Great-Aunt Elsie? You loved her best, didn't you?' Mr Iredale seemed to grope for his handkerchief. 'Come, let me.'

She took it from his pocket. 'If only we could... But it's no matter. I must put it out of my mind. Perhaps some day...'

A feeble outbreak of coughing overcame her. She sank back against the cushions.

'You're not feeling worse, my love?' he asked, instantly perturbed, then burst out, 'If it would make you happy... I've been thinking. It would not be a great matter to make the alterations.'

'You don't mean – restore the house to what it was when you were a boy? What a beautiful thing it would be! A kind of memorial to Aunt Elsie – and Great-grand-mother.'

'It would mean doing without the study but that wouldn't matter. Francis can have his books in here or in his room. We could take out the wall.'

'Grandfather!'

He chuckled at her rapturous exclam-ation.

'You'd like that, wouldn't you?'

There came a pause. I glanced up from my needlework and found Lilian's eyes upon me. She looked away.

'If only the cottage had been empty,' she said. 'It does seem a shame to give up the whole scheme. If it hadn't been for...'

'Old Nancy Rigg?' Reminded of her ex-istence, Mr Iredale reduced her to an out-worn relic difficult to discard outright but not unworthy of a place in the lumber room. 'We can find somewhere else for her to go.'

'It certainly is too big for one woman. But I'm afraid Francis may not like it.'

'Francis!' Mr Iredale's mood changed. He sat up abruptly. The newspaper slid from his knee. He grabbed at it irritably. 'Why should he not like it?'

'Might he not think – we have a duty to let Mrs Rigg stay?'

'Might he not think' – Mr Iredale took some satisfaction in the grim repartee – 'that I have a duty to my own granddaughter?' He fumbled with the newspaper, reducing its sheets to disarray. 'When I'm dead, then it will be soon enough for Francis to exercise his authority.' He grew incoherent. 'For that matter – it would be as well – Cordwell from Whingate – I'll go and have a look. It was a mistake ever to put a partition there...'

He groped his way across the room, bumping into the furniture and stumbled over the threshold and along the passage.

Lilian stretched out her arms with a wide satisfied gesture and reached for *The Gentlewoman at Home* which at that time supplied the whole of her reading matter. Feeling that I could neither discuss the plan amiably nor leave it alone, I took the opportunity to slip away.

'They would never give notice to Mrs Rigg,' Miss Abbot said when I anxiously

177

mentioned the matter. 'She has been there so long. It would break her heart to leave. But Mr Iredale can be a hard man when his own interests are involved. Lilian does seem to have set her heart on a higher style of living. It's wonderful, really, considering her state of health.'

'Where would Mrs Rigg go?'

'Mr Iredale has other cottages, at Groat's Gate, but they're all in ruins except the old forge house and that's nearly a mile out of the village. Oh dear! And Mrs Rigg has nursed every baby and laid out every corpse in Asherby for thirty years. But it's always the way. Good deeds only bring their reward in the next world.'

I was to learn how easily objections to a course of action can become the very reason for carrying it out when later in that same afternoon I called at Sacristy House to return a pair of curling tongs Lilian had lent me. The sound of angry voices in the parlour made me hesitate to go further than the hall.

'It must not be, sir. I cannot allow it.' Francis, it seemed, could be imperious too. He sounded furiously angry. 'It would be altogether heartless and cruel – and what's more, unnecessary.'

'Allow? Unnecessary?' Mr Iredale wheezed and choked. 'Don't take that tone with me. How can you begrudge your cousin a little happiness – and at such a trifling expense? Think of all she suffers. You must understand that I shall do as I think fit.'

There was a tightness in his voice as if he were being strangled. Then there came a crash. Something – his small table – had been overturned.

'Francis!' Lilian sounded alarmed. 'You're upsetting him. Sit down, grandpa. Come along. Let me help you, dearest.'

The door opened and Francis burst out of the room as if to go upstairs.

'I was returning these...'

'Maggie.' He stopped as if relieved to see me. 'Here's a wretched business.'

'About Well Cottage?'

'You knew? We cannot disturb Mrs Rigg. It's out of the question.' We both turned as Lilian joined us. I had the impression that she disliked seeing us together. 'I say it's out of the question, Lilian. Grandfather doesn't know what he's doing. The old lady is wretchedly unhappy as it is.'

'I understand how you feel,' Lilian said without even knowing how untruthful her remark was. 'But I must say that is a good reason for encouraging her to make a change.'

'Encouraging her? You mean evicting her.'

'For all we know it may be the very best thing for her to have new surroundings. That is something I understand, Francis.

179

You spend so little time here. You cannot know how tedious it can be to spend one's life in the same room, day in, day out. This scheme of grandfather's would do us both good, Mrs Rigg and me.'

Francis's high colour had faded. To my dismay he was listening. His fatal inability to see only one side of a question – in this case the right side – kept him silent. I nerved myself to intervene.

'Johnny said he was sure that Mr Iredale would look after Mrs Rigg. He felt that she would be content without him so long as she had her house and garden.'

I should have known better. It was no business of mine and it had been a mistake to mention Johnny. The anger in Lilian's eyes, the flare of her nostrils, had not lost their power to daunt me.

'Content? Is she content? She has never settled for an instant since – since he was drowned. And as for the garden, can she not have a garden at Groat's Gate, and a much bigger one?'

'A nettle patch,' Francis said unhappily, 'and the forge house is no better than a cow-shed – and a full mile from the village.'

'You're exaggerating. It will suit her well enough with a few improvements. Cordwell can see to them too. It will be an opportunity to improve both properties at the same time. Her cronies will flock to see her.

One would imagine' – she patted his cheek and smiled indulgently – 'that we were sending her to the workhouse.'

'Don't say that.' Francis spoke sharply and drew away from her. In me too the word awoke a shudder. It threatened the ultimate disgrace. Nothing aroused more passion or despair among the poor at that time than the dread of such a fate. Not a soul in Asherby but would gladly have died rather than make that last journey up Asherby Bank in the ill-omened springless cart from the Whingate Union. All the same, Lilian had achieved her effect. In comparison with a fate so dire the removal of Mrs Rigg from one cottage to another seemed much less harsh; and Lilian's tone had been so sweetly reasonable that Francis so far forgot his first blunt refusal as to suggest: 'Could we not have her here instead? There would be plenty of room. In fact there will be more rooms than we can possibly need. Where are we to find servants to keep up such a mansion? Mrs Rigg might be helpful. She could give Jael a hand.'

Lilian was clearly taken aback.

'We must see. Mrs Rigg would not like to be dependent. A place of her own would suit her better.' She looked down, suddenly tearful. 'It was such a wonderful scheme. Grandfather quite longs to restore the house to what it was and I...'

She leaned against the wall as if weary to death, her hand held to her side. How convenient her delicate health had always been! If only one could face her, just for once, on equal terms! For Francis it was impossible.

'I don't know. You must let me speak to Mrs Rigg – to sound her feelings – and prepare her.'

Lilian's smile as she nodded her approval was particularly charming.

'You wouldn't care to come with me, Maggie?' Francis caught up with me as I went down the steps. 'Not if it would embarrass you. But you have a way of comforting people; and honestly I don't know what to say. Is it at all possible, do you think, that she wouldn't mind?'

Mrs Rigg was just setting out on one of her countless pilgrimages to the gate as we came up the path. At the sight of us she waited, holding the door ajar. Her face had lit up. I believe it flashed into her mind that by some miracle we had brought good news of Johnny. She looked uncertainly from Francis to me and the hope died.

During the past few weeks I had seen little more of her than the flutter of her apron as she made her restless journeys to and from the gate, and I had expected to find her more altered. But grief, having found that one harmless outlet, had left her otherwise unchanged except that she was wretchedly thin and shrunken. She scanned our gloomy faces with all her native shrewdness and by the time she had ushered us into her kitchen, had leapt, I believe, not to the precise reason for our visit but to somewhere near it.

'You've not brought good news by the looks of you,' she said bluntly. 'Pull them two chairs up to the fire, Mr Francis.'

But I sat down on the fender and warmed my hands. The room was ruddy with the light of burning logs. The canary fluttered in its handsome cage. It was difficult to know where to begin.

'How well it draws, the fire.'

'Ay, and I keep it going. For anybody coming home after a long journey there's no sight like a red fire.'

Francis caught my eye, his expression as heart-sick as mine must have been.

'Come on then.' She sat down in her Windsor chair, or rather on the edge of it, and clasped its arms so firmly that her knuckles whitened. 'Tell me what's to do.'

'I've come without telling my grandfather,' Francis began, 'to prepare you. He'll be wanting to see you.'

'He's waited long enough. It'll be the first time for over thirty years.'

But for all her tart humour her face had blenched. Her stumpy figure seemed to retreat into its ample skirts.

'He wants me out, is that it?' She looked sharply at Francis who nodded.

'It's what I've always dreaded.'

'It's not settled, only talked of.'

'Once or twice I've dreamed of such a thing happening. But Johnny always said... He wouldn't believe it if he knew. Nor would Rigg. "It'll never be the workhouse for us, thank God," Rigg said when we first came here after he was lamed for the Queen. "They're good people, the Iredales." There were silences as she struggled to keep some outward dignity, drawing upon reserves of strength that made me feel puny and ashamed. 'If you were to tell Rigg, or tell Johnny, they'd never believe it. Never. You might as well take that sword' – she pointed to the shining sabre hanging on the chimney breast – 'and cut me in two, Mr Francis, as send me to the House.'

'No, no,' Francis said. 'There's no question of that.'

Many a time I had sat in her lap and slid from her too smooth apron. Now I went and put my arms round her and held her close.

'You shall never go to the workhouse, Mrs Rigg. It isn't to be thought of. It's just that Mr Iredale wants to extend the house by taking in the cottage. So far he only talks of it. Francis wanted to find out how you feel about it.'

She laid her head on my shoulder and I

184

could almost feel how awful a thing it was to be old: how wearisome and hopeless to be old and poor and lonely.

'It would mean finding somewhere else for you to live.' Francis explained the possibilities. She grew quiet, and presently sat up, patted my hand and made an effort to regain command of herself; with success. The lines of her brown face had already hardened in response to a new fortitude, though fortitude was not new to her... 'At Groat's Gate, or we could find you a room somewhere. You'll never be in want.'

'You've been good to me already, lad. Without what you've been giving me I'd have had to use the last of the savings.' It was the first I had heard of this. Francis looked embarrassed. 'I know you do it for Johnny's sake. That makes every shilling worth twice as much to me.'

'If you could choose, Mrs Rigg' – it occurred to me that Miss Abbot might take her in – 'would you prefer a room if we could find you one, or...'

'I want nobody's room and no more charity than will keep me alive; and I hope and pray that won't be for long. The old smithy at Groat's Gate is lost in muck and wide open to the wind and weather but I'd rather be there, if I could have it to myself, than under somebody else's roof.'

Relieved of the dread prospect of ending

her days in the workhouse, she could now face a change which only an hour ago would have been unthinkable. She recovered sufficiently to fill the kettle and make tea. We talked of old times and the very sadness of recalling them made this fresh disaster shrink a little, to become one more set-back in her seventy strenuous years.

The details of the cottage were familiar but now I looked round with a more discerning eye. The ground floor rooms were large and well proportioned. When it was time to leave she took us with a pride that was touching in the circumstances into her best parlour, apologising for the lack of a fire.

It was certainly chilly and dark but she carried in the lamp and set it on the round table; and there in its yellow light were the panelled walls: there, barely recognisable behind the green serge frill was the fireplace in the style of Adam with its fluted white columns and acanthus leaves and on the mantel-piece vases of dried lavender from the famous hedge. With the addition of the study it would make a handsome apartment where Lilian could sit with as many as a dozen guests.

Who would they be? My eyes fell upon a photograph in a fretwork frame along the ornaments on Mrs Rigg's brown plush table-cloth: a dim sepia-toned likeness of

Johnny. In the low light of the lamp his cocksure brightness was lost. There remained a look of grave confidence as if he belonged there and would be difficult to displace. It seemed likely – the cold room with its haunting scent of dried lavender had given a superstitious turn to my thoughts – that among her guests Lilian might harbour one uninvited visitor.

For wherever he was, under the sea or up in the sky – a star pricked the deepening blue as we went out – Johnny would know that it was all Lilian's fault. He had always known everything. Whatever change he had undergone, even though he had put on celestial garments and mingled with the blessed, he would never forgive her. Some-where in the unimaginable vast blue vault above the cold sweep of hills would persist a spark of light and heat which would be Johnny's unforgiveness.

A current of dank air rose from the culvert as we crossed the beck; and all at once on the topmost branch of a naked birch a missel-thrush burst into song. The urgent notes thrilled through the dusk like life out of death. It my troubled mood I heard them not so much as an assurance of spring, rather as a warning; and now I remembered – in this very spot – the startling execution of the cat and saw it lying limp on the grass whose winter damp struck cold through the soles of my feet to my very heart. 'It's my nature,' Johnny had said, and his nature had been to snuff out without pity the creature which had threatened his grandmother's peace of mind. He had been so strong and free from all constraint, so swiftly calculating and sure of movement, that I could not imagine him made ineffectual even by death.

We turned along the path, leaving behind the dark bulk of the barn, more massive than ever in the fading light. The disapproval I had come to feel for Lilian melted a little. How sad, how fearful a destiny to people one's world with ghosts: reproachful – or revengeful – shadows of those one had wronged!

11

'I really am going home at last, Francis.' We had reached Miss Abbot's gate. 'The day after tomorrow.'

'I can't imagine what it will be like without you. But you've had enough of us, Maggie.'

'Of you, never.' Why did I not say what I so deeply felt? It should have been easy, as natural as the clasp of our hands and his grateful brotherly kiss on my cheek, especially as he seemed loth to leave me. Instead, I submitted wordlessly to the pain of letting the precious minutes pass. We had been together so little, and soon there would be no more time.

'Don't go in, Maggie. Need you?'

We crossed the green and turned back in the direction from which we had come but this time by way of the road, past the church on our left, under the larches and out into the open. The windows of Comfrey Farm stamped tiny squares of light on the dark moor rising austerely bare, empty of life, above all empty of Lilian. We were escaping together, leaving her behind. My spirits rose and suddenly all restraint was gone. We could talk freely as we had not talked for months.

'You're happy to be going home?'

'Oh yes. There will be so many things to do.' I rattled them off: the visits, calls, shopping, my singing and drawing lessons, my mornings at the Home for Ailing Gentlewomen, lectures at the Mechanics Institute. Having dreamed of escape for the whole winter, I must be happy in the prospect of going home; and all the time I knew that it was nonsense: there could be no happiness if Francis was not there.

On our right swelled the sombre curve of Groat Moor. There was still enough light in the sky to blacken the horizon and reveal on its smooth line the low arc of Hagg Barrow.

'We've never been.'

'Where?'

'To the Barrow.' Some day we would go there together and everything would be different.

'You're not suggesting that we should go there now.' Francis's tone was discouraging.

'Miss Abbot will be expecting me. It's too late.'

'It will be dark in half an hour.'

'There's someone there.'

I pointed. A tiny figure, thinned by distance to nothing more substantial than a rush-stem, moved against the sky. We stopped. It had gone. There was nothing to be seen, no movement in all the wide moor.

'There couldn't be at this time of day.'

We walked on arm in arm until a curve in the road brought us in sight of the derelict hamlet of Groat's Gate and presently to the forge house with its black doorway and paneless windows, its humped roof of reed thatch, and to the right the yawning cavern of the doorless smithy.

'It's impossible.' Francis's face was pale and glum.

'We're seeing it at its worst. In daylight...'

'I wish the place were mine now. I must have a word with Cordwell. It may be possible to delay things. Grandfather is failing. He's already past making decisions about the property.'

'It's lovely here in summer,' I said cheerfully. 'Remember, we used to sit on the wall for a rest before climbing the hill to the Toll House.'

But it was hard to recall the heat of summer days, the smell of wild thyme and the flash of lapwings tumbling over the marshy patches on the moor's edge.

'What a comfort you are, Maggie. You listen so patiently to all our problems. I can talk to you as to no one else.'

The sympathy between us was far more than the absence of discord: it was a positive, growing harmony as I now know; but my sense of being always an outsider, a witness, whose role it was to come, look on for a while and then depart, robbed me of confidence even though I knew in my heart that Mrs Belfleur had been right. There is no virtue in letting happiness slip away, only weakness. It seemed to me that the pattern of our lives was set. It did not occur to me that I could alter their course. If only there had been more time, if it had not been for Lilian, if only she... I felt the lowering shadow of the thought that must never be expressed and strove to think instead only of Francis and the joy of being with him.

We had almost reached the village, walking slowly in spite of the cold, when a faint sound made us turn. At first there was nothing to see but the flickering light of a lantern. Someone left the road and stepped noiselessly along the path by the beck. We saw her flit across the stepping stones to Sacristy House, a slender figure blacker than the shadow of the trees or the silent church above them. In the unmoving scene the one moving shape, frail as a bird, impressed me with a feeling of its significance. It conveyed a message, a reminder, as though without even knowing that a solution was needed, I was offered a clue.

'It's Jael. She's been – no, it couldn't be – alone at this time of night. But I thought I saw someone up there by the Barrow.'

Francis did not answer. I had never known him so unresponsive. Groat's Gate had evidently depressed him.

We saw her presently at the lamplit window of the kitchen. She took off her bonnet, smoothed the strings, hung it on a hook and disappeared, then returned to lower the blind. She must be the loneliest creature in all the world.

'You look half frozen,' Miss Abbot said. 'You must take some mulled wine. I believe you're thinner. I don't know what your father and mother will say. We have all been selfish and imposed on you. It's high time you went home.'

On the morning of my departure I was driven into Whingate in a hired cab. Francis had gone off much earlier but he left his desk and came to the station to say goodbye and present me with a great bouquet of hot-house roses. We wrapped the stems in our handkerchiefs soaked in water from the drinking fountain, and I laid them on an outspread newspaper in my empty compartment. When this small commotion was over, Francis took the corner seat opposite mine. He was looking drawn and tired.

'You didn't sleep well.'

'I lay awake, thinking.'

'You're worried about Mrs Rigg?'

'Yes. This business has set me wondering about the whole question of the property and oh, all sorts of things. The future.' The roses had been freshly cut. Their perfume filled the compartment. I could have stayed there for the rest of my life, endlessly prolonging the misery of leaving him. 'I wish we could have talked more. In all these months we've scarcely...'

'We've both been so busy.'

'Now that you're going, there'll be no one to argue things out with. I've come to rely on you, Maggie, for so much. Still, summer will soon be here.'

'I'm not sure that mother will want to come. It won't be the same for her without Mrs Belfleur.'

'I suppose not. And you too.' He hesitated, unexpectedly shy. 'You may have other plans this year now that you... I mean, you have other obligations.' The engine let off steam. A latecomer ran along the platform. Francis got down. 'You've never talked about your – attachment – and I haven't liked to mention it.'

'Attachment?'

'Lilian told me, of course. I wish you joy, Maggie dear.'

'Stand back, sir, please, if you're not travelling.'

A hand slammed the heavy door between us.

'Lilian was quite mistaken.'

The engine screamed again.

'What did you say?'

'If there had been any attachment, I would have told you.'

He smiled, unconvinced. It was neither the time nor the place for explanations. I was too flustered to express a denial forceful enough to remove the impression Lilian had already far more forcefully conveyed.

'Come in the summer all the same.'

'I'm not sure...'

It was too late. He could not hear. He shook his head, deafened, and seemed to sink through clouds of white vapour as though dissolving before my eyes.

It was a luxury to travel alone. I could cry for miles of the way. Station after station passed me in a tearful blur; and yet, agonising as it had been to leave Francis looking anxious and harassed as the train drew away, in some mysterious way I took him with me. He never left my thoughts or ceased to haunt those regions of the spirit more retentive than the mind.

'You've been away too long, Maggie,' mother said. 'You've only half come back. Sometimes I wish we had broken our connection with Asherby long ago.'

I had been at home less than two months when the sad little drama of Well Cottage reached its last act. Miss Abbot had written regularly and kept us informed. We knew that alterations were going briskly ahead so that Mrs Rigg could move to Groat's Gate by Whitsuntide. Mr Iredale behaved as if there were no time to be lost, whether to thwart Francis or because he felt his own days to be numbered.

On the Tuesday after Whitsuntide Mrs Rigg moved to the old smithy with all her goods and chattels – and without fuss or any word of complaint. But a few days later she fell ill of a chill and ague. Since there was no one at hand to look after her, Dr Slater, hastily summoned by a passing shepherd, himself took her to the Poor Law hospital at Whingate where she grew rapidly worse; so that, after all, her worst fears were fulfilled: she died in the workhouse.

Having been neighbours for so many years, the two old people were not long divided. Scarcely had the wall between house and cottage been removed when Mr Iredale, after a heated quarrel with his grandson, suffered a fatal stroke. He lay unconscious for a few days and so presumably never knew the consolation of dying in his own home, soon to become a very comfortable and dignified country residence.

12

'It was a wicked will,' mother said. 'He was a wicked old man. I regret having been polite and considerate to him all these years.'

'You might have made him worse by being rude,' father said.

'It's no use, Edward. You can't tease me into a good humour.'

'I must confess he has shown more cunning than one might have expected. He obviously knew his grandson through and through and yet was clever enough to give him no legal grounds for complaint. The will is more than generous to Francis, on the face of it.'

To hear them speak of Francis gave me a

hollow kind of pleasure. It was like talk of food to the starving. There had scarcely been an hour, a minute since my homecoming when I had not thought of him. My dreams of home while in exile had been transformed long before I reached Broomwood Place, into dreams of Asherby; dreams far more vivid and painful than ever before. How had I fallen into this dual non-existence; this limbo: divided in spirit between the two places? All my life I had loved Asherby best; no longer could I live there in any peace of mind; nor could I separate myself from it except in body.

When Mr Iredale died, mother was quick to see – had long foreseen – the problems at Sacristy House. I was grateful to her and father for their constant open thrashing-out of the Iredales' affairs for I could neither bear to speak of them myself nor stop thinking about them; and so hung unhappily on the fringe of their discussion, passionately speechless.

'Not a penny to Cynthia,' mother said. 'Not that she needs it. But after all she is his daughter. And think how he has tied Francis's hands. The old villain has moulded the lives of those two young people since they were babies and this is the last straw.'

The house and other properties with the land attached to them were left to Francis together with one half of Mr Iredale's capital.

The other half of the money was to be held in trust for Lilian until she reached the age of twenty-five or until her marriage. In the meantime she was to have the income from a small investment amounting to little more than a hundred pounds a year. She would be too poor to set up home on her own, nor could she stay on in the only home she had known, without Francis's permission and under his protection.

'In other words,' mother said, 'as his wife. How else could the two of them live together? Francis cannot turn Lilian out...'

'Oh, he never would,' I cried and sank back instantly into tongue-tied misery.

'Nor would she let him. If only it had been the other way round! If the house had gone to Lilian, Francis could have moved elsewhere; except that she wouldn't have had the means to run it. As it is, Mr Iredale has hung her like a millstone round Francis's neck. Who else' – Mother seemed to speak with deliberate clarity – 'would marry Francis with Lilian always there?'

'No girl in her senses,' father said with equal deliberation. There followed an impressive pause, long enough for the most slow-witted of girls to receive the message. 'Is there no hope that in time Lilian will fall in love with someone else, poor fellow?'

'In time perhaps.' Mother's eyes narrowed in calculation. 'She knows so few young men and no one suitable in Asherby, needless to say. Of course she's devoted to Francis and he to her but as for falling in love... Francis has made her completely dependent on him and in her state of health she cannot make a life for herself as some girls do. According to Miss Abbot, Lilian's distress at her grandfather's death is terrible to see.' How well I could envisage the distressful scenes and their effect on Francis! 'If only he will do nothing in haste! I wonder if we should invite Lilian here for a long stay.'

'Do you not think, Elinor, that Maggie may have had enough of Lilian for a while?'

'I never stop thinking of Maggie,' mother said and put her arms round me.

Nor did I stop thinking of Francis. With astonishing persistence he went with me everywhere. The house where he had never set foot was steeped in his personality as if he had lived there all his life. Sometimes in a shadowy way he almost took shape, at my elbow or behind me; opposite, while I had my eyes on my needlework; vanishing as I glanced up.

Mother understood too well to try and comfort me and respected my inability to confide in her. Instead she provided distractions: an orgy of shopping; visits to dressmakers; calls; drives; and wherever we went, an insubstantial Francis went with us, commenting on my new dresses, influencing my choice, theorising on every topic, advising on the new carriage horse, handing me bouquets of pink roses.

It was not surprising that one morning I looked down from the drawing room window and with a great leap of the heart saw him on the other side of the street; or thought I saw him. A baker's van slowed down and stopped in front of the tall figure in a grey frock coat and grey hat. Then a waggonette went by crammed with children on an outing. When they had gone, Francis had gone too; if he had ever been there. How could it have been Francis, sauntering in that indecisive way in his best clothes and gazing up at the doors as if in search of Number Eleven? He never came to Martlebury.

I went to my room to write letters, and fine rubbish they must have been. A stirring of hope and excitement had scattered my wits. Sure enough an hour later came the tread of feet on the stairs. The housemaid tapped. There was a caller in the drawing room, a young gentleman, but since the mistress was out... I didn't even glance at the card but flew downstairs in the kind of swooping rush one experiences in dreams, to find him standing at the window.

'Mr Barnard.'

If somehow with a huge effort I concealed the shattering disappointment, the credit must be his. He turned, scarlet with pleasure, and in a trice I felt again his remarkable niceness, his modesty, his self-forgetful interest in and enthusiasm for – well – for me.

'I dared not hope that it would be you, Miss Ossian.' Blushing, he relegated poor mother to the social oblivion where everyone but me belonged. 'It has been such a long time. You heard perhaps that we were obliged to go abroad in November? No, it was not for mother's health. She is well. But her brother, my uncle, was ill in Cannes. We stayed the winter. Otherwise I should have taken the liberty of calling long ago. But I hoped you would have heard of the change in our plans from Mrs Blower.'

I had not heard. I had forgotten Mrs Blower and her friend, Mrs Barnard; and almost, Mr Barnard. Even now that he stood before me, smiling, a little sunburned and really rather handsome, it was as though from a distance of two or three feet I could not quite see him. Save for the tiny morsel of consciousness that kept me chatting decorously, all my faculties were devoted to Francis and the possibility that he might be in Martlebury. At any moment he might knock.

I could not drag myself from the window but motioned Mr Barnard to the other chair in the bay. It wasn't easy to see past the asparagus fern and then through the lilac boughs to our own steps; or between the dusty lime trees to the street.

'...our walks at Bonchurch... Lord Tennyson... I remembered your quotation ... "bowery hollows crowned with summer seas"...'

It was from Francis that I had learned the line, raptly listening on the stone seat while he read the poem aloud and the beck murmured a placid undertone.

'...I thought you might like to borrow this.'

Mr Barnard produced a volume of the *Idylls of the King* in limp leather, brand new, I could tell.

I thanked him and glimpsed a movement between the trees; a hint of grey? It was Mario with his barrel organ. The 'Letitia Waltz' came thumping through the open window.

'How appropriate! You liked to dance, Miss Ossian, I remember. Perhaps some day ... we may...'

'Dance?' I recollected the activity with the distant interest an obscure tribal custom might arouse and moved the asparagus fern to the right.

'You have never visited Mrs Blower at Cotsdean? She has often said how much pleasure it would give her to receive Mrs Ossian. Cotsdean is only a mile from Stone Barnard.'

A breeze lifted the lace curtains and brought with it Martlebury's curious blend of lilac and bad drains; and suddenly I knew that it had only been a fancy. Francis had not been there. He never came to Martlebury. I could have died of grief. Nothing in the world could be sadder than the scent of lilac unless it was the toneless jangle of a barrel organ. Mario was moving away.

'I must give him something. He'll expect it.'

'Let me.'

He followed me downstairs and out into the veiled sunshine. Mario swept off his hat of battered black and flashed us a smile of flawless white. The monkey sadly held out his scarlet hat for Mr Barnard's lavish shilling. Mario bowed and gave me a conspiratorial nod as if attributing his good luck to me.

'Why is the monkey looking so miserable?' Mr Barnard asked. 'Does he want another shilling?'

'I expect he knows how sad life is.'

'Not on a morning like this surely. It has been the happiest morning of my life – to find you again. Shall I tell him?'

'Oh, do look. You've dropped your glove and you're treading on it.' He picked up the crumpled doe-skin and stuffed it unheeding into his pocket. 'You haven't changed a bit.'

We laughed. He went away. At the corner by the Botanical Gardens he paused and raised his hat. I waved and turning, saw a young man in grey walking in the opposite direction on the shady side of the street.

'Francis.' I darted off in pursuit. Mario had stopped at the lower end of the street where it turned into the busy thoroughfare of Church Road. Children were dancing to his music on the pavement. I stepped on to the cobbles almost in the path of an approaching water cart, recovered myself and hurried to the corner, brushing the water drops from my hair. Church Road was full of pedestrians. He had gone. I was not dressed for the street and could go no further.

A terrible heartache seized me, a regret so intense that it was an effort to move from the spot where I had last seen him. I felt too an anxiety out of all proportion to the event, if it could be called an event. Why had he gone away without calling? How I hoped he had not seen us laughing on the steps! It would confirm his absurd idea – fostered by Lilian, I thought furiously – of an understanding between James Barnard and me. Yet if he had come to make an ordinary call while in town on business such an incident would not have deterred him. Some other motive had brought him, some need. His manner had been tentative, uncertain. I looked down from the window and seemed once again to see him dissolving from sight, a grey shape vanishing into the grey-green shade of the dusty lime trees. From far away came the sound of Mario's music, its hammered notes suggesting a tune, as barrel organs do, without ever quite reaching it. The drain-polluted lilacs smelt of decay like flowers at a funeral.

Lilian's letter reached us at the end of the week. She and Francis had been married two days before; a quiet wedding; there were no guests apart from Miss Abbot.

'You must come and see us,' she wrote and lest there should be any misunderstanding, signed herself Lilian Iredale.

13

Stone Barnard can never have looked lovelier than on the summer day when I first saw it: a Georgian house of rose-red brick and white-painted windows, the symmetry of its south façade softened by twisting wistaria boughs hung with pale mauve blooms.

From the shade of the cedar on the lawn where we had tea the sunlit house had the still permanence of a picture: or perhaps the backcloth of a stage; for there seemed a quality of illusion in such unflawed charm. On the other hand, my sense of unreality was not confined to the house itself.

The three ladies in their wicker chairs, for instance, had combined to perfection their concerted manoeuvres as both scene shifters and participants in the action. For a time they had come to rest, looking amid the spreading flounces of their summer dresses, in their cascades of lace and wide, gauze-trimmed hats, like the magical shapes in *The Tempest* who laid out a banquet with inviting gestures. That banquet too was unreal.

Mrs Barnard poured tea from a pot of fluted silver while mother and Mrs Blower talked of begonias, flannel shirts for market porters, winter coals, soup and candles for the needy, and William Morris curtains; their voices soft and light, without resonance in the warm air. And when tea was over, without haste or any sign of acting together, they rose from their chairs and drifted away in an apparently spontaneous fashion to look at the peaches. Yet as they passed one by one through the archway in the wall, their blue and grey and mauve zephyrs and voiles brushing the brick path, their withdrawal was so positive – it emphasised my duty so firmly – that it was necessary to overcome a flutter of nervousness now that James and I were alone.

'I'm glad they've gone,' he said at once. In his own home he had an assurance he had not shown before. 'I was afraid there wouldn't be time to talk to you. As it was, I could only look. You'll forgive me, Maggie – you must know how I feel towards you – if I tell you how lovely you look. And to see you in our own garden at last! Only,' he moved to the vacant chair next to my own, 'there's a sadness too, isn't there?'

Totally unprepared for such directness, I was taken aback and forced, to my own amazement, into a similar directness.

'Yes,' I said. 'I'm dreadfully unhappy.'

I had not confessed it openly even to mother, had confided in no one, had not intended to do so now. It was not for this that the ladies had left us alone together. It must have been the utter sincerity of his concern combined with the special nature of our situation that made concealment impossible. He was so whole-heartedly on my side. Here was the one person to whom it seemed not only natural but right to open my heart. 'It's about Francis,' I said and poured it all out: how much I had cared for him: how inevitable it had been that he would marry Lilian: how difficult it was to change one's feelings.

'But they do change,' James said gently. 'I thought myself in love with someone else until I met you and realised how trivial my feelings had been. And your feelings will change, Maggie. Now that he is married, it cannot be otherwise. I don't mean that you should forget. You've loved Asherby and the people there too long ever to forget them. But there comes a time when one has to say the thing is finished, and put a frame round it, like a picture. I won't urge you: you are in no mood for it. I love you and want to ask you to be my wife; but I must wait until your own judgment tells you that there can be no happiness for you in loving a man who belongs to someone else; nor for him if he should ever find out that he might have had the dearest and best wife a man could have – and let her go.'

I had not thought of that. How good and wise he was!

'When things go wrong we must pick ourselves up and begin again. Do you not think, Maggie, that we could be happy together, some day?'

I looked at him, at his handsome honest face; at his mouth, its corners upturned with a winsome pleasantness. I liked his deprecating smile when he spoke about himself. Was this then to be my husband? The last few minutes had brought us closer than had all his attentions during the past weeks. It really was – possible. Francis and Lilian had taken the momentous step into marriage. Why should I not take it too?

The ladies came fluttering back through the archway. Seeing us absorbed in intimate conversation, they vanished obligingly into the house, their back flounces expressing, one could have imagined, a ripple of applause.

'I'm glad you told me.'

'There is no one else I could tell.'

In his modesty he was delighted. A feeling of peace stole into my heart. Beyond the sprawling shadows of the cedar on the emerald lawn, the rose-red house was warm and welcoming. The veil of unreality had lifted; had floated and settled upon Asherby Cross. Its tree-filled hollows and bare hills wavered with dreamlike inconstancy. Here was my own life, here and now. The ladies – they had come out on to the terrace – knew what was good for me, what was essential. Father would approve, had already approved or I would not be here.

'You'll come again? I haven't shown you all the house or the garden. There's so much to talk about. You'll think it over? You aren't sorry that I spoke as I did?'

'No, I'm not sorry. Not sorry at all.'

For the life of me I could not say more. It was too soon to root out the lifelong habit of loving Francis; but like an apostate confronted with a new religion, I found in its message some promise of salvation.

'You'll be at Mrs Blower's for some time?'

He knew precisely how long. Mother would return home next day to prepare for father's annual holiday in Scotland. It had been settled that I would stay for another two weeks at least.

'I'm afraid they're thinking of leaving,' James said. There was a gathering up of parasols; a maid appeared with capes; the landau was being brought round. 'But we'll meet again soon?'

I took my seat opposite mother and Mrs Blower. The smooth flow of their conversation continued uninterrupted as the landau rolled rapidly down the drive. I composed my features into a deceptively attentive expression, fixed my eyes on the filigree cone of Mrs Blower's hatpin and began cautiously to replan my future.

'There's no need for haste,' mother said when she had heard a carefully edited version of my talk with James. 'You've all the time in the world. But you're much too sensible not to realise that such an opportunity may not arise again.'

I had never felt more sensible. Common sense had not been in the past a quality I had much cared about or shown signs of possessing; but during the next ten days following mother's return to Martlebury it dictated my behaviour to a degree that must have gratified Mrs Blower after all the trouble she had taken. James called every day; we went again to Stone Barnard where he showed me his old nursery and schoolroom; we explored the shrubbery, the conservatory, the church, chatted to the gardener, looked at family albums, discovered common ground in our dislike of cucumbers and shared a weakness for marmalade pudding. I felt increasingly at ease with James and with Mrs Barnard whom I had always liked.

'And that,' Mrs Blower couldn't help saying, though she was the soul of discretion and had given no sign of conniving, 'is most satisfactory, that you and she should get on so well together. The post is here, I see. There's one for you, dear.'

She skimmed her own letters. I opened mine, from mother and written in haste to tell me of a change of plan. Father would break his journey in Edinburgh to meet representatives of a Danish firm who were his customers. Mother would go with him. It would be an opportunity to visit the art galleries.

'You could probably stay longer with Robina,' she wrote. 'Indeed I should prefer you to stay in the country as Martlebury never does suit you in warm weather. Explain the position and leave it to her to suggest an extension of your visit. I have asked Cousin Constance to come and take charge here while we are away. She always likes to come. Let her know when you will return. I can rely on you to do the most sensible thing.'

'How nice! News from the Warnolds.' Mrs Blower had come to the end of her letter. I knew the Warnolds, a Martlebury family, and waited, prepared to be interested. 'Annie is to be married. She will sail for India in August.'

Faint as the echo of an old tune came the memory of another August wedding; another bride sailing for India; and with it, other echoes, other memories.

'I can rely on you to do the sensible thing,' mother had written. There it was again, the most sedate of words. It reminded me of my new role. But it did not prevent me from returning my letter to its envelope without telling Mrs Blower that it was from mother; nor from saying my goodbyes to the Blowers and Barnards with genuine gratitude at the end of the fortnight, but with no reference to my parents' absence from home; nor from waiting on the platform at Cotsdean Junction until the Martlebury train had left and then taking a slow train to Whingate instead. Common sense played no part in this strategy. The fact that I could perform the office of a friend by collecting Mrs Hart's tapestry and delivering it into the hands of Annie Warnold was no more than an excuse. It would be a simple matter for the Iredales to send it by rail unaccompanied.

Yes, it was a rash impulse that drove me to Asherby Cross to risk again the old torment of jealousy and love. And yet some vestige of reason – an instinctive wisdom – seemed to justify what on the face of it was sheer folly. I could not give James Barnard the clear answer his patience and goodness deserved until I had seen Francis just once more and got it into my head through the evidence of my own eyes that he belonged now, inescapably and for always, to Lilian.

And to be at Asherby again in summer time! I saw it – as the slow train bore me to Whingate – a vignette in a border of leaves, larch, birch and rowan, enclosing a quiet hour; Francis with his book, I with my pencil drawing the blue flowers of monkshood; sweetness and poison intermingled as they had been in all my days there.

It could do no harm to go. Nothing else could happen now that they were married. Nothing of interest could happen in the whole dreary expanse of our three lives. And if the visit should prove a mistake, no amount of pain could outweigh the happiness of seeing Francis just once more.

14

At the Toll House the driver stopped to check the traces before the long descent.

'You won't be wanting to get down here the way you used to,' he said. 'There's nobody here now.'

It had not been my intention but during

the seven-mile drive from Whingate a fit of cowardice had come upon me and I was glad of an excuse to postpone my arrival. The delivery of my luggage would at least warn Miss Abbot that I was descending upon her in this high-handed manner.

'The walk will do me good,' I said – and watched the four-wheeler creep round the first curve of Asherby Bank. When the grating of its wheels had died away, the familiar quiet enclosed me, deeper now than ever. Without Daniel's goats to graze it, the wayside grass had grown long. Birds had spattered the window sills. Above the sunblistered door and fading inn sign a strip of guttering had come away, dislodging the martins' nests.

It was the garden we had always loved best. With some hope of finding it less desolate, I pushed open the wicket and felt once more the unique blending of openness and seclusion; across the valley the heather was turning purple again; within the stone walls larkspur and lupins grew tall among the weeds; apple and damson trees leaned low above the unmown orchard grass.

And yet the place was less overgrown than might have been expected after almost a year's neglect. Someone had tied back the honeysuckle. A heap of weeds, still green, lay in a shaded corner by the wall. Ahead of me as I walked up the path a slender figure moved. Jael was cutting blooms from a rose-bush. Her thoughts had been far away. The rustle of my dress startled her. She turned and smiled.

'You're quite a stranger, Miss Maggie.'

'Jael.' I kissed her. Her pale cheek coloured faintly. She was, if possible, thinner than ever. Her dress under a Holland gardening apron was still of unrelieved black. 'Your mother's white roses.'

'It's best to cut them.'

Her self control was unshaken. Suffering had taken her far beyond the nostalgia that had brought me to this scene of happier days. All the same I suspected that she felt at peace here. When she had laid her flowers in a willow basket and we went out through the gate, she closed it slowly and looked back as if a last glance at the garden might fortify her in all that she must endure when absent from it.

We walked to the village by the woodland path. Mrs Iredale, she explained, was spending the day at Jasmine Lodge and Miss Abbot had suggested that Jael might like to have a few hours to herself. I learned that Mrs Iredale was often at the Lodge.

'Mr Francis is away from home a good deal,' Jael told me. 'He's staying in Whingate until Saturday.'

It served me right. I swallowed the disappointment as best I could and would have felt more dispirited with any other companion than Jael. Her fortitude must be my example. It impressed me all over again now that I saw her after a lapse of several months; and as we wound our way between the trees, I became aware of something else. Nothing could have been more mundane than our conversation: commonplace questions on my part: factual replies on hers: she had always been sparing of speech. But her brief remarks came with the effect of leaving undisturbed a portion of her mind devoted to other – and higher – things.

I stole a glance at her hollow cheeks and temples, her slender innocent-looking neck. In her black straw bonnet of nun-like austerity she had an intense, withdrawn look as if, especially now that she was for once not at work, her energy had turned inward and found some volatile fuel that made her spirit burn with a bright pure flame; as if she found the world harsh and retreated from it into a private existence with nothing sensuous in it. A feeling that this was not a sociable quality made me ask if she had made friends in Asherby.

'There isn't much time for making friends.'

It was not a complaint. My feeling that I should have – or that someone surely could have done more to make her happy, seemed all at once impertinent. She had found her own solution to the problem of loneliness.

As to what the solution might be I hazarded a guess.

'Do you find comfort in your religion, Jael?'

'I read my Bible.' Her tone conveyed no more than the fact.

I asked when she had last visited her Aunt Effie and was dismayed to hear that she and her husband had recently emigrated to Australia.

'You didn't think of going with them?'

'Aunt Effie wanted me to go. She was afraid of being lonely out there.'

She offered no reason for remaining behind.

'Some day perhaps you may join them.'

'I won't be going to Australia.'

We had left the green shade and come out into a clearing. The full light from the west fell on her face. It looked ethereal. She had spoken with simple finality as if she had other plans which could not be altered. A raptness in her expression made me catch my breath in momentary awe. We stepped into the shade again and her face took on the luminous delicacy of white jade, rare and beautiful. Yet as a child she had been plain.

I was so taken up with these discoveries that our arrival at the village took me un-awares, still not quite prepared for a meeting with Lilian. Jael took her flowers to the

217

churchyard, and I followed the path along the beck with the sensation of bracing myself to face an ordeal. But Lilian and Miss Abbot saw me from the window and came hurrying out. Their embraces and kind enquiries were as welcoming as ever. I forgot the awkwardness of having come unexpectedly and almost forgot my precious excuse, the tapestry.

'We hoped you had just come to see us,' Miss Abbot said in her gentle way when I explained. 'It wouldn't be summer without a glimpse of you or your dear mother. Lilian and I are always glad of company.'

The table set for three, the smaller teapot, reminded me that our numbers had certainly shrunk. The two houses must be quiet now, each occupied for much of the time by a solitary mistress and maid; at Sacristy House, Lilian and Jael. How odd that seemed! Especially now that the house had been extended. I was struck by the feeling of spaciousness when after tea Lilian took me to see the alterations. For all my disapproval I was dying to see the new rooms and would have said so had not Lilian forestalled me.

'I suppose you can't wait to see the drawing room after all the fuss.'

The approach was awkward along a narrow corridor leading from the hall to the door of the former study. Lilian flung it open with a flourish. I breathed the smell of damp plaster and new paint and was bewildered at first by the transformation.

'It's just as you wanted it,' I said, over-whelmed by the profusion of buttoned velvet chairs, rosewood tables, bamboo plant-stands and wicker jardinères, wax fruit and feather flowers under glass shades, alabaster swans on an étagère, peacock fans outspread on the wall, a pair of silk screens sent from India. They were all so perfectly in keeping with our taste at the time that I suffered a pang of envy; and not only on account of the room. Lilian had indeed achieved everything she wanted now that she was Mrs Francis Iredale and mistress of a fine house. Since the earliest days of our rivalry she had always won. A distant memory of her tapering fingers as they closed on my knave of hearts made me almost expect to hear her say, 'Snap.'

She had knelt down on a prie-dieu chair as if trying it out; but instantly got up again and walked about the room, her mauve skirt brushing the brass clawed feet of tables laden with ornaments and setting the china knick-knacks a-quiver.

'You must be very pleased.' I sat down rather unwillingly on a two-seated sofa. For all its elegance there was no feeling of com-fort in the room. A pallid shower of paper frills occupied the grate. My eyes came to rest with relief upon the mirror above the secretaire. Its carved and gilded frame gave back the lightly moving reflection of leaves outside: a welcome picture of living green amid so many unused and useless things.

In the long room, among so many new possessions, Lilian herself had a new look. She seemed to have thrown off her invalid ways. Had she discovered that there was no point in being ill without a sympathetic audience? Though inexcusably malicious, this conjecture may have held a grain of truth. In my ignorance I did not recognise her sunken eyes and over-delicate skin as signs of grave physical malady but I could not overlook her feverish restlessness. She had never been tranquil but her vivacity had always found expression in talk or activity. The new nervous unrest which set her pacing about the room seemed of a sterile kind that could have no fruitful outcome.

'Do come and sit down. Where do you usually sit?'

'Oh, I don't know.' She had come to a halt by the empty white fireplace. 'We never sit here. Francis can't bear the room.'

'But when you have visitors?'

'Visitors? I don't have any. I haven't been in the mood since the funeral – or the wedding.' She laughed and was suddenly serious again, her eyes appealing. 'Besides I have the most peculiar feeling sometimes. All these things...' She looked slowly round the room, at the swans and fruit, the screens and feathers...

'They're all here because I chose them.'

'Well, naturally.'

'But I have the oddest feeling that there's something else here as well.'

Something she had not chosen and would rather be without? One might have wondered what additional thing the fashionably crowded room could accommodate.

'I can't settle. And it's never warm. I open the windows to let the cold out.' She did so. The new painted woodwork resisted but she pushed defiantly and leaned, panting, against the frame. 'And in comes a dampness from the back. It's too near. Just there.'

Mrs Rigg's thick thorn hedge had been uprooted. Her plot of land now formed part of the Iredales' garden. From close at hand came the soft rushing sound of water until Lilian dragged the window shut again and restored to the room its own lifeless chill.

'Now that all this trouble has been taken,' I said after a thoughtful pause, 'you must try to enjoy the room. Otherwise it will all have been for nothing.'

'It has all been for nothing. There, I've said it. You're the only person I can tell and if you ever mention a word of it, I'll kill you, Maggie Ossian.' At this descent into the language of our nursery days we both giggled though shakily. She flopped down beside me, taking more than her share of the sofa as usual. 'Poor grandpa. He did so want me to be happy. If we had left things as they were, he might have been here still. It was all too much for him.'

With an heroic effort I refrained from pointing out that it had been too much for Mrs Rigg as well. Some vestige of her old magical charm held me captive still with at least an air of listening sympathetically. I could never really quarrel with Lilian though there had often been cause and she was to give me cause again, quite soon.

'You've been to Stone Barnard?'

'Yes. Why did you tell Francis that there was an understanding between James Barnard and me?'

'Well, isn't there? Has he asked you to marry him?'

'Yes, but only recently.'

'And you've accepted?'

'I don't know…'

'There you are then. You haven't refused. I was right. It's just a question of making up your mind. But if you take my advice' – her hand closed on mine – 'you'll stay as you are. I envy you your freedom.'

'You aren't happy in your marriage?' I said slowly.

'Happy? I hate every minute of it. It has changed us both, changed everything. It's no good looking at me like that.' For all the petulance of her manner, there was no doubting her distress. 'It's no use feeling sorry for us. After all it's partly your fault.' I stared at her in dismay. 'If only you hadn't always wanted Francis so much, I would never have wanted him at all.'

My peace of mind, already threatened, was not unnaturally shattered by this outrageous speech. She had no idea of its effect. Her blue eyes met mine with a look of incomprehension that was oddly innocent. In a confused way I understood that she did not see me. It was as though, looking outward, she was always afflicted with a partial blindness. Instead of other people she saw faceless shapes, blank areas like mirrors giving back only pictures of herself. How isolating that must be! How withering to the spirit! Especially when turning inward she found only the arid desert of her own selfishness. No wonder she reached out to suck dry the vitality of others.

'Do you remember when we played at seesaw?' Her cool voice held a note of desolation like the night breeze beyond a closed casement. 'It was the perfect game for us. I knew that when you went up, it would be my turn next – to look down on you.'

Was it possible that in all the years of our uneasy friendship she had suffered a jealousy similar to mine? There was no need to ask.

'I've always envied you, I suppose. You're so self-contained and patient, with your soft brown eyes and your soft brown hair.' She stroked it lightly. There was no rancour in her tone. 'Those nightdresses you had with the frills at the neck – they made you look like the good little girl in a Sunday story book. Everyone liked you best. Except grandpa.'

All this washed over me unheeded. One single fact was all I cared to know.

'Then you married Francis without really loving him?'

'Love? I care for him. He is part of my life. But as a wife should love her husband or as a woman can love a man' – her eyes clouded in recollection – 'no, of course not. All my life I never needed to think about him. Even when we walked to church to be married I wasn't aware of him as a being separate from myself. It was when I found myself making the promises – I realised that they were being made to another person, a stranger standing at my side. It was like stepping into prison, for life, fettered to another prisoner. I felt the chill of stone walls closing round me. And if it's any consolation to you, so did he.'

Did she really imagine that I could find consolation in that – or in anything?

'In those few minutes my blood turned to ice and so did his. Marriage is supposed to unite people. It has divided us. We have nothing to say to each other. But what else could we have done? It was all arranged, all contrived. Nothing could stop it.'

I leaned my head against the green brocade of the sofa, sick at heart. Suppose Francis had known of her wanton adventure with Daniel Hebworthy, would he still have married her? Keeping the secret had done no good to them or to me. By blurting it out I might have saved them from such a joyless marriage as theirs must be and at the same time altered the course of my own life. Even now I had only to tell her what I knew to frighten her to death, I thought, with a coldness of despair that alarms me when I recall it. The shock of it would probably kill her...

The evil impulse passed. It was no more than a glimpse into noisome depths. We were united, Lilian and I, by strands of affection and resentment so entangled that from years of practice I could long for her to suffer and at the same time love her still.

'I shouldn't have told you all this,' she said. A pulse quickened in her throat. I felt her sudden anxiety. 'You'll tell Francis. You and he always tell each other everything.'

'You're mistaken,' I said. 'There are things I have never told Francis. And you must try to be happy – now that you're married.'

'It's for all our lives,' she said as if I had not spoken. 'There's no way of undoing it. Except to die.'

We both started as the door opened and in a moment Jael came softly in carrying a bowl of flowers which she placed on the pedestal table by Lilian's couch.

'The room is cold, ma'am. I came to see if you would like a fire.'

With the self-confidence of the perfectly trained servant she seemed without moving to withdraw, as she stood, her hands at her side, waiting for Lilian's answer.

As she became still, the flowers sprang into prominence. The word is not too active for the way in which, despite its multitude of objects, they dominated the room: a wide-spreading, many coloured array of cultivated and wild blooms: larkspur and pinks, big white daisies, poppies, roses and purple bells of foxglove. Jael had used nothing so wearisome as artistry. She had brought them effortlessly together with a strangely dedi-cated love. They had unity. My own mood was such that I felt their collective mood with something less than pleasure. They expressed a native spirit, original and unpredictable which might – how absurd a fancy! – become active. Jael had admitted the countryside into the house: but all is not sweet and fragrant in the country. There are other influences, baneful and hostile and vigorously alive. Beyond the flowers the clut-tered ornaments, the swans and wax fruit in all their dreadful newness seemed not only dead but embalmed.

Such thoughts could only spring from my

own disturbed state of mind. In an effort to shake myself free of them I got up and bent over the flowers to enjoy their perfume. A hundred petals shivered in response to my movement; and now I caught, breathed from the very heart of their fragrance, a hint of rankness from some bloom by no means fragrant. I thought it came from a spray of dull purple flowers drooping on curved stems that intertwined the straighter stalks with a wholly natural effect.

'Those aren't our roses.' Lilian touched one lightly, her hand only a little less white than the petals.

'They're from the Toll House, ma'am. I took the rest to the churchyard.'

'Don't bother about a fire.' Lilian's voice had lost its casual note. 'We'll go to the parlour.'

I went quickly to the door but Lilian seemed overcome with lassitude. I heard the slow dragging of her skirts behind me along the corridor as if they were holding her back.

Her little couch, the shabby wing chair, the tumbling piles of *Oddities of the Law* – remained unaltered. They seemed to reassure her. We talked until dinner time about trivial things like people addressing each other from either side of a sulphurous pit and pretending not to notice it.

15

It was not only for my own sake that I longed for Saturday to come, but for Jael's too. Life must be easier for her when Francis was at home. Inevitably, selfless as she was, she fell victim to Lilian's often unreasonable demands. Some inkling of what she had to put up with came to me the next morning when I arrived at Sacristy House to witness the tail-end of a commotion.

Lilian still used the old morning room on the ground floor. The door stood open.

'You stupid girl. Do you realise what might have happened? And it would have been your fault.' Lilian's voice rose thin and cold like a winter wind. It had already blown Hetty to the door where she stood blubbering with fright. Lilian was still in bed wearing the same amber-coloured peignoir. Her breakfast tray had been removed. She sat propped up by four pillows, her fair hair rising like an aureole; but any hint of sanctity in the room came from Jael who stood with her capped head bowed before the storm.

'It will never happen again, ma'am.' Her voice was low and respectful as ever. The quiet submissiveness brought a touching

228

memory of Agnes – and with it a tantalising sense that in recalling half-forgotten scenes at the Toll House, I ought to recall something more, some small but significant event which had altered things; or – to be more precise and more puzzling – which would alter things.

'We've always tried to put the bed back in exactly the same place when it has been moved, ma'am, but it isn't easy when it's so heavy with just the two of us.'

'It wouldn't matter about the bed if you moved the table too. As it is, the medicine glass is quite out of reach.' Lilian stretched out her arm. 'See. Oh, there you are, Maggie.'

'Still the same drops,' I said in an attempt to restore a reasonable atmosphere. 'Not the very same bottle?'

'As a matter of fact it is. The drops have always been a stand-by, thank goodness. I haven't needed them more than two or three times. But when the pain comes on – it's a kind of stiffness in my arm and side – I can scarcely move, much less stretch half-way across the room. Oh, go away, Hetty. And you too, Jael. I'll get up.'

Hetty vanished with rare speed.

'No wonder you were upset, ma'am.' Jael moved the heavy side table nearer to the bed. Her wrists were as thin as sticks. 'You might have died if you had needed your

229

drops and not been able to reach them.'

She gave me a shy smile and went to the door.

'I behaved badly.' Lilian's pout of contrition disarmed me. 'No, I'm not ill. There wasn't even that excuse. In any case I have more faith in this than in Dr Slater's potions.' She produced it from under the pillows – the hare's foot the gipsy had given her. 'Francis put this silver mount on it – he took it from an old whip – to make it more respectable.' But in fact it looked incongruous, a handsomely chased handle for a shabby dead thing. 'You remember what the gipsy said. So long as I have this, I simply can't die.'

A movement behind made me turn quickly. I had thought we were alone but only then did the door quietly close; and I remember – brief as it was – the mysterious chill of anxiety that set me shivering.

'It's the dread of illness that makes me waspish – the terror of dying – alone.'

'Don't think of it. Dr Slater has always said...'

'That I shall live for years. Imagine living to be an old woman. Years and years of being oneself.'

'It's what everyone has to put up with. Only I wonder that you risk upsetting Jael. Whatever would you do if she were to leave?'

'She won't leave. She has nowhere to go.

Still, I must say she works hard and does her best.'

She got languidly out of bed. I left her leaning against the cupboard in the wall, white-faced and golden-haired against the black oak door. The incident had revived my concern for Jael, friendless, put upon, with no other prospect than to work her fingers to the bone for Lilian. There seemed little I could do to help: but an impulse to single her out by some special favour moved me to make a surprising gesture: surprising to me, that is. I could at the very least give her a present; one that she would really like. Fortunately, as it happened, in spite of my earlier resolutions, I had been obliged to leave some of my possessions at the Lodge when I went home in April as they were too many and too awkward to pack.

Back in my room, I considered them: a carved ivory jewel box: a set of blue glass toilet bottles: neither of them of much use to Jael: a gilt-framed picture of cherub heads, a birthday present from Mrs Belfleur. It would have been difficult to explain my conviction that the chubby guileless faces would not be quite to Jael's taste. In fact, remembering the severity of her hollow cheeks and finely chiselled lips, I was suddenly irritated by the cherubs, cloud-borne, limpid-eyed and smug. No effort would be needed to part with them.

A loftier martyrdom was required. I had merely been postponing the decision. It had been clear to me from the first what the gift must be.

The fact that it would be a fearful wrench to part with it made me all the more determined. Bursting with sacrificial zeal, I emptied out its contents and rushed to Sacristy House without giving myself time to repent.

Jael was not in the kitchen, nor in any of the ground-floor rooms. She must be in her own room. It was at about this time that she usually changed from her morning prints into her more formal black. The room at the top of the back stairs was empty. She would be here presently. I marched in and set down my gift on her window sill: the miniature chest of drawers Johnny had made me. It really was a charming little piece: of walnut with two tiny half drawers and three full length ones, each fitted with a keyhole scutcheon and drop-handles of brass. I turned my back on it with a sigh.

As might be expected, the room was a model of neatness. The last time I had seen it was on the night before the wedding. The memory strengthened my weakening resolve to give the chest to Jael, absurdly inadequate as it was in way of recompense. It would not, as it happened, be the first gift I had given her. On the simple deal dressing table stood an almanac with coloured pictures which I had given her soon after she came, having pleased Ada with a similar one at Christmas. There was a separate page for each month: a picture in the upper half, a calendar below and a border of tiny scenes appropriate to the season; in this case of harvest fields, reapers and gleaners and at the top Father Time as a harvester bearing a sickle.

We were then in the second week of August. Was it just another sign of Jael's methodical nature that she had pencilled a diagonal mark across each day of the month so far? Or had she some reason for marking off the days? The possibility had not occurred to me. It seemed in direct contradiction of my assumption that for her there was no future: no hope to distinguish one day from another. With a slight feeling of guilt, I ventured to turn back the previous pages which she had folded neatly over the cardboard mount. Every day of July, June and May was similarly crossed off and so on back to the day early in January when she had come; though it was in fact later in the month when I had given her the almanac.

Yes, it was like her to be painstaking and accurate; and yet it puzzled me. Most people ticked off the days that lay between them and some unfulfilled desire: the holidays: a birthday. I replaced the almanac and saw a pencil dot above some date later in the month.

She was there, already unhooking her cotton dress when she saw me.

'I was waiting for you, Jael.' Her eyes had travelled to the almanac. 'You find it useful? You've been crossing off the days.' I blundered on in some discomfort. 'That's what I used to do, mark off the days until it was time to come to Asherby.'

'But you'll never do that again, will you, Miss Maggie?'

It was the last thing I expected from her, the calm pity in her face. She had found time, overworked though she was, to observe the moods of those she served, even mine; or was it through a natural delicacy of perception that she sensed the feelings of others? Whatever inspired it, her remark altered the balance of our relationship. It was she who was sorry for me.

'Well.' I recovered myself. 'I'm glad you have something to look forward to.'

Needless to say she offered no clue as to what it was, but stood with her hands clasped, waiting to hear why I had come.

'I want to give you a present.' So far I had stood between her and the chest. 'Look. Do you like it?'

'It's lovely.' Her beautiful eyes had brightened. 'It's a lovely thing.'

'You could use it for your sewing things.'

'Yes.' She went across and carefully pulled out one of the smooth-sliding drawers. 'But you don't want to part with it, Miss Maggie.'

'It was made in Asherby and it belongs here as you do.' The fanciful notion was easier to express than my real reason for wanting her to have it, especially as that now seemed inexplicably patronising. 'You knew the person who made it. Johnny Rigg. He gave it to me when I was a little girl.'

'Poor Johnny! And Mrs Rigg!' She had raised her head quickly and looked, not at me, but at something unseen that influenced her thoughts. It is no exaggeration to say that her spirit left me as if her attention had been unexpectedly recalled to another region, summoned by the ghostly ringing of a bell. She replaced the drawer.

'Thank you, Miss Maggie. You and Mrs Ossian were always kind to me. But I can't take it. You must keep it. It was meant for you.'

'Oh please…'

She looked at me from a great distance.

'I won't be wanting it. It would be a shame.'

Again she spoke with foresight as if her future had been arranged: a future in which emigrating to Australia and rearranging her sewing things were equally trivial.

She held out the chest with a gentle smile but so firmly that I had to take it. She was taller than I. Her grey eyes looking down had taken on a brilliance that roused in me a vague sad disquiet, whether of apprehension or from the stirring of an old fear, or of both. She had sounded so clearly the note of renunciation – it echoed in my mind as I went back to the Lodge – as to suggest the giving up of more than the walnut chest. Was she bent on renouncing the world? I thought of her already as a creature set apart. How, I mused, did a person set about becoming a nun? Some Anglican sisterhood devoted to caring for the sick and poor might provide a haven for such a girl as Jael. If my ideas of the cloistered life had been at all romantic, they now lost their glamour. The fierce purity of Jael's spirit and her rigorous self-discipline were realities strong as steel.

During the next few days I saw her more than once go up the steep path to the lychgate. By the end of the week the stone vase on Agnes's greening grave had been refilled with fresh flowers: larkspur, pinks and foxgloves. I made this discovery on the Saturday afternoon as I loitered out of doors in a mood of nervous expectation. Francis would be home in an hour or two. I had actually set off towards the turnpike road to meet him in the old way until I remembered that the old ways were over and done with. The unthinking friendship of childhood was no longer possible now that he was married to

Lilian. But I resolved to stay out of doors until he had arrived and learned that I was in Asherby.

From my vantage point on the church knoll I caught sight of Jael returning from one of her walks. She came down the farm track, stepped out on to the short stretch of road, then darted in among the trees and over the beck to Sacristy House as if afraid of being late. She was so regimented in all her ways that even these forays into wild moorland during her precious hours of freedom seemed part of the purposeful routine she had imposed on herself.

Whereas for me – my feet led me unconsciously up the same path past Comfrey Farm and out on to the moor – for me such an outing was a piece of idle indulgence. Lost in thought, I paid little heed to the bright pink bells of heath, the wheatears frisking ahead from stone to stone, the freshening breeze as the cart road dwindled into a steep footpath and then a sheep track; until the sudden consciousness of having fulfilled a purpose long ago relinquished, brought me to a halt. A few yards to my left rose a circular mound; a hillock with the top cut off to leave banked-up walls of stones and turves enclosing a shallow depression: Hagg Barrow without a doubt. I climbed the little escarpment to the edge of the tumulus itself where I could command, rather breathlessly, a wide view of rolling hills, desolate and wild.

In contrast to the pearl-like lustre of the sky, the earth had a sombre darkness. It was here on this remote moorland spur that the ancient folk of Asherby had buried their dead: not the common men: they would not merit so laborious a funeral; but the leaders, fierce, unyielding individuals whose spirits would not willingly leave the territory they had won and toiled to keep. It was best to bring them up here; and as Francis said, it would be a splendid place to haunt: to swoop low over stretches of white cotton grass shining like water in air so pure that even the earth-bound body might take wing.

So I thought, and felt no fear of Bronze Age ghosts; then looked down into the shallow pit and turned faint with sudden terror; not so much at what I saw as at what must be there unseen. For there was nothing macabre in the stones carefully laid out on the turf in the form of a simple cross; nor in the earthenware jar of flowers; larkspur, pinks and foxgloves; nothing fearful; only their incongruity in that unhallowed place and the swift message they conveyed: that Daniel Hebworthy was here at my feet.

16

I stepped back hastily and would have run away, down the long track at full speed to the safety of the village, had not the thought of Jael restrained me. The tragic solitude of her plight impressed me as never before. To think that the one outlet for her affections was to tend her family's graves, especially this one – and in this pagan wilderness! The thin black figure in silhouette against the sky when Francis and I had walked to Groat's Gate had been hers. She had come here even in winter.

As to how it had been contrived, this latest lawless addition to the tumulus, the startling light of comprehension fell not only on Jael. Her innocent flowers revealed more than the whereabouts of Daniel's body. Scarcely daring to turn my back on his grave and equally unwilling to face it, I slithered down the slope and pondered the grisly facts. The body had been stolen from the Fleece after the inquest while it awaited its unsanctified burial. Someone had brought it up here to this desolate spot. A choice of place so apt could only have come from a daring imagination – and an unusual one. It was the freakishness of the exploit that startled me. Absently wiping the clay from my Louis heels, I remembered the kitchen-maid grumbling over Francis's boots. 'Every morning this week,' she had complained, 'and he wasn't home till cock-crow...' But there was no need of circumstantial evidence. It could only have been Francis. I was sure of it – even though the certainty altered beyond recognition the Francis I had known.

More than one person must have been involved but I could think only of him. What nerve it must have taken, what cold courage of a kind that Johnny, for all his spirit, was not capable of! And it was such a long way – in the dark – with such a burden.

And yet the grim journey to the barrow was the same that the Bronze Age men had undertaken. A movement to the right drew my attention to another track apparently leading up from Groat's Gate and less steep than the one past Comfrey Farm. A horse was even now plodding up it and a vehicle of some sort. That would be the way they used to come.

I chafed my cold hands. It was as if Daniel had stepped out of the earth to revive the horrifying memory of my last glimpse of him: not leaning against an ash tree in May time nor distantly through the uncertain glass as he clasped Lilian in his arms, but face to face as I had last seen him – at the end of a rope. With the same shock of reality there had emerged a more disturbing view of Francis. Tender memories, long associations, familiar looks and words fell away useless. They failed to compose the whole person. Even while I admired and applauded what he had done, I could, with a shiver of premonition, have been a little afraid of him – as Lilian was.

Where this curious train of thought might have led me there is no knowing. The horse and gig had drawn near enough to be recognised.

'Maggie!' He jumped down and came to me through the heather. 'I saw you from Asherby Bank. What on earth are you doing here?'

'You promised never to come here without me – and you broke your promise.'

'And what about your promise?'

His smile was the same but his eyes had a guarded look which made them unexpectedly like Lilian's; and not only the eyes. Apart from their fairness of hair and complexion I had never seen any resemblance between them; but now an indefinable combination of feature and expression stamped him not as Francis – not Lilian's husband – but Lilian's cousin.

'I've found out what you did.'

'How?' His brow contracted, in displeasure, I thought.

241

'Come and see.'

At the sight of the cross and flowers his face relaxed in a wry smile.

'Jael, I suppose. She shouldn't draw attention to the place. After all it was a crime to steal a body.'

'Jael has known about it all the time?'

'I didn't mean to draw her into it. She found out.'

'But surely you didn't do it all by yourself?'

'At first I thought Johnny would help but he couldn't face it. The whole thing upset him. Daniel had been a friend. But I happen to know a fellow who would do anything for a sovereign – or less. He helped me to dig a grave…'

And here it was! I looked at it in a trance of amazement. Here we were – together at last at Hagg Barrow but not alone. How could I have dreamed that it would be in such company?

'We hid the body for one night at the old forge. The next night, while I was waiting for him, Jael came. She just appeared out of the dark. I had the impression that she had been hanging about keeping an eye on her father. She was always his shadow. I told her what we were going to do and sent her home. As it happened the fellow didn't come. I managed it myself.' He turned, measuring with his eye the long uneven path. 'From there where I left the cart was the worst part. It took all my strength.'

For a time I could not think what was wrong in his manner of telling the story. It occurred to me that it was the lack of feeling. And now for the first time there had stolen into his voice a note of warmth, of eagerness.

'In a way I enjoyed it, Maggie. No, that isn't the word. But it was a thrill to break the rules. There was a feeling of release in it. It was like turning back in time, away from respectable nineteenth-century England – to battle with darkness and death. Can you imagine how bleak, how terrifying it must have been for the men who made these barrows? For a few days I felt the bleakness and terror. And after all this is a burial place. "A place in which the remains of a person might by the laws or *custom* of England be interred." If he couldn't have a Christian burial, it seemed reasonable to give him a heathen one.'

'Reasonable! Only you, Francis, could be reasonable about such a thing.'

Some half formed notion that it was even more unusual to translate so rational a judgment into such a hare-brained action made me thoughtful. And yet to marry as he had done from motives of bloodless chivalry – was not that the same kind of oddity? Could it be that I was actually finding fault with Francis? The unfamiliar experience troubled me. I had always dreamed that some day we would stand here together and afterwards, in some mystical way, everything would be different. It hadn't occurred to me that we might be different too.

With a sudden longing to restore him to his pedestal I said eagerly: 'I believe it was really because you were sorry for him too.'

'Yes. It was unjust to go on punishing him after he was dead even if it was legal. He had suffered enough. Practising the law has taught me how little it has to do with justice. But it wasn't only the injustice. The sight of him – and what he did – he had suffered more than he could bear.' He turned to me so quickly that I had no time to prepare myself. 'Did you know, Maggie – perhaps I shock you to speak of it – that there was – a woman.'

'There was talk,' I said.

'She drove him beyond endurance. It's unfair, I suppose, and unreasonable to feel that she was the more guilty of the two.'

'You feel that?'

'It's partly because I knew him and know the price he paid; but mostly because one expects a higher standard of conduct from women. They must keep us on the right road, not lead us off it. There's no excuse for him and the shameful way he used Agnes but that woman whoever she is' – his tone was cold, his face hard with contempt – 'no one seems to know. They kept their secret well, she and Hebworthy. She must be a woman of these parts. She must have known his circumstances: a man with a family. What can one say of such a low wretch as she must be?'

I stooped and picked a sprig of heather and stared at it as if my own last hope of mercy depended on a knowledge of its structure.

'You said – he was punished enough here on earth, in his life. Do you not think she too...?'

'We must all pay for our sins, she as well as anyone else. But why on earth are we talking of such things? I haven't greeted you yet. It's a delightful surprise to find you in Asherby.'

With a certain lack of candour I explained about the tapestry.

'That was thoughtful. Such an opportunity may not come again.'

He turned away from the barrow, but I climbed back up the slope and laid my sprig of heather beside the flowers.

'If there's to be punishment,' I said breathlessly, 'there'd be forgiveness – for her too – wouldn't there?'

'Who?'

'The woman.'

'Don't think of her, Maggie. Your paths will never cross, please God. Some wretched slut at one of the out-lying farms.'

'You would have mercy on her, Francis, if ever it was found out – who she is?'

'It would not be for me to exercise mercy or withhold it. I'm not likely ever to be in her company, whoever she is.' There was no charity in his voice. 'By the way, I've never spoken to Lilian about this affair. The slightest mention of the subject upsets her. You know how sensitive she is.' He said it almost mechanically as if in response to a deeply implanted habit. Then suddenly he smiled. 'You're looking at me hard. Surely you know me well enough by this time.'

He was the same, I assured myself, the same good and gentle companion. He must be. It was just that our meeting had taken an unexpected form. Yet what form ought a meeting with Lilian's husband to take? The thought roused such a bewildering conflict of emotions that I cast my mind back with relief to an earlier occasion.

'Did you come to Martlebury, one day in May?'

'You saw me?'

'Why did you not call?'

An impulse, he told me, had made him step into a train. He had wanted very much to talk to me before the wedding.

'But finding you with Barnard brought me to my senses. It would have been too bad of me to burden you with my problems.'

'I wish you had.'

'In any event there was no solution. I must tell you, Maggie, that this marriage is not a success. It hasn't made Lilian happy. Oh, I should have foreseen. And yet what else could I have done?' He stood staring at the dark skyline with a look of hopeless resignation.

There was nothing to be said. The wind stirring the long grasses seemed the only thing of purpose in a place of death. In another three thousand years, I thought, what will have become of us? If no more than to become part of this impartial earth, what did it matter who married whom; whether a man did what he thought to be his duty, or whether he flouted it as Daniel Hebworthy had done? Any attempt to impose order on our lives seemed to me then no more than a handful of flowers and stones laid on a barren waste.

And in the depths of this sombre mood stirred an even more sombre fear: a conviction that bad as the situation was, it could be worse. I remembered hints, pronouncements about the Iredales made by my parents. 'A person can be too kind.' 'The old man has moulded their lives.' What if the mould should be cracked by pressure from within? I was still too young to understand that a dutiful nature too sternly repressed might erupt and find expression in some wild and uncharacteristic act, even though proof of it lay at my feet in Daniel Hebworthy's grave. That adventure had been an act of defiance from a man whose life was one long imprisonment to duty even before his marriage.

But what I did not understand, I felt. Suppose, confined for life in the bondage of their marriage, Francis should ever see Lilian in a different light and come to hate her. Would he face the crisis with the same weird logic, the same ice-cold courage as when he consigned Daniel to the earth up here alone in the dark? With the thought came a disturbing sense of Lilian's predicament, an anxious dread on her behalf. He must never know. Oh, Francis must never, never know.

He held out his hand to help me as we stumbled through the heather but I drew away, troubled and apprehensive. His own mood was no more cheerful.

'I don't want to go back,' he said, as the cob took its own way down the bumpy path. 'This affair of Well Cottage has made us unpopular in the village. They're blaming us for Mrs Rigg's death – and in the workhouse. That loud-mouthed wife of Ogshaw the carpenter called after me the other day: "I hear you've a fine new parlour, Mr Iredale." I turned on her and snarled – Yes, I felt myself snarling, "Hold your tongue, woman." "You can't frighten me," she said. "You're not my landlord. Our house belongs to the squire." I've come to dread the place. There's no direction in which my mind can turn for comfort. Except to you, Maggie.'

'It's too late for that,' I said.

The air in the valley felt thick and warm. I sat inert, submitting to the movement of the gig with as little interest in reaching a destination as the gnats what hovered in meaningless eddies under the low canopy of trees.

'Mr Iredale.'

Elias Hardy the postman had been standing in the road by the gate of what had once been Well Cottage. He came puffing alongside as Francis drew up.

'There's a letter come for Mrs Rigg. I don't know what's the right thing to do with it. Whether it's a case of "Returned to Sender". Norwich, it's come from. There's never but once before been a letter for Mrs Rigg in all the years I've walked these roads. You being in the legal way it might be all right for you to open it,' he concluded doubtfully, and dabbed his brow with a red spotted handkerchief.

'Let me see.'

At the sight of the handwriting Francis turned white. He tore open the envelope.

'It's from Johnny,' he said. 'He's coming home.'

17

'But how can he? The *Emma Gray*...?'

'He left her – at Yarmouth. He's been in prison for refusing to sail in her.'

I scanned the letter. One glance at the confident, slapdash sentences written in hot haste – and Johnny was alive, was there with us, miraculously unchanged.

'...I misliked the look of the *Emma* the minute I clapped eyes on her, she was so deep in water. The first day I worked on her she made eighteen inches. "If she leaks like this lying at anchor, what's going to happen when she's labouring in a storm?" I says to the master. "You'll find that out when the time comes," he says, "for you've signed on and there can be no backing out now without you want to go to gaol." He was a decent skipper and knew as well as I did that she was no better than a leaking old kettle but he had to take her or never be given another ship...'

'Johnny knew, you see,' I cried bursting with astonishment and joy. 'Wasn't that like him?'

The letter did not tell the whole story. We heard the details later.

Two days out the *Emma Gray* had nearly foundered off Yarmouth where a similar vessel had gone down with all hands in February of 1870. That was enough for Johnny. By good luck – for him – they were forced to put in for repairs and to land one of the deck-hands suffering from a fever. Having failed to persuade the crew to band together and refuse to sail, for the poor fellows dared not risk being gaoled, knowing they would never be signed on again, Johnny insisted on going ashore and facing arrest; was handed over to the police and taken handcuffed before two magistrates appointed to deal with seamen's cases. The usual term of imprisonment for breaking articles was three months. Johnny was given six, and always declared that the magistrates were themselves ship-owners and wanted to make an example of him.

As to why there had been no word from him, the explanation was tragically simple. Knowing what distress his imprisonment would cause his grandmother, Johnny had intended to keep her in ignorance of it as long as possible. One of his cronies on the *Emma Gray*, a man from the Asherby district, had promised to let her know of Johnny's plight when the ship docked after the return voyage: a promise never to be fulfilled. Johnny had come out of prison, half starved, filthy, penniless; had fallen ill, recovered, supported himself by making dolls' furniture for a dealer in Norwich from bits of wood left over when the choir stalls were repaired – until he could make himself presentable enough to come home. But only two days ago by chance he had met the sailor who had been put ashore suffering from fever. From him he had heard for the first time of the fate of the unhappy *Emma Gray* and was coming home at once.

'He's safe. But think of those poor men! Twenty-three of them. But isn't Johnny splendid? I knew he was much too clever to be drowned,' I sobbed absurdly, hysterically, passing from utter joy to pity for the lost men, from admiration for Johnny to distress for Mrs Rigg whose instinct had not failed her: and gradually when the first transport of incredulous delight had passed and Elias, scarlet as his handkerchief, had puffed away to spread the glad news, it was Mrs Rigg who stole upon the scene and silently occupied the centre of the stage.

We had got down from the gig in a daze. The dramatic turn of events had occupied only a few minutes.

'Look at that.' Francis turned over the last sheet and pointed to the concluding sentences.

'I can hardly wait to be back home. I've fixed up to leave here at the end of the week. Keep a look out for me.'

'She did. Oh Francis, she did.'

'…We'll sit by the fire like old times. It will be good to see Francis again.'

Involuntarily, as if revolved on a spit, we both turned to face the new wing of Sacristy House, formerly Well Cottage. A faint rectangular outline on the south wall where the new stone had not yet blended with the old showed where Mrs Rigg's front door had once been.

'If ever in my life I have regretted anything,' Francis said with such seriousness that I thought he would weep, 'I regret that' – and in a voice trembling with anger as well as sorrow – 'and it was so absolutely, criminally unnecessary.'

'It was Mr Iredale's decision.'

Already I found myself assuming the role of counsel for the defence in the forthcoming trial, against Johnny's furious prosecution. He would also be judge, too deeply embittered to be impartial, merciless in his condemnation. I remembered his capacity for swift action and saw again the cat lying dead and Lilian's face, white as her dress as he thrust her, half crazed, into the barn. Francis had seen neither of these things. His vision of Johnny's homecoming might be less dramatic than mine but it must have been painful judging by his expression.

'I should have stopped it somehow. How can I face him? His home gone – his grandmother dead – like a pauper in the workhouse. Thank God the furniture is still there at Groat's Gate. I haven't been able to decide what to do with it. The fact is' – as might be expected Francis had already conducted his own inward trial – 'to be completely honest, if we had known that Johnny was coming home, I would have moved heaven and earth to stop grandfather from making the alterations. Mrs Rigg would still have been here. Could anything be more base than to betray a friend because he is safely dead?'

'He will know – oh, he'll be disappointed and sad but he'll know that it wasn't your fault,' I said and mentally added that Johnny would know exactly whose fault it had been. For the first time I faced the full implications of his return. He would take a terrible revenge. Nothing now would stop him from disgracing Lilian. Why should he protect her? There'd be a scandal. It would ruin her life. She could no longer live in Asherby when it was known that the woman who had turned Granny Rigg out of her home was the same woman who had broken Agnes Hebworthy's heart. I closed my eyes and seemed to hear the whole valley echo with the bloodcurdling clamour of savage dogs, set upon Lilian.

And Francis? His face was set in lines of severity I had not seen before. Only half an hour ago he had denounced 'the wretched slut' who had driven Daniel Hebworthy to his death. 'I'm not likely ever to be in her company,' he had said. What would he do when he found out that he had married her?

If only Johnny could be appealed to before it was too late! If only he would hold his tongue!

'Lilian had no idea of the suffering it would cause.' I continued my silent pleading at the bar scarcely knowing which of her offences I was defending. 'Remember, she had been very ill and had lost touch with the world outside as sick people do. Mr Iredale only wanted her to be happy and get well again.'

The argument struck me as almost indecently flimsy, especially as Johnny too had been ill and – far more drastically than Lilian – had lost touch with the outside world. His recent experiences were not likely to have made him more reasonable or more sympathetic to the Iredales.

There would be no shortage of witnesses for the prosecution. The village was stirring. We walked a little way along the road and saw Elias installed in state on the seat encircling the chestnut on the green. Mrs Ogshaw, clearly audible even at this distance, was handing him a brimming tankard of home-brewed. Children were scurrying off to bear the tidings to the men in the harvest fields. From the sexton's cottage old William Laidler appeared and stumped up to the lych-gate with the obvious intention of ringing the church bells. I saw Ada run along the path from the Lodge to Sacristy House, all agog no doubt to share the news.

'We must tell Lilian,' I said slowly.

'You tell her. I may say too much and upset her.'

Francis went off glumly to the stables. I found Lilian in her new drawing room.

'Ada has just told me,' she said. 'You know about it. I saw you reading the letter.'

'It's wonderful news, that he's alive.'

'Yes, it's wonderful. I'm glad.' She emphasised the word and at once contradicted it by adding. 'We should have been so happy to have him back.' Her eyes – their blue was of a depth I had not seen till now – moved slowly from the peacock feathers to the silk screens, from the acanthus leaves of the fireplace to the wax fruit and feather flowers under their glass shades. 'This dreadful room. I'd like to set fire to it. But it's too cold to burn. If only it would disappear in a puff of smoke and Well Cottage come back with Mrs Rigg inside instead of me. If only I could have vanished like the wicked fairy by the time Johnny comes home. It's all my fault. I made grandfather do it. I deserve every cruel word Johnny will say to me.'

Some magical transformation had already been at work. In this softened, chastened mood she looked not unlike a forlorn figure in a fairy tale with her upspringing fair hair and pale dress of trailing muslin, and the impression she gave of having suffered the sinister effects of her own magic and lost her way. As we stood, troubled and anxious, amid all the paraphernalia of the disastrous room, the same supernatural element must have been at work on me, transforming me too. My heart melted. All jealousy and resentment left me. By some gift of grace I have always been thankful for, I cared for her again; not quite as of old when she had charmed me into a half-mesmerised affection, but with understanding and pity; with a consciousness of all she had missed and lost and all that she had to face; and with the old instinct, stronger now than ever, to help and protect her.

'Johnny always disliked me. Now it will be worse than ever. When he comes home – he will make Francis hate me too.'

'How can that be?'

'There are other things that you don't know about. Things I'm ashamed of. He will tell Francis, to shame me.'

'Could you not tell me – what they are?'

Her face was strained with nervousness. We were whispering.

'Perhaps I could tell you, Maggie. Some day I will. You would never tell. I'm so tired of carrying it about all the time, shut up inside my own self. You wouldn't despise me, Maggie, if I told you?'

I put my arms round her, uncertain how to act, knowing my own unworthiness. In continuing to love Francis I would be no better than she had been in loving Daniel Hebworthy. She had been bolder, more ruthless because her will was more vital than mine. Who could blame her if she had grasped at the opportunity of happiness, living as she had always done in the shadow of death? Was this the moment to tell her at last that I knew and sympathised – or would it only add to her distress? I evaded the decision.

'There's no need to tell me,' I said, feeling humbled and ashamed, 'unless you want to.'

As usual, having condemned her again and again, I rushed to the opposite extreme and exonerated her from blame. Others must take their share of it: Daniel, Mr Iredale, and even Agnes. Lilian had become in some mysterious way the victim, she who had so often been the offender. If afterwards, in a calmer mood, I have re-adjusted the balance of our ever changing relationship, I am glad if for once I was too generous. No, I cannot be sorry, in view of what happened, that my uncertain sympathies became fixed once more upon Lilian.

In unspoken agreement we turned our backs on the wax and alabaster, the feathers of dead birds, and the pall-like velvet draperies, to find what comfort we could in the trees, the gable end of the barn, the church, the tilted headstones and silent mounds. Francis had come back from the stables and was pacing gloomily up and down by the water's edge. He glanced towards us and remembered no doubt that he had not yet greeted Lilian since his return. Unfortunately his nearest approach was by way of the path between Mrs Rigg's lavender bushes which now led – maliciously one might have fancied – only to a blank wall. Faced with this dead-end, he stepped across a flower bed to the window. It was as if this small inconvenience brought to a head all the spleen and anxiety he had been suffering. His face, looking in, was unsmiling and hostile.

'I hope,' he said to his wife, and his tone must have cut her to the quick, 'when Johnny comes home you'll make a point of receiving him in your new drawing room.'

Lilian flinched and drew one of her gasping breaths.

'Yes,' she said softly, 'I shall make myself sit here until he comes' – and when her husband had left us – 'I can bear Francis's anger but if he should ever lose his respect for me, that would be more than I could bear.' With a touch of her old childish mischief she went on, 'I shall sit here for the rest of my days as a punishment for my sins.'

She installed herself on the damask sofa, her mauve skirts outspread, her feet on a stool, her lace ruffles drooping over her slender wrists, her long fingers clasped in an attitude of half mocking martyrdom.

Throughout the following day at least she kept her word. It was Sunday, a day of such interminable length that by evening we all seemed to have grown older. I sat with my back to the window where I could see the leaves move in the gilt-framed mirror until it seemed as if not just a day but a whole summer had passed. Lilian and I might have fared better on our own but Francis stayed with us, glued to a Bradshaw and scarcely speaking except to speculate on the time of Johnny's arrival which would almost certainly be on the next day.

If he travelled by rail he would either come to Cantleton by the coastal line; or, more likely since Cantleton was nine miles to the north of Asherby, he would come to Whingate. Francis proposed to meet the late afternoon train there and if necessary the evening one. Whatever our secret thoughts, on one point we were unanimous: the necessity of breaking the news to Johnny before he actually arrived and discovered for himself the changes wrought in his absence.

The nerve-racking day was so uneventful that tiny incidents seemed significant. Lilian and I had got out our desks and were writing to our mothers.

'It will be your mother's birthday on

Wednesday,' I remarked without looking up as I wrote the date. 'Did you remember to write to her in good time?'

Lilian murmured an assent. The birthday was easy to remember because we had always celebrated it in style: a drive to Cantleton Rocks, tea at the Toll House, charades in the evening, and last year of course there had been the wedding. Mrs Belfleur had married on her forty-second birthday. That had been Lilian's idea. With these recollections was mingled one more elusive; some more recent reminder of the date. 19th August. It appeared to my inward eye in bold black figures, not written but printed, to tease my memory and then fade.

'Do tell your mother that Annie Warnold will bring her the tapestry.'

There was no answer. Lilian was turning out the contents of her velvet bag on to the table. Then she thrust her hand into her pocket and brought out one by one a handkerchief, a gold pencil and a vinaigrette, put them back and looked about her anxiously.

'Have you lost something?'

'My hare's foot. I've never mislaid it before. Have you seen it, Francis? I must ask Jael. I gave her some old petticoats and things to take up to the attic. It may have got caught up in the bundle.'

'I should let it stay there,' Francis said. 'It's high time the thing was thrown away.'

'How can you say that? You know what it means to me.'

He smiled coldly. Everything in the room was cold. Jael had lit a fire. The pale flames reached up bravely only to sink down disheartened by the surrounding morgue-like chill. In my thin summer dress I felt as inadequately clothed as the porcelain cupids on the French clock, whose fingers might have been frozen, so slowly did they move. Even with my head bent over my letter I felt the silent presence of the flowers massed in great bowls and vases like an attentive crowd. The white roses at my elbow smelt of white paint.

It must have been at about ten o'clock the next morning when I took the green path to Sacristy House and saw Francis driving off through the front gates. I had got as far as the stepping stones when Lilian came out of the house with a letter in her hand. Seeing me, she came quickly across.

'This has just come. It's for Francis. From Johnny, I think.'

'It's too late. Francis must be well on his way by this time.' We gazed at the letter in consternation. 'Perhaps you'd better open it.'

She hesitated, turning it over and over, then tore open the envelope, glanced at the contents and handed the letter to me. It was simply to say that he would be arriving at Cantleton on the eleven o'clock train. He had obviously written in the hope that Francis would meet him.

As it was, he would be upon us before Francis came back from Whingate, having waited to meet the later train. Johnny would arrive unprepared, tired, disheartened, to find his home gone, his grandmother dead. It was the very situation we had hoped to avoid.

Lilian seemed absorbed in some anxious calculation. It didn't take me long to make up my mind. I must go myself to meet Johnny. Unlike Francis, I knew the whole story; could point out to him the harm he could do to Lilian and Francis; beg him to have mercy.

'Yes,' Lilian said after a thoughtful pause when I made the suggestion – though without giving all my reasons – 'perhaps that would be best.'

There was no question of her going. The strenuous walk would have been far beyond her strength. Already she was looking exhausted. Her helplessness was, as always, touching. Moved as I was by it, I could still see how effective it had always been. If only…

'Of course the best thing of all,' I said, 'would be for you to tell him all about it yourself.'

She looked at me, suddenly attentive.

'You're so clever,' I said, half teasing and certainly without the least notion of the effect my remark might have, 'and so charming. No one can resist you.'

We exchanged the grimaces proper between friends on such occasions. I rushed off to the Lodge, gabbled an explanation to Miss Abbot, pinned up my skirt, put on thick shoes and came back to find Lilian crouched on the turtle-shaped boulder trailing her fingers in the water in the old way and watching them change under the stealthily moving current into sharp white claws.

'I shall be waiting in the drawing room,' she said with an attempt at lightness; and with an irony I can appreciate more fully now as I look back, remembering her cool voice. If it came as always with an effect of emptiness, it had pathos too. For some reason I hesitated to leave her, as if we were parting for a long time.

'Dearest Maggie. What should I do without you? I can't think' – a look of wonder dawned in her blue eyes – 'why you care so much.'

As I stepped from the path into the road, I turned to wave but she was not looking. She had made her way to the barn. Through the leaves I saw her with arms outspread as she leaned with all her weight against the wall. The sun brightened her cloud of fair hair so that her head took on once more the look of a sculptured angel's head; but from this distance I could not see her expression; and perhaps that was just as well.

18

The way to Cantleton, like all Asherby's roads, was rough and steep. It wound uphill between high hedges for a mile or more until wild rose and hazel gave way to stone walls and wide grass verges. I paused for breath and instantly saw, in the more open country, the figure of a woman walking ahead: a plump, middle-aged body in a brown shawl and bonnet: Mrs Ogshaw, the loud-mouthed wife of the village carpenter.

Here was a dilemma. It might be possible by a superhuman effort to overtake her but there would be little hope of leaving her behind. She would pant along at my side, talking all the way. Her conversation at best was not pleasing. On this occasion it would be insufferable. She would have but one topic: the adventures of her husband's former apprentice and how he had been wronged by the Iredales. On the other hand by lagging behind I risked the possibility that she would meet Johnny before I did and deliver her version of recent events in Asherby with as little delicacy as could be achieved with a sledge-hammer.

The white road climbed steeply in the full

glare of the mid-day sun. Instinctively I ducked down in the shelter of the wall as Mrs Ogshaw stopped and took off her shawl. She would be going to visit her daughter, a farmer's wife living somewhere between Asherby and Cantleton. I hoped, not only for Mrs Ogshaw's sake, that the journey would be short. She was moving on more slowly. I followed cautiously and at the next bend was happy to see, a quarter of a mile away on the left side of the road, a red-tiled farmhouse amid its barns and byres: a pleasant and even enviable home for Mrs Ogshaw's daughter.

It seemed a good idea to rest for a while and so give Mrs Ogshaw time to reach the farm gate. I clambered over the wall into a stretch of rough pasture where a busy stream gushed down the hillside between bracken and bog myrtle, and saw that by following its course uphill I could cut off a wide loop and save almost a mile: but soon the bank of the stream became less defined and I plunged over my shoe-tops into a treacherous morass of water-logged sedge. Regretting the loss of time, I scrambled out and ran back to the road only to see Mrs Ogshaw, now twice as far ahead, relentlessly passing the farm gate. Another minute and she had vanished round the next bend.

Johnny would probably travel from Cantleton in the carrier's wagon, which would stop to pick up and set down parcels at the Travellers' Arms, a humble wayside inn about four and a half miles from Asherby. I could only pray that Mrs Ogshaw would turn aside at some nearer point; otherwise she and the carrier would converge upon the inn at the same time. There was nothing for it but to put on a tremendous spurt, over-haul her and go firmly ahead with no more than a word of greeting.

Another twenty minutes brought me, breathless, to the brow of a hill where I could look down on the whitewashed walls of the Travellers' Arms and Mrs Ogshaw plodding resolutely towards it. It was impossible to get there before her. Even if I did, she would arrive hot on my heels. How was the meeting with Johnny to be managed in her presence? Must we besiege the carrier's cart together, each clamouring to tell her story? The one hope was that she would even yet turn aside along some field path.

The hope died as she drew level with the inn, set down her bass bag and sank grate-fully on the wooden seat by the door, where she was immediately joined by a woman in an apron, presumably the landlady. They settled down to enjoy a chat.

Disconsolately I sat down on a milestone marked: Cantleton: 5 miles; took off my shoes and stretched out my feet to dry in the sun. A grasshopper alighted on my skirt; far away a dog barked; and Mrs Ogshaw and the landlady disappeared into the Travellers' Arms. Now was my chance. In ten minutes I could be past the inn with Mrs Ogshaw safely inside. Beyond it the road climbed, turned west and climbed again to the top of the last hill above Cantleton. And now I caught a distant movement close to the sky as a hooded cart hove into view and stopped after the long upward haul. My heart beat fast at the thought of Johnny inside, or more likely seated beside the driver, eagerly scanning the familiar landmarks, impatient to be home.

I had hustled my feet into their stiffening shoes ready to make a desperate dash past the inn when the exasperating Mrs Ogshaw reappeared with two or three other people: the landlady, a stout man in shirt sleeves and a villainous-looking tramp. Mrs Ogshaw sat down on the bench; the stout man carried a few packages to the road side as if for the carrier; the tramp took his leave and set off in my direction. He was such a rough-looking vagabond in his short tattered coat with a white hat above his black-bearded face that I shrank from meeting him and was once more on the point of climbing a wall when he forestalled me, leapt over the near-est gate and went striding downhill, follow-ing the stream with such reckless speed that

I wondered he did not fall. In no time he had come to the patch of bog, made no attempt to avoid it but plunged in over the ankles with no more concern than if he were walking on a lawn and went on in a stumbling trot, his coat flapping, like a scarecrow run amok; a desperate fellow whom I had been lucky to avoid.

These evasions had ruffled me a little but after all they were to be crowned with success. Not only did Mrs Ogshaw gather up her bass bag and shawl and lumber off; but almost at once she left the road for a rough track which led her into a stony hollow and out of sight. I shook out my skirt, straightened my hat and presently took her place gratefully on the bench. The inn was a poor, bare place, no better than a pothouse but I was determined to stay there until the carrier arrived.

Instantly the landlady appeared. She was a thin woman with pale prominent eyes which gave her a look of startled surprise; but we had exchanged no more than a few words when I detected in her manner a suppressed excitement. Something unusual had happened. But in that quiet spot to have two or three callers in one afternoon must in itself be an unusual experience.

'You've come from Asherby as well then?' Her eyes expressed an amazement disproportionate to the simple fact. She pursed her lips, nodded knowingly and was about to speak when I begged her to make me some tea. 'There's a pot just made with no more than two cups poured out – and one of them hardly touched.' She darted off and returned with a thick white cup brimming over into its saucer.

'If you've come from Asherby, you'll know Mrs Ogshaw.'

No confirmation was needed: Mrs Ogshaw was well known. Discouraged by my silence, the landlady left me to drink my tea, watch the green hood of the carrier's cart crawl like a caterpillar above the limestone walls – and prepare myself for the meeting with Johnny, now only a few minutes away.

'Mrs Ogshaw paid for it. But nobody likes to see money thrown away.' The landlady had come out again carrying a moustache-cup of tea and cast its contents on the grass. 'He'd no more than wetted his lips.' Her startled eyes explored the cup in disbelief. 'And a good meal would have done him no harm, by the looks of him. He was naught but skin and bone.'

She must be referring to the tramp. It was indeed surprising that he had not drunk his tea but had apparently rushed off after a single sip and gone crashing down the hill like a madman. A faint uneasiness hovered about the memory. Yes, the combination of heedlessness and haste had given an impression of insane purpose.

'"Here," I says to him, "drink your tea. It'll do you good and Mrs Ogshaw'll settle for it." For that matter it wouldn't have been the first time I'd given a cup of tea to such as him for nothing. "I can't wait"' he says – and claps his hat on his head. "As for settling, I've got some settling to do myself." If you could have seen his face when Mrs Ogshaw told him.' Her pent-up longing to tell the story showed signs of breaking forth. 'Funny her knowing him. You're not going already?'

Like a sleepwalker obedient to some mysterious compulsion I had got up, rummaged in my purse for a sixpence and silently laid it on the tray. She looked, transfixed with astonishment, from the coin to my half empty cup.

'There surely can't be anything wrong with the tea.'

I shook my head and in the same trance-like mood took to the road again.

'You'll never walk all the way back? Wait for the wagon. It'll be here directly.'

Her voice grew fainter as I trudged away into merciful solitude. Tears blinded me to ruts and stones: tears of distress and helpless sympathy. Could that be all that was left of Johnny Rigg, that man of rags and bones? Against all likelihood I had expected to see him smiling, cocksure, debonair. There had always been a touch of the dandy about his neckties, I remembered. He had certainly grown a beard: that was why I hadn't recognised him; but far from growing rich, he had lost all he had, even his home. He hadn't waited for the carrier but had rushed headlong across country from Cantleton, hoping all the time to see Francis coming to meet him with the gig, only to be confronted instead with Mrs Ogshaw and her story.

There was no hope of catching up with him; yet I could not bear to be overtaken by the carrier and so walked quickly, risking shortcuts and sometimes running; and step by step Johnny's image grew more insistent, more grotesque and wild; step by step I feverishly touched up the picture, darkening its mood, underlining the anger and despair, strengthening the purpose that drove him headlong down the hill to Asherby as if no hedge or wall or ditch could even for a moment hold him back.

At the top of the last incline I stopped to rest. Soon the hedges of wild rose and hazel would enclose me again but from here I could look down on the village, half submerged in thick foliage. A deadly weariness came over me: a depression so deep that for all the light and warmth of summer, the heather-scented air, the harebells blue as the sky, I stared into darkness and saw no chink of light. The change in Johnny, though the most spectacular, was only one of many changes. Once, long ago in another age, under those sheltering trees by the friendly beck, the timeless days of childhood had slipped by as if in one unbroken summer. Now ill luck seemed to have fallen upon us. The churchyard, the Barrow, the forge, the Toll House chimneys – from this high point I could see them all and interpret their silent testimony. Sacristy House was out of sight, hidden in its hollow.

With the sudden lurid clarity of a lantern slide another picture took shape; of Lilian's drawing room in all its hostile newness, cold as a tomb; and on the sofa, Lilian waiting as she had promised, her light skirts outspread, her hands as I had so often seen them, bloodless and waxen as if all life had left them. It was for her sake that I had come on this wildgoose chase, wanting only to protect her, to shield her from distress. It must have been the tiredness, the heat, the disappointment that suddenly sharpened my anxiety and turned it into fear. My heart beat so wildly that it agitated not only my own body but the whole scene. Hills and sky seemed to move, in defiance of the laws of nature. There were no laws, no rules that could not be broken.

Far below, across the stretch of rough grass at the moor's edge, a tattered figure was moving rapidly towards the village.

19

There was nothing I could do, only watch. In all my days at Asherby I had been nothing more than a looker-on, seeing more of the game perhaps than the others did but taking no active part in it. My only claim to involvement had been that I cared so much for all of them – and for the place, more ravishingly beautiful than ever seen from this high point in this moment of heightened perception.

With all the land falling away into a blue-green hemisphere of meadows and copses, pastures and lanes, I saw everything: not only Johnny drawing steadily nearer to Sacristy House but the whole chain of events his arrival there would set in motion like falling ninepins. In this way God must look down on the world. 'Now,' He must sometimes think 'now is the time to intervene.' And He would reach down and with a benign hand move one of his creatures and set him on another course. That was what He must do *now*.

I looked up into the vast and mighty sky. It wouldn't only be for Lilian, I pointed out, but for Francis too. But I saw the difficulty.

He was all-powerful, so powerful that He could extinguish us all as easily as a man might kill a cat. All the same it was difficult to see how with a single gesture He could make us all happy. Whatever He did, somebody would be left out; unless, stooping low with a mighty breath like a great wind filled with the smell of peat and heather, He could re-arrange the entire scene.

Reeling from my contemplation of the enigmatic heavens, I looked down. Johnny had reached the gate opening on to the lane that led to the village. As if in response to some unseen influence he ignored it, went past without slackening his pace and made his way westward along the green fringe of the moor towards Groat's Gate. I saw his head bobbing above the tall bracken.

There was still time.

He woke to see me looking in over the half door. He was lying on the mat by the hearth where he had kindled a fire. Without the ragged coat, in a shirt once white, he looked less like a scarecrow. His black-bearded face broke into a smile.

'It's me. Maggie Ossian.'

'So I see. I hadn't forgotten you.'

He got up and unbolted the lower half of the door.

'I've been looking for you all day.'

'That was nice of you, Miss Maggie. I had

no idea that you were at Miss Abbot's, or I would have called.'

The words – politely conventional – might have been droll in view of his vagabond state but they were perfectly sincere and instantly re-affirmed his social confidence.

'I saw you at the Travellers' Arms. I thought you were a tramp.'

'You were there? A tramp? That's what I am. You've never walked all that way?'

'I went to meet you,' I broke out wildly, 'to explain. But Mrs Ogshaw saw you first.'

'Come and sit down. You've got yourself into a state.'

He moved Mrs Rigg's chair to the window.

'Oh Johnny, you haven't changed. I'm so happy to see you – and so dreadfully sorry…'

'I'm glad you think I haven't changed,' he said grimly.

'Only in your looks. That's nothing. You see, I thought…'

He listened while I unburdened myself pell-mell of all my fears. My well-rehearsed pleading for the Iredales lapsed into hopeless incoherence. There was no tact, no wisdom and little sense in what I said.

'What exactly did you think I would do?'

What indeed? I looked at him. His face was thin and lined, all the paler for the blackness of his beard. His dark eyes were sunken. Their expression was different. In their depths burned a flame of – was it passion?

276

Some new purpose? But in his immediate grasp of the situation he was himself, unchanged.

'Did you think I would lay hands on Lilian and strangle her in revenge for what she did to my grandmother? Don't cry,' he said gently. 'Tell me, was it because you thought I had the instincts of a murderer or because you thought Lilian deserved it? You thought that turning a good old woman out of her home was about as bad a thing as a spoilt young woman could do, didn't you? I honour you for that.'

'I never thought you would be cruel to her physically,' I protested. It wasn't true, though the notions I had entertained had been too wild to be called thoughts. 'But you treated her roughly – the day Daniel Hebworthy died; and I did think, and so did Lilian, that you might punish her by telling Francis about Daniel, and that might have brought on one of her attacks. She's afraid of you.'

'I'm not sorry for that. But you were mistaken. I would never have told Francis. He hasn't behaved like a friend but there's no need to add to his miseries. He's too good at making himself miserable to need any help from me.'

'Then no one need ever know but you and me.' He looked at me sharply but did not contradict.

'She told you?' he said instead.

'No. I found out. They were in the barn that morning, weren't they?' I looked away, embarrassed.

'Poor Lilian!' he said unexpectedly. 'It disgusted me at the time and made me angry with them both. She always had to have what she wanted. But that was her only escape from all the pampering and cosseting Francis gave her. And now she's tied to him for life. It wasn't Daniel that ruined her. It was Francis. Marriage has turned them into a pair of waxworks, according to Mrs Ogshaw. Still, the Iredales would rather be miserable together than happy with anyone else.'

The reversal of so many of my ideas left me bewildered and weak. I discovered that I had not eaten for hours; nor had Johnny. To my surprise he told me that he had found the door unlocked and food on the table when he arrived but he had been too tired to eat. We sat down and shared a meat pie, bread and cheese. I suggested that he should come back with me to Jasmine Lodge where he would be more comfortable but he declined.

'There isn't time,' he said. 'Now that there's nothing to keep me here.' He swallowed a lump in his throat, the one sign of personal distress he had shown. 'I'll collect a few things and move on. There's so much to be done that can't wait.' His seriousness was almost ferocious. I remembered his remark to the landlady about having an account to settle and realised that I had misinterpreted it. 'You weren't mistaken about my murderous intentions. I want revenge all right. But not on the Iredales. Their kind are not worth wasting energy on. They've done me a good turn by hammering home the lesson that the poor have no chance against the rich. The only thing is to make money and make better use of it than they do. No, my revenge will be on the godless villains that let the *Emma Gray* go to the bottom with twenty-three decent men on board. I'm going to find the owners, Miss Maggie, and hound them. It's them I'm going to frighten to death.'

He would succeed. I quailed myself before the ferocity of his dark scowl and burning eyes. He explained how the ownership of a vessel was divided into sixty-four parts bought in various proportions – sometimes by a number of owners. To my surprise they were often small speculators: comfortable drapers, village schoolmasters, single ladies with legacies to invest. His plan was to find and confront every individual who had shares in the *Emma Gray* and bring home to each of them the effects of their indifference and greed.

'A man doesn't go through what I've been through this last year without having his mind sharpened – and hardened. I've shed one thing after another until there's nothing left but the one thing that matters: to save poor folk from being treated like dirt. It's too late to save my old granny.' He looked round at her simple possessions as if trying to identify acquaintances in a strange place, then went on with bitter sadness. 'And it won't hurt me too much to cut the Iredales out of my life. But there is something I can do for the seamen. Do you know' – he spoke so sternly that I flinched – 'that there are laws to stop horses from being overloaded, but overloading ships – that doesn't matter. It's only men that go to their deaths.'

He turned, caught sight of himself in the glass of his grandmother's sideboard and gave a rueful grimace.

'In prison I used to imagine myself in decent clothes again, smartened up. But I've changed my mind. This is how I'll go, like a tramp, and let the world see what they've done to me. I'll stand at the street corners and shout it to the high heavens. What's the use of looking respectable when you're talking about a massacre?'

He intended to seek out all the dependants of the dead men, raise funds, get up subscription lists.

'I'm glad you're here in Asherby.' I felt flattered until he added, 'One of the things I planned was to see your father. You said he knew Mr Plimsoll. You can give me his address. Plimsoll's the man I must see, and I'll write to the editor of *The Lifeboat*.'

He pulled out one or two drawers as if looking for paper and pen.

'My father will give you money – and Francis.'

'If Francis feels he owes me anything, he can give me money for the widows of the *Emma Gray*'s crew. I'll take nothing else from him. Who left this pie?' He stopped chewing and looked at it suspiciously.

'Mrs Ogshaw perhaps,' I tactfully suggested. 'I'll help you. I'll make people give money.' An endless pageant of bazaars and musical evenings marshalled itself in my imagination. But oh, how dull a woman's part would be in such a stirring enterprise! 'You'll do it, Johnny. You'll succeed.'

And indeed when an amended Merchant Seamen's Bill was passed in the following summer I was not the only one to feel that Johnny Rigg had had his share in it.

I went to the door. The day had mellowed into early evening. Trees pointed their long shadows towards Asherby. The air was still; but I felt that a mighty wind had indeed blown down from the moor, transformed the scene and purified my soul. The very largeness of Johnny's magnificent purpose, his freedom from self-interest and meanness, reduced the affairs at Asherby, so momentous an hour ago, to no more than the murmur of gossip at the parish pump.

'You won't go without saying goodbye?'

'What's that?' He looked up absently from his letter, saw that I was leaving and got up. 'I'll be going first thing in the morning. The sooner the better.'

We shook hands.

'You'll come back, Johnny?' His haggard face and beggarly look still troubled me. 'Why don't you marry and settle down.' Inspiration came to me. 'You could marry Jael.'

'Jael!' He looked positively startled. 'Jael Hebworthy?'

'She would look after you. She's a wonderful housekeeper – and she needs someone...'

'You've seen her?'

'Why, she works at Sacristy House. Quite by chance she saw the advertisement in the *Courier*.'

'She came – in answer to an advertisement?'

He seemed strangely impressed. Her coming had been a coincidence: I had felt it to be so myself. But his look was one of consternation; at my suggestion that he should marry, presumably.

'Think about it,' I said, pretending to tease but rather taken up with my idea.

'No.' He spoke quite vehemently. 'No.'

'She's a perfect treasure, Johnny.'

'She's a Hebworthy,' he said slowly and for some reason I felt the smile fade from my lips. 'And I can't understand why she – oh well!' He shrugged as if deliberately dismissing a problem. 'Goodbye, Miss Maggie.'

At the curve in the road I turned. He was watching me from the half door – and waved. In the circumstances it was good of him to spare the time.

My mood became less uplifted as I trudged along in the dust. When I left behind the great purple swell of Groat Moor and stepped into the shadow of the larches, a new kind of depression subdued my spirit. The disaster had been averted. The ninepins need never fall. The circumstance which might have alienated Francis from his wife was buried now for ever. But after all what joy was there in that for me? It had been easy to plan Johnny's future. The complications in my own life were less easy to resolve. There hovered too on the very fringe of consciousness the notion of some additional anxiety; an impression of random facts ignored like straws lifted by a wind too light to direct their movement steadily in one direction. Troubled by these undefined anxieties, I felt an unfamiliar distaste for Asherby: an impulse to throw off its entanglements: to be done with it; especially as the air here in the hollow below the church was stagnant and heavy. The streams crept sullenly between the stepping stones. In the hall I had to stop to draw breath, half suffocated by the scent of flowers. Tired as I was, I found them all at once overpowering. There seemed to be more of them than ever. They were everywhere, bowls of them on the chest, the window sill, the Pembroke table. It was as if they had moved into the house of their own accord bringing with them the primitive power of the countryside, sinister and sweet. Cornflowers and scabious, hollyhocks, cranesbill and foxgloves – all the crimsons and blues and purples of high summer gathered in a triumphant assertion – of what? The watchful confidence of their petalled heads made me suddenly, irrationally, nervous. I think of them now as an interested audience gathered to see the last act.

'Lilian!' I took refuge in the passage leading to the drawing room where they couldn't see me. 'Lilian!' How long the day must have seemed to her? 'Are you there?'

She didn't answer. I burst into the room. She was there on the sofa just as I had pictured her. She did not turn her head or speak. Her skirts were curiously entangled, her feet oddly splayed as if they could not find the footstool. Her head lay askew. She seemed to look at me sideways from under her cloud of golden hair and her expression did not change.

I raised her head. It lolled back to rest upon her shoulder. Her arm was outstretched, the fingers reaching out as if for help; or as if even to the very end there was something she had failed to grasp.

20

In all my life I have never felt again so sharp a grief. Pure sorrow brought me to my knees at her side to weep my heart out for the loss of my first and closest friend. It was as if a light had gone out, a flame which had warmed and brightened even if it had also seared and scorched my childhood.

'She's dead,' I told some unseen, unbelieving listener. 'Lilian's dead' – and looking at her wan face could only feel her persistent vitality. It filled my whole being and overflowed the room: the silent room.

When the first agony of tears had passed, I became aware of the total absence of other sounds. The fingers of the clock had finally frozen at four o'clock. It must be a good deal later: the sun was far to the west, the room in shade. Flower petals littered the carpet. Lilian's little writing desk had fallen from her lap. The pen had lodged its nib in her skirt. By her left foot lay the still un-finished letter to India. If only her mother were here! How strange! – I seized upon this additional strangeness as if it offered an escape from the mournful scene – it was almost exactly a year since she had left.

'Be well and happy and good,' she had decreed sweetly, uselessly, without reference to probability from the cloudless peak of her idyll.

I got up, my teeth chattering, and laid the desk and letter and pen carefully on a chair. Lilian's form had become an object quite separate from the spiritual presence pulsat-ing in the air and in my heart and mind: a thing of light hair and crushed muslin and blanched skin, limp, consigned to death, abandoned.

At the same time I recognised another feeling. It had been there from the moment I found her, a troubled undercurrent to my grief: a sense of something that demanded my attention. I looked stupidly round the room, half conscious of some abnormality among its crowded contents: some small significant thing which altered the situation; then stole another glance at Lilian. The look of feline grace cruelly halted, the poise of the fingers like open claws set me shudder-ing again.

Tragic, shocking as it was, Lilian's death was not unexpected. The sword had hung above her head all her life and now it had fallen. If I had never quite believed that it would happen, that was because even at the worst crises of illness she had always been more full of life than anyone else. Like her great-aunt she had been doomed to die young. But surely she need not have died like this, alone: she who had always dreaded solitude and clutched at other people for support. The white fingers outstretched to the limit of their slender bones symbolised that need; and yet the glass was there on the table and beyond it, the bottle, but just too far for her to reach. The irony of it after all the care we had taken! An inch or two nearer and it might have saved her life. The frustrated hand was unbearably pathetic, as if she had been pleading, entreating – though there had been no one to hear.

A sudden doubt seized me. I stumbled to the door and in so doing discovered the peculiar thing that made the room different: a blankness on the wall opposite the window where the mirror should be giving back its green reflection of leaves outside.

The glass had been turned to the wall.

I had not forgotten – indeed it came back to me with piercing sharpness – the last time I had heard of the country custom.

'Stop the clock, Effie,' Agnes had said, 'and turn the glass to the wall.'

That had been when her baby died, a year ago almost to the day. Some one had already done the same thing for Lilian. Some one had been here. The simple ritual enlightened me, teaching me the truth I should long ago have grasped; so that I knew not only who had been here but much, much more. I knew how it must have been even before Jael silently appeared.

She closed the door behind her and stood, hands at her side, in the attitude of a perfect servant. But there was no servility in the look that irradiated her delicate features. It was a look of exaltation.

'You found her – dead?' I said, still unwilling to think the worst.

'I found her – ill.'

My eyes travelled to the bottle, less than a finger's length from Lilian's grasp, then back to Jael's face. Her marvellous grey eyes blazed with all her father's intensity – and more. What folly to have thought of her only as Agnes's daughter! She was Daniel's child, his second self, his shadow. She had followed him everywhere, known everything he did, seen everything – and what she had not seen, sensed with the cruel pain a loving child would suffer, tongue-tied. Those meetings, day and night…

A weird sense of the impropriety of speaking or even thinking of such things in Lilian's presence made me motion Jael into the narrow corridor. We faced each other, so close that her white face and light-filled eyes appear before me even now, bringing the same awe and fear I felt then.

'You could have saved her.'

'It was what I came here for, to see her die. It's what I've prayed for every day and every night.'

'You've been waiting – all this time – while you...' I was far beyond tears now but a deep sob rent my whole body. 'Oh Jael, had you no pity?'

'No more than she had.'

Her face was ruthless as steel. I looked away.

'It was wicked, to let her die without comfort or help.'

'That was how my mother died.'

Her white face changed a little in response to an inward pang, but of the spirit not the flesh. She seemed hardly to belong to the physical world at all. But I guessed from that barely perceptible change that she was remembering the Toll House; and how childishly young she looked! Not much older after all than when she had snatched the baby out of the wicker cradle and carried him away from Lilian's baneful influence; or when she had sat under the churchyard wall clutching her flowers, knowing where her father was – and with whom. How could I have failed to see that of course she had known the whole story, always?

'You've been waiting for this to happen.'

'The Lord has done it. He answered my prayers.' The flame burned again in her eyes. 'He has saved me at the eleventh hour.' She gazed beyond me into whatever mysterious realm her spirit inhabited. 'If He had not, I would have done it myself, soon, tomorrow – or the next day.'

With a chill of horror I pictured her relentless hand as she marked off the days on the almanac. The wedding meant nothing to her. The coming anniversary would be of her father's – and mother's – and brother's death.

'I prayed for the strength to do it. To poison her. Time and again courage failed me. That's why I made a promise to myself. "It'll be on the same day come a year," I said, "if I haven't done it before." Then, as if sensing the question I could not bring myself to ask: 'I meant to do it with the flowers.'

She relaxed a little as if speaking of friends. With a tremendous effort I told myself that she was unhinged, distraught, in need of help. Someone should have known, have helped her, rescued her from the terrible flower-filled world she had made for herself and from the pagan god she had turned to. Her view was distorted, her morality a rank growth sprung from suffering. It was too late. There was no reaching her now.

'You mustn't say such things.'

'It's true,' she said with a faint hint of reproach. 'And it was you, Miss Maggie, that first gave me the idea.'

'I?'

'You came running up to the Toll House one day – a long time ago – to show us a drawing you had made, of monkshood, you said. But Mother called it wolf's bane. "You should learn the plants that are poisonous," she said to me when you'd gone, "if ever you want to work in a stillroom else you never know what might happen." That's where she learned them. I know plenty of them, Miss Maggie. There's cuckoo pint and night-shade, baneberry and hemlock, bear's foot and kingcups.' In her low voice, the names as she recited them were like a quiet spell. 'Whenever I arranged the flowers, I tried to put in one of the poison kind to remind me how easy it would be... But with some it's only the berries and I couldn't wait for them. With wolf's bane it's the whole plant. I found it down there by the beck in the spring. That's what I meant to use. It was only finding the courage.'

As it was, she had not needed it; not active courage. She had made do with the implac-able hate that enabled her to watch, rejoic-ing, as Lilian died, even when she pleaded, reaching out in agony for her medicine. I wondered, and put the thought from me, whether that avenging hand had actually moved the bottle further away, inch by inch. Had it been so? I could not, dare not, must not ask.

'You could not have done it,' I said, trying to reach out across the grim abyss that separated Jael from the rest of us. 'It would have been a terrible crime. To poison someone! They would have hanged you.'

Her neck was frail and slender. Above it her oval face was calm.

'I would only have died like my father,' she said. A tremor shook her whole frame. I thought her eyes filled but no tears fell.

She had been prepared then to face the consequences; had been steadily preparing herself to leave the world. I had not been mistaken about that. I could scarcely have envisaged the motive and direction and means of her departure. The life of a convent, I could now see, would scarcely have suited Jael; an altogether too safe and sedate a retreat for a girl who could look steadfastly into the fires of hell and face damnation without turning aside. As to whether the crime of withholding aid while Lilian died was less heinous than the crime of poisoning her, I have never been able to decide; any more than I have ever been able to bring flowers into the house without a sickening qualm. Whatever the morality of it, one thing was certain: the Hebworthys were not like other people. Local opinion had not erred in that respect. Even now Jael could still astonish me.

'What will you do?' I whispered, in the presence of her appalling guilt.

She withdrew her gaze from the infinite and gave her attention to the future.

'I can go now,' she said and added with a correctness grotesque under the circumstances, 'when it is convenient to Mr Francis. I would not like to desert him at a time like this.' Then with a sudden change to the likeness of the ardent child she might have been in another untroubled, different existence, 'It will be better here now that the evil is gone from the house. You'll see. She was evil, Miss Maggie. Everyone suffered because of her. Not only me. You, Mr Francis, Mrs Rigg... But it will be better now.'

The uncharacteristic spate of words ceased. She was as quietly composed as if she were bringing in the tea, in her snowy muslin apron, with her hair neatly braided under a cap of virginal white, her eyes luminous with the remote, uplifted look that had become habitual. It had indeed intensified so that it seemed as if her narrow shoes of shining black were her only contact with the earth.

'She's wicked,' I thought. 'No better than a murderess. She's lucky to have escaped the gallows.' But I didn't believe it, couldn't feel it to be true.

The ache in my head and shoulders, the trembling in my knees, recalled me to the immediate situation and its demands. It would be hours still before Francis came home. He must be sent for. At the thought of his return and all the problems it would bring, my head reeled.

'Jael, you must do something for me.'

She gave me all her attention, watching my lips as a foreign person might do.

'You have told me all this' – if I spoke deliberately as to a child, it was because I could not tell what strange inhuman attitude she might adopt – 'because we are friends.'

A faint flush stained her cheeks.

'But it would be best not to speak of it again. It would distress Mr Francis to know how you felt. He might not understand – as I do.'

'I was never one to talk,' she said. 'But you were always good to me, Miss Maggie.'

And after all, I thought bitterly, it was only natural for her to confide in the one who had inspired the whole diabolical scheme. The thought of what she might have done made me urge: 'You should pray for forgiveness, Jael. God will forgive you and cleanse your heart if you ask Him.'

'I have nothing else to ask God for. He has done everything I wanted already. How could it be wrong to wish her dead when He has killed her Himself?'

Her fearful logic silenced me. There was indeed an aptness in the time of Lilian's death that seemed to support Jael's simple reasoning. I was too tired to tell her that she was wrong. It was too late to reach her, to melt her frozen heart or re-direct her mis-guided conscience.

'We must send for Dr Slater.'

'I have sent Hetty for the doctor, miss. He should be here soon. There will be a good deal to do.'

She went quietly back to the drawing room. I had no doubt that she was equal to all that was required of her. She was already familiar with death.

I did not follow. I felt a weary longing to find Miss Abbot, to bury my head in her lap and feel her kind hand on my hair and be reminded of the normal ways of thinking and feeling.

In the dim hall the flowers met me again; impassive, unjudging faces in hushed ranks and tiers and long drooping sprays. They had watched all day, not caring… It was my turn to lose touch with reality. In a sudden frenzy of passion and grief, I swept the china bowls and vases one by one to the floor and trampled furiously on the fallen blooms until the polished boards were wet with their spilt juices and oozing stems and crushed petals; until my skirt and stockings were dyed with their deadly blues and purples.

Then, appalled, as if I had shed blood, I fled to Jasmine Lodge.

21

I can look back with something like gratitude to my first outburst of grief for Lilian's death. The sense of loss was never again to spring with such loving simplicity from the heart, untainted. It was not long before I discovered that in dying, Lilian had by no means ceased to be; nor had our intricate relationship been simplified.

Until the funeral was over I devoted myself to Miss Abbot. She was deeply distressed and grateful for my company. We comforted each other and it was agreed that she should come home with me to Martlebury at the end of the week and spend some time with us. Meanwhile she understood the niceties of the situation and the demands of propriety. Consequently I hardly saw Francis and then only in company. A few relatives, all Iredales, came for the funeral, which Miss Abbot and I did not attend.

'If your mother had been here, it would have been different. As it is, it would not be quite suitable. There is no kinship; and you are very young – and so is Francis.' She sighed. 'All this has made me feel old, Maggie.'

Sitting well back from her parlour window, we saw no more than the carriages and black-plumed horses as they came down the drive of Sacristy House and past the green. I had begged Miss Abbot to let me open the blinds by the merest chink, not to look out but to let in a meagre portion of the August sunshine. It was a hot afternoon.

'We knew that this must come.' Miss Abbot's hands in their black lace mittens seemed to have taken on a life of their own. They shook and jerked and clasped each other without reference to her wishes. 'And yet one went on hoping that she would be restored to health. A quiet life was what she needed. Dear Lilian! Too much excitement has taken its toll. I can see now that the past year has been too eventful: her mother's marriage, her grandfather's death, her own marriage. She lived so intensely.' She paused, wondered whether the next remark would be suitable and decided in its favour. 'One thing I give thanks for. They had not seemed altogether happy in their marriage, Lilian and Francis, until that last day. Seeing them together, I ventured to hope, from their – behaviour towards each other, that the future would be brighter. Only of course there was to be no future.' A tear rolled unregarded down her cheek and into the ruffles of her chemisette.

My own recollection of the last day they had spent together, that long silent Sunday, were so different that after a puzzled moment I asked: 'Which day was that, Miss Abbot?'

'Let me see, it would be Monday, wouldn't it? The very day dear Lilian died.'

'I didn't think Francis and Lilian had seen much of each other that day. Francis had left some time before I went to meet Johnny and that was quite early.'

'It *was* kind of you, dear. Such a long hot walk. It was too much for you and quite unnecessary. We are all sorry for Johnny Rigg but it was a not altogether suitable thing for you to do. I didn't quite hear when you came rushing in or I would have persuaded you not to go. Francis should have gone.'

'But how could he, Miss Abbot? Francis had left for Whingate, before the post came.'

'Not for Whingate, dear. Ada tells me that he went to Groat's Gate with a hamper of food for Johnny. He insisted on going himself to make sure that the place was comfortable. But he came back.'

And meanwhile – I considered this revelation as coolly as I could – Johnny's letter had arrived, addressed to Francis.

'Lilian cannot have known that he was

coming back.' She would have told me, I assured myself, with diminishing certainty. 'I'm sure she thought he had left for Whingate and would be there until evening.'

Otherwise why should she have opened the letter instead of waiting until he came back from Groat's Gate?

'What did you say, dear?'

I said it again, more loudly and less confidently.

'Oh no. He was expected. Jael was grilling chops for his luncheon when Ada called. She's much too fond of dropping in at Sacristy House as you know, Maggie, but it's very quiet for her here and she's such a good girl. Francis didn't leave for Whingate until after luncheon.'

She brightened a little at having found the sort of topic which in other circumstances might have absorbed us peacefully for the rest of the afternoon. It neither brightened nor pacified me. The room had become stifling. I got up abruptly and went to the window. Between the slats of the blinds I saw rectangular sections of the carriages moving back to Sacristy House; black strips of panelling, half wheels and headless people. They had left Lilian behind; but I did not think of her as lying passive in the dank earth: rather as she had been when I last saw her by the boulder, trailing her claw-like fingers in the beck with a look of calculation. 'Francis will be back presently,' was all she had needed to say, leaving the letter unopened. Instead she had read it. If Francis had seen the letter, he would have driven off at once to Cantleton, not Whingate. For some reason she had preferred to let me go toiling up the hill in the noon-day heat and had not shown Francis the letter at all.

'I think perhaps,' Miss Abbot said, 'we might ask Ada to bring tea a little earlier. It has been a trying afternoon.'

I rang the bell. It dawned on me that the letter had given Lilian an unlooked-for opportunity. Confined as she was to the house and garden, she had perforce to be patient, to sit with her hands folded, and do nothing; until suddenly the chance came to see Johnny before he met Francis. What luck then that the letter had come while Francis was at Groat's Gate! Had she quickly planned to be open with Johnny, to plead, to throw herself upon his mercy? How she would hate that, knowing that nothing would shake Johnny when his mind was made up! I believe it came to me gradually that there was an alternative or at least that there were two stages to the plan. Thanks to the letter she could now see each of them separately before they met. Suppose she had seen – and seized – the opportunity, the last chance before Johnny came home and as it happened, the last chance in her life, to break down the barrier that separated her from Francis. But she could have done that before – at any time: after all she was his wife. Then I recalled that it was only on Saturday that she had heard of Johnny's return; only since then had she been desperate.

Miss Abbot had closed her eyes. I stealthily raised the blind an inch or two and saw Mrs Ogshaw's dog idly gnawing a blood-stained bone on the green. Yes, Lilian had been desperate. And on Sunday there had been no chance to speak privately to Francis because I was there, an intruder as usual. But surely after I had left them in the evening... Nevertheless I felt sure that it was only after the letter came that she had laid her plans, whatever they were.

'It's all over, ma'am.' Ada was spreading the teacloth. 'They're back at the house. The flowers are beautiful, as you would expect.'

'Perhaps you would pour out, dear. My hand has taken to shaking so stupidly and this is a fresh cloth.'

Lilian had always been quick to act in her own interest; in this case unusually quick. Just how had she used the respite that chance – and I – had contrived for her? My mind was drawn again unwillingly to the time she had spent alone with Francis when he came back from Groat's Gate.

'They had luncheon early,' Miss Abbot remarked, having taken a first refreshing sip, 'though neither of them ate much, according to Ada. The clock was striking two when they came out on to the steps. What a lovely day it was! And dry enough under foot for me to take my walk by the beck instead of on the road. It was so still and peaceful. Jael was quietly gathering flowers by that willow tree, the twisted one. This – the thought flashed through my mind – this is England at its dearest and best, land of our beloved Queen. As Mr Browning puts it, "All's right with the world."'

Miss Abbot set down her cup and recollected the tranquil scene with misty eyes.

'As I said, it did my heart good to see how lovingly they parted. I looked away, naturally, in case they saw me, but I couldn't help noticing, well, the tenderness of their embrace, Maggie. Their last embrace as it happened.'

It could also have been their first. The ice, it seemed, had mysteriously melted. Exercising all my generosity, I tried to be glad for their sakes, to rejoice in the belated tenderness and harmony, vainly resisting the temptation to dwell instead on the indifference, oh more than that, the ruthlessness with which Lilian had watched me go. Of course I had offered. She had not needed to ask.

'You're *helping* me, Maggie, and I'm *letting* you,' the cool voice assured me again.

Calculation and cunning had served her before. The suspicion that they had served her to the end has given them for me an enduring quality like that of dead, unsightly things preserved in amber.

For all that, now that I remembered her more clearly as she leaned over the beck and traced inscrutable patterns in the water, I saw her as by no means on the point of death but alert, resourceful, attentive. What was it I had said to rouse her to full attention, right at the end?

When at last I escaped from the parlour and could walk in the cool of the evening along the green path, I somehow failed to find there the quiet peace to which Miss Abbot had so poetically responded. As always in the evening the rush and swirl of the stream seemed louder than by day. Listening to its many voices united in a single mood too urgent to be soothing, I was startled to find Francis at my side without having heard him come.

'Maggie! I've been wanting very much to see you.'

His black clothes and the deep band of crêpe on his sleeve emphasised the fairness of his hair and skin; but – and this was unexpected – they did not subdue an unusual restlessness in his manner or a slight flush on his cheeks.

'Do you feel like talking?'

He put out a hand to guide me to the boulder near the willow.

'No, not there.'

He scarcely noticed as I pointed instead to one of the little paths under the trees but came with me in an absent way, oblivious of his surroundings, absorbed and oddly – the word seems as unsuitable as the mood was incongruous – uplifted. I tried, wretchedly, to express some sort of consolation. The words died away as if from a helpless sense of their own inadequacy. Was it safe – I was suddenly inspired – to speak of Johnny, of his mission at least? But no, there would be too many areas to avoid, too many possibilities of involving Lilian. And yet she was the only possible subject of conversation. What else would Francis want to talk about?

I sat down on the stone bench and looked up at him; and with a start realised how like Lilian the new spark of animation had made him: the blue eyes, the full lower lip, a touch of self-absorption, above all, the restlessness. A wild fancy darted into my mind, to lodge and cling there with surprising persistence: that if ever Francis should marry again, and if he should have a daughter, she would be like Lilian. Not like her mother, the dimly imaginable, unimpressive second wife. She, poor creature, would be the odd man out, the necessary but insignificant third. My sympathy for her was unaccountably tinged with rebellion.

'Lilian never came here on her own, did she?' Francis looked round at the trees, the barn, with an understanding smile. 'She was a creature of light, Maggie.'

The earth was so thickly strewn with dead leaves that they rose almost to the level of the seat. Idly probing their mysterious depths, I remembered the hard, sharp teeth of the comb I had unearthed and got up quickly, wiping my fingers on my handkerchief.

'How little we know of those who are closest to us!' It sounded like another of his generalisations but it rang truer than most. Indeed his next words showed that it was no theory. He had found it out from experience. 'Am I such a cold, distant sort of fellow, Maggie, that she could never confide in me? Poor girl! I thank God that at last she did.'

'Confide in you?'

Involuntarily I had come to a halt on the west side of the barn, patterned now with the shadow of branches and the golden light that stole between them. A cat was sunning itself by the great door. Either a memory or an inkling of what was to come quickened my pulse.

'Yes. On that last morning. "I want to tell you all about it myself, dearest," she said.'

How appealing the words would sound in Lilian's voice, wistful as a wind at the keyhole; but the idea had been mine. 'The best thing of all would be for you to tell him yourself,' I had said. 'No one can resist you.' And she had looked up, suddenly attentive. But the confession I had had in mind was to be made to Johnny, not Francis.

'How she had suffered! And I had no idea. "If only you had come to me before – and told me," I said to her. Believe me, Maggie' – his voice broke – 'had it not been for the anxiety and distress – and she bore it so bravely, alone – she might have been with us now. She blamed herself, you see. Imagine it. She lived under the shadow of her self reproach.'

He paused, savouring the phrase. I waited to hear for what particular thing Lilian had blamed herself. There were several possibilities.

'But of course you don't know. The most extraordinary thing! I don't suppose you remember, but when we met at Hagg Barrow, I said some harsh and cruel things about the woman – whom Daniel Hebworthy had loved.'

'I do remember.'

'It was unpardonable prejudice and ignorance on my part to condemn her out of hand. Unjust too. The fact is – this will astonish you, Maggie, as it did me – the woman he loved was none other than – Lilian. Oh, there's no need to look shocked. It was a situation in which any beautiful young girl might find herself: to be adored from a distance, indeed, worshipped, by a man of inferior station. The poor fellow couldn't help himself. He haunted her. Wherever she went, he would appear. It was a tragic passion on his side; on hers, nothing but innocent regret. She blamed herself for having inspired it – and for what he did. As if it could be her fault! She was filled with pity for Agnes and the suffering it must have caused her, to see the change in him.'

'Yes,' I said. 'Agnes died of it,' and just caught a flash of resentment in his eyes as he said quickly:

'The tragic injustice of it! That Lilian should ever be caught up with such people as the Hebworthys. He made her life a misery. In her innocence she dreaded lest anyone should find out. In fact, as she told me, Johnny Rigg once saw her with Hebworthy. She was only reminding him of his duty. But ever afterwards she feared that Johnny might have misinterpreted what he saw. You know Johnny. A good fellow but coarse-grained, naturally.'

Flabbergasted as I was, I could not speak. Was that really how it had been? It had never entered my head that she would tell. To hear the secret, kept for her sake with so much pain and anxiety, to hear it from the lips of Francis, of all people, was like a physical shock; and to hear it in such a form. She had at the last, the very last, told her story. With growing agitation. I realised that a story like a landscape changes with the point of view and Lilian's view of the events was vastly different from mine. But then – a terrible doubt seized me – I had seen nothing that could be called an event. I had supposed that certain things had happened because I had seen what seemed to be their effects. Could anything be more intangible, more misleading?

We had strolled into the wood. From time to time the path twisted so that we faced the blinding light only to turn again into the shade. The alternation of dazzling gold and dense green made my head ache; and as from moment to moment the scene changed, so did the memory of Lilian flicker and shift, lose its shape and re-form. Seen through the eyes of Francis she was pure and good, innocent of selfishness and deceit. Could it be that jealousy had warped my judgment, not once or twice, but steadily, consistently, so that I had misinterpreted her every act, seen guilt where there was none? Was it, not the telescope, but my own imperfect vision that had distorted a harmless meeting into a guilty embrace? Lost in astonishment and dismay, I tried to recall the evidence against Lilian. All those times, those scenes... The barn? I had *seen* nothing. An empty bed? She could have been anywhere and alone. For the rest there had been only her moods, her manner, or more precisely, my interpretation of them. There never had been the smallest proof that Lilian's acquaintance with Daniel Hebworthy had been other than innocent. I had wronged her deeply and could only be thankful that I had managed to keep my shameful suspicions to myself.

With relief I remembered Johnny; and was instantly ashamed. It ought not to be a source of comfort that he had thought her guilty too. Besides – the relief was shortlived – had not Francis dismissed Johnny as a coarse-grained fellow, likely to take a coarse view of any meeting he might have witnessed between a beautiful girl and an inferior who adored – indeed worshipped her – from afar? But surely the term was figurative. It had not always been from afar.

'It's fanciful, I know, but I find myself thinking of her as Diana,' Francis said whimsically. 'The moon goddess. A woodland spirit. And he was Actaeon, the hunter, who stumbled into her sacred grove.'

In my remorse I strove dutifully to remember the tale and seemed to recall that Actaeon too had come to a terrible end. The inconstant light in which I had always seen Lilian seemed to settle and burn bright upon a picture of her, goddess-like, or with the look of a bright-haired angel as she leaned her head against the white stone.

A remarkably competent angel! My mood underwent a sudden change as we came out into the orchard. She had put those last hours with Francis to very good use. Her exit had been accomplished with a brilliance that left me breathless. Having buried the unsavoury facts and lived in terror of their discovery, she had boldly unearthed them – somewhat altered – and presented them to Francis in the form of a myth whereby he saw her in a new light, more tender, more beautiful than an honest wife could kindle in a lifetime of constancy. And after that to die! – and place herself beyond all doubt, all criticism, all reproach!

Yet with all her craft and cleverness she could not have known that she would die that very day; unless from some foreboding. The half empty bottle testified to other attacks. Her manner, if not her nature, had grown softer, more penitent – *apparently*, I added with growing disillusionment. Suppose she had guessed that the end was not far off. Suppose that from the tissues and organs and nerves of her body she had received a warning. If one knew, what would one do before the clock measured the last minute?

Small things would cease to matter. Un-important people would be swept aside; or moved quickly – and pleasantly – out of the way. In extremity the mind would be wholly fixed on whatever one had cherished most jealously: the thing it would be hardest to give up. In Lilian's case, for all their recent estrangement, that would be Francis.

'The strange thing' – Francis turned his back to the sun. His shadow fell upon the seesaw, long abandoned – 'well, the wonderful thing really – was that as she faltered out her story, I saw her with Hebworthy's eyes, as he saw her. Do you know, Maggie, I had never before realised how beautiful she was, how desirable. It was quite simply miraculous the way my love for her sprang into life right at the end, with such force, as if it were meant to sustain me for a whole lifetime without her.'

One of the stones supporting the wooden plank had fallen away so that the seesaw lay tilted, one end on the ground, the other pointing skyward: Lilian's end, I noticed without surprise.

'We must never forget her, Maggie. We must cherish the memory of her as she really was.'

I ought to tell him what she was really like. It was wrong to let him stray from reality into illusion. But how could I tell him the truth when I no longer knew what the truth was? As always my confidence wavered, browbeaten by Lilian's. How was she, really?

As difficult to transfix as the moth that hovered and then settled on Francis's dark sleeve. Untouched, it lay mist-white and still. I understood that death had given to his vision of Lilian a lasting form, a final touch of perfection, unchanging, unchangeable, like a work of art. No matter what I said, he would never believe me.

'That's unjust,' he would say, 'to speak ill of her now that she cannot defend herself.'

'People tell me that the grief will pass,' he actually said, 'but I cannot bear to think that time will take her farther from me even than she is now. I want to hold fast to the memory – especially of the last morning when there was perfect confidence between us. There was something about her... Oh, it's no wonder that everyone loved her.'

We had neither of us heard the light footsteps approaching. Framed in the taut ropes of the swing, Jael was coming towards us across the grass, dressed as if for a journey. She wore her black straw bonnet and carried her reticule in her gloved hand. She walked steadily. In my uncertain mood, it was her unflinching certainty that impressed me again, more forcibly than ever. Her spirit may have strayed into forbidden realms but her conduct was founded in harsh and absolute reality. Jael would never confound fact with fantasy.

'You're going now, at this time of day?'

Francis turned to me. 'You may not have heard. Jael is leaving me.'

I met her splendid gaze, grey, luminous, fearless, and did not doubt that she would have gone to the scaffold with just such composure if a mightier hand had not intervened; mightier but not steadier than hers would have been as she mixed the fatal draught.

'Where are you going, Jael?' I asked.

'To Whingate Hall, Miss Maggie. The housekeeper told me when I left that there would be a place for me if ever I wanted it, for my mother's sake as well as my own.'

'You mustn't walk all that way,' Francis said.

'Mr Ogshaw will take me, sir, in the trap.'

I hesitated, then kissed her; not warmly, not kindly, but timidly, with reverence; and looking into her face saw her eyes swim with tears. They wrung my heart. She turned and walked away without speaking. Her anguish had always been beyond words.

'She's just a girl,' I said as she passed under the trees and out of sight.

'I didn't urge her to stay,' Francis said, 'when she told me she was going. I understood her feelings. It wouldn't be the same for her without Lilian. She didn't want to take the quarter's money. "It wasn't for money I came," she said. Of course I insisted. Nor did she even ask for a character though

I gave her one.'

It would not be easy, I thought, to express the essence of Jael's character in a few lines.

'She was an exceptional servant,' I felt it safe to say.

She had gone; and Johnny had gone. They had each accepted the necessity of breaking their ties with Asherby though both had loved it as I had loved it. I looked round, aching with regret, at the secluded acre where the most vivid moments of my childhood had been spent; and knew that like the innocent years themselves, their haunts must be left behind. Times can be outgrown, and places, and – even more painfully – people.

'...That is what I fear most,' Francis had returned to the only theme that interested him, 'that I should ever forget her. All my life she has been here – we've been here together...'

My purpose in coming again to Asherby had been fulfilled. I had seen for myself, more clearly than ever, beyond any shadow of doubt, that Francis belonged with all his heart and soul to Lilian. All the physical bonds, all the years they had shared, had united them more closely than cousins, than brother and sister, than husband and wife, in an intimacy so mysterious that they could never be parted. And yet, seeing him caught up in an unearthly loyalty, his cheeks flushed with an unnatural elation, I knew with the bitter sweetness never absent from my love for him that he needed me now as he had never done before. What would become of him, alone?

'You must help me, Maggie. We must talk of her often, you and I. We knew her best. Whenever we are together, she will be with us.'

Between the orchard trees the shining rifts of sky had lost their gold. Close at hand an apple dropped, too soon, and lay buried in the long grass. The moth clinging to Francis' sleeve was scarcely more substantial than the gathering twilight. Trembling with nervousness, I grasped the rope of the swing for support, gathered all my courage and faced him.

'Dear Francis, we've always been – friends. You've scolded me sometimes for keeping things from you.' He smiled with the gentle understanding which had first made me love him. My heart smote me at what I must say.

'There is something I ought to tell you. I haven't told it to anyone else.'

'What is it, Maggie?'

Still I hesitated. I had half known it for some time but only as I found the words did it become true: and miraculously, though it was evening, the truth brought a sudden bright glimpse of morning, a distant, unbelievable flash of relief and joy.

'I'm going to be married, to James Barnard.'

I looked up quickly and caught in the blue depths of his eyes, fleeting but unmistakable, a flicker of disappointment; and I was glad to know that he needed me, sad that I no longer needed him.

'That's wonderful news,' he said at once. 'He's a lucky fellow. I wish you all the happiness you deserve, Maggie dear.' He took my hand and kissed it and I felt again, more than the joy of escaping, the anguish of leaving him behind; and told myself that he was not desolate even when he spoke of grief. The elation was still there, the secret confidence in Lilian's continuing presence; and almost at once he said: 'Lilian told me, you know, that it would happen. She was sensitive about such things.'

So that it was of Lilian we talked as I swung gently in the twilight until the bats came out and the birds went to roost; until it was time for me to go. I left him there. From the yew hedge I looked back and saw him absently push the swing. It went on moving with surprising force. It was not just in fancy that I saw her floating there with no touch of earth – ethereal, golden, triumphant. It was more than fancy. There was no doubt as to who was having the last – and longest – turn.

We were almost at the top of Asherby Bank when I remembered the tapestry.

'Is there time to turn back, do you think?' Miss Abbot undid her cape and peered at her watch.

'We can't go back now,' I said.

Behind us the white road wound bracken-fringed down to the deep valley. Beyond, rising from fold to fold of purple and blue, Groat Moor soared to the sky. Here on the brow, moss-grown garden walls enclosed a sanctuary of flowers and bees. The horses breasted the hill and there was the Toll House, dreaming in the green shade of its great chestnut.

All this I knew though I neither listened nor looked but gazed steadily at the level road ahead without a backward glance.

'I don't ever want to go back,' I said.

22

But now that I can look back more calmly on the events of that last year of my girlhood at Asherby Cross, I have been trying to recapture the mournful mood in which I left; trying without much success. It must have been shortlived. There was grief, naturally, for the death of my closest friend;

and surely I must have felt the passing of a whole epoch of my existence. It must be assured that I suffered a suitable regret. The fact is, I have forgotten it.

Instead I remember an entirely new pleasure in being at home again. There was Miss Abbot to be settled in her new quarters – permanently, as it proved, for she stayed with my parents for the rest of her life. There were subscriptions to be collected for the Relief of Merchant Seamen's Dependants Fund. Above all, as the empty horizon was immediately filled by James, there came the thrill and fuss and bustle of being engaged and – in no time at all, it seemed – married.

Was this the lightness of a shallow nature, this hasty turnabout from melancholy to joy? I put the question to James, confident that his reply would be, as usual, all that I could wish.

'Shallow? You, my dearest Maggie? Never. It wasn't a sudden change of attitude, remember. You had been growing away from Asherby and the Iredales, for some time, hadn't you?'

The greatest of our blessings was – and has always been – the openness between us. I told him everything: how I had bungled and blundered and misunderstood – and cared. He was an interested listener but not, I am happy to say, an impartial one. He saw everything from my point of view. It was James who summed up the whole painful subject and helped me to put it from my mind.

'So far as I can make out, it doesn't matter now what happened or didn't happen – except to Iredale. He's the only one concerned and for him there's only one version: Lilian's. You did right, Maggie, to let her have the last word.'

The episode was closed. Its scenes gradually took on a distant quality, fading slowly like the pictures in Mrs Hart's tapestry.

When we were first married, James's mother stayed on at Stone Barnard and we lived in the little dower house across the park; until our third child – James Edward – was born, when we exchanged houses; and we were still at the dower house when my attention was drawn to Asherby again and in rather an arresting manner.

One morning in the summer of 1884 James opened his newspaper and gave a startled exclamation.

'Good heavens! Look at this, Maggie.'

I leaned over his shoulder and together we read the black headline: SUSPECTED MURDER IN MOORLAND VILLAGE.

In the smaller print, I caught sight of a familiar name.

'Police are investigating the discovery of human remains at a remote moorland spot north of the village of Asherby Cross, by Mr Arthur Tunbridge, the distinguished historian and archaeologist, author of *Bronze Age Relics* and other works.

'Mr Tunbridge, a guest at Asherby Hall, took the opportunity while in the neighbourhood to visit some of the ancient barrows or howes which are so noteworthy a feature of the area. At the tumulus known locally as Hagg Barrow, Mr Tunbridge noticed an abnormality in the vegetation, suggesting that the barrow had been disturbed more recently than the year 1805, when the last known excavations were made. His suspicions were confirmed when bones were unearthed forming the complete skeleton of a man judged to have been in the prime of life...'

'Daniel,' I breathed. 'Oh James, what will they do?'

'...At an inquest held in the Fleece Inn, Asherby Cross, a verdict was returned of 'Murder by person or persons unknown' and Coroner Pearce directed that the remains should be given decent and proper burial in Asherby churchyard. Exhaustive questioning by the Whingate police has produced no information as to the possible identity of the murdered man. According to Mr Francis Iredale, a lawyer and landed proprietor resident in Asherby Cross, no living soul has disappeared under suspicious circumstances in recent years. The last known murder in Asherby was in 1792 when Amos Atkins of Comfrey Farm was cudgelled to death by a highwayman near the hamlet of Groat's Gate...'

'How extraordinarily interesting!' James observed. 'Two inquests on the same man.'

'It was rather clever of Francis to put it like that, when he said that no *living* soul had disappeared.'

'Surely someone would remember that a dead one had, and then put two and two together.'

'Of course they would. But no matter what they suspected no one in Asherby would tell. It says here that the funeral of the unknown man was well attended. I'm perfectly sure that some of the people there, besides Francis, would have a good idea who was being buried.'

And they would be glad that Daniel had at last been given Christian burial, I thought, especially the women.

We talked of the strange affair, so typical of Asherby, until other interests took its place. It would have remained as no more than a topic of conversation if one of the ripples it set in motion had not touched on our own concerns.

The mystery caused a flutter of public interest and Asherby enjoyed a brief notoriety. Until its steep hills and inhospitable residents discouraged them, visitors drove there to look at the church and Hagg Barrow and exclaim over the rural charm of the district. The upshot was that father's solicitor received an attractive offer from a would-be purchaser of Jasmine Lodge.

It had become a problem. We discussed it at every family gathering. Since Miss Abbot left, it had been let several times but had now stood empty for two years. Father had always been in favour of selling. But Mrs Hart had begged Mother not to break her ties with Asherby. The Harts would soon be coming home for good and half thought of settling in the neighbourhood.

'You and James must decide,' mother now wrote. 'Your father thinks we should sell. As you know he has no sentimental attachment to it. If we keep it, it will be yours some day. It would make a nice little nest egg for one of the girls. Meanwhile it would have to be let again...'

'It would be a shame to let it go,' I said, feeling all at once overcome with affection for the house I had forgotten for ten years. 'Mother obviously wants to keep it in the family. It's a dear little house. You haven't seen it.'

'That could easily be remedied, my love. Would it upset you at all to go and have a look? I should be interested to see your old haunts – and to meet Iredale again, I must confess. He strikes me as an odd fellow.'

I wrote to Francis and to Ada. We made a little holiday of it and took the girls. Nell was then eight and Cynthia a year younger. We put up at an hotel in Cantleton and drove over to Asherby from the north, so that it didn't feel the same, though the passing of a decade had left the landmarks unchanged; if not the people.

Heads appeared at cottage windows and doors opened surreptitiously as the carriage drew up by the green, where an immensely plump old woman was drawing water at the pump. Beside her, lying as heavily as a stone, crouched an ancient, overfed dog.

'If it isn't Miss Ossian.' She dourly observed the carriage and its three other occupants and grudgingly made the necessary amendment. 'Miss Ossian that was.'

At the sound of her voice Cynthia, who was passing through a nervous phase, jumped visibly. It had lost little of its raucous volume; but like the dog, which rolled a still vicious eye and looked at us obliquely, it's owner had lost some of her teeth and most of her power to alarm me.

'...only a short visit, Mrs Ogshaw...'

We were rescued by Ada who was waiting at the Lodge gate to welcome us. We were to have luncheon there and spend the afternoon at Sacristy House. Scarcely were we settled in the parlour when Francis arrived.

323

It ought to have been a poignant moment. Indeed I had dreaded it. But it so happened that it was Cynthia who stood directly in his way as he came in. His face lit up.

'Why, it's little Maggie all over again.' He swept her up in his arms and kissed her. To our delight she forgot her shyness and smiled and blushed with pleasure. 'You know, it was always the same. First the swallows came, and the cuckoo. Then Maggie came and we knew it really was summer.'

'How do you do?' Nell held out her hand formally. 'My sister's name is Cynthia. Not Maggie.'

Only then did he turn to me.

'I wonder you didn't name one of them after Lilian.'

'There could only be one Lilian,' I said quickly.

He nodded and his smile was tender. He put Cynthia down and took my hand.

'You haven't changed, dear, except for your hair…'

He looked vaguely at my upswept curls. There had been ample time since we last met for me to dispense with my old-fashioned chignon, once my pride, and to blossom into puffed-out sleeves and the new style of bustle under my green watered silk (for I had not been able to resist the impulse to wear my best); but he seemed to me to be wearing the same black coat as when I saw

324

him last and he was still clean shaven. His brows had grown a little spikier; and he had developed a habit of looking away while he talked as if he had grown unused to company; or, perhaps – it was no more than a fleeting thought – he had grown used to other, more absorbing company. Still, he seemed to enjoy ours. James and he were on easy terms at once (no one can resist James); and we were only halfway through luncheon when Nell wondered if she and Cynthia might call him Uncle Francis.

We talked of Johnny. He had settled in Norwich in partnership with the cabinet-maker who had helped him when he came out of prison, and was prospering. It didn't surprise me to hear that he had developed a talent for public speaking and was generally in the thick of one Radical movement or another.

When we went by way of the green path to Sacristy House we were greeted – and this did surprise me – by Bella. She had evidently returned from her self-imposed exile soon after Mrs Iredale passed away; and had been elevated to the position of housekeeper. It appeared to suit her well and I must say the house was clean and comfortable.

'He's no trouble,' she confided. 'So considerate. Always was. It was never him… No, it's the parlour today, ma'am,' as I turned towards the narrow passage from the hall.

'The drawing room is rather large for a gentleman living on his own. He doesn't have many visitors. Today is quite an exception.' Her tone conveyed a faint tolerance. 'Yes, he still reads a lot. He was always a thoughtful gentleman.'

She ushered us into the old room with its horsehair and red serge; still the murmur of the beck through the open window and the moist smell of leaves; still the pipe racks and overflowing bookcases. A precarious pile of law books and *Field and Furrow,* long on the point of falling, came tumbling down in response to one of James's sudden movements (for he had not improved in this respect and never has done).

He picked up a calf-bound volume, well worn, but I will say for Bella, free of dust. (I never liked her).

'Just how would you define an oddity of the law?' he asked with a glance at the title.

I had often wondered and listened with some mystification as Francis enlarged upon the subject.

'I take it,' James said innocently, 'that it would be a legal oddity to disinter a man who had died by his own hand and give him Christian burial on the grounds that he had been murdered.'

Francis smiled.

'And so grant him the justice he was denied,' he said.

His sympathy for Daniel may well have deepened. They had worshipped at the same shrine.

James and I left the girls with him while we strolled about the village, then climbed the path to the lych-gate and passed between the dark yews into the churchyard. Agnes Hebworthy's grave was bright with flowers: lupins and marguerites, sweet William and snapdragons, Canterbury bells... A similar burst of colour drew our attention to another newer grave where we found an identical spray under the inscription:

Here lie the mortal remains of a man
   unknown.
God grant him Everlasting Rest.

The flowers were freshly cut. I felt sure that the two graves were seldom bare despite the seven long miles from Whingate Hall. She would never forget. A spray of columbine fallen from the stone vase and not yet withered, showed that she had recently been here – and gone. There was no one in that quiet place of birds and trees but ourselves and a moorland sheep or two nibbling the rich turf.

The stone had weathered above a third grave where one white lily marked the resting place of Lilian, beloved wife of Francis Iredale, who died in her twentieth year: a single perfect bloom of matchless purity. How long ago it all seemed, how distant, seen down the vista of mellowing years!

A breeze tugged at my gauze scarf like a playful hand and pulled at my skirt – light but insistent and cool enough to set me shivering. The weather was changing. The sky had clouded; the trees crowded in; a few drops of rain, the first of a heavy shower, sent us hurrying across the beck to take refuge in the house.

It was too wet for the children to play out of doors. At Francis' suggestion I took them up to the attic and left them to spend an absorbed hour or two amid its lumber. I contrived too as I came down to take a quick peep into the drawing room where the furniture and fire-irons were shrouded in dust sheets. The musty smell of a room un-used for years, a slight, stealthy movement of leaves in the mirror above the secretaire, were enough to make me close the door quietly and go back to the comfortable parlour. I sat by the window in Mrs Bel-fleur's chair.

'I have told Francis that we intend to keep on the Lodge,' James said. Indeed he had taken a liking to it and resolved to take over the expense of maintaining it until the girls grew up.

'Then you'll come again every summer, Maggie. It will be like old times.'

'Not so often. We're so very busy, Francis. But sometimes...'

'Of course I must not urge you,' he said quickly and looked downcast.

I was regretting my lukewarm reply when James with his usual tact broke in heartily.

'You have an advantage over us, Iredale. We have no trout stream at Stone Barnard. Maggie tells me you rent a stretch of the Cantle. If you were to invite me for a fort-night's fishing now and again...'

'The water is yours, my dear Barnard, whenever you care to come.'

'It's a very interesting attic, Uncle Fran-cis,' Nell told him politely when the bright-ening sky brought the girls downstairs. 'Cynthia has found such a funny thing among some old clothes.'

'Let me see.'

Overwhelmed at being the centre of atten-tion, Cynthia held it up rather doubtfully: a shabby, uncouth object terminating incon-gruously in a handsome silver handle.

'The hare's foot!' I exclaimed.

'So that's where it was. It was clever of you to find it, my dear.' He took it reverently and turned it over with a sigh. 'She believed in it implicitly, poor darling.'

'And wasn't it strange, Francis, that she should lose it only the day before...?'

For an instant the shared memory united us. Then my attention wandered – far away

329

down that long vista of years where I caught again a glimpse of a silent listener and heard a door quietly closed. And I guessed that Jael had not relied only on prayer. She had left no stone unturned. She had always been thorough in everything she did. And who knows what power the grisly talisman possessed...?

Francis seemed to ponder over it with something of his lawyer's expression as though considering all sides of the question before making a decision.

'Finders are supposed to be keepers,' he said at last. 'Would you like to have it, my dear?' His tone bestowed upon it the priceless worth of a sacred relic.

To my dismay the child shrank back and turned to me.

'I don't really want it, mother.' Her whisper was dreadfully audible.

'Come, Cynthia. That is ungracious,' James said.

'It was Lilian's,' Francis said gravely.

'I think that's why Cynthia doesn't want it,' Nell said candidly and clearly.

The extreme inappropriateness of this remark together with Francis's look of wounded reproach robbed me of all presence of mind. James took pity on me.

'But that is the very reason for accepting so kind a gift,' he said. 'Lilian was Uncle Francis's wife.'

'Oh, I know that.' Nell glanced at her host anxiously. 'And so does Cynthia.'

'She was also your mother's dear friend.'

'But she wasn't–' Nell paused in conflict, conscious of giving offence but aware of the need to rescue her sister, and consequently pitched her voice low, to such confidential depths as to sound almost sepulchral – 'she wasn't a good girl. She did wicked things.'

I held my breath as if walking again on the edge of a familiar precipice. One can over-estimate the calming effect of time. The room grew still, the air heavy again with the burden of old secrets.

'Whatever makes you think that?' Francis pretended, rather weightily, to take this piece of childish nonsense seriously. I waited for him to put the question I would not have dared to ask. 'What did she do?'

The answer came with a rush.

'She threw your dictionary in the kitchen fire. She said so herself. Well, she wrote it down in a book. We found it in the attic.'

I breathed again.

'So that was what became of the diction-ary.' There was a wealth of indulgent love in his voice. 'And I never knew.'

'That was because mother never told. You were a true friend, weren't you, mother? It says so in the book.'

'Then it must be true.'

Francis laughed and slipped the hare's

foot into his pocket. James caught my eye and smiled. A rush of happiness brought tears to my eyes. She had always known, then, that I loved her.

Into the leaf-shaded room came the murmur of the stream, the sweetness of the air after rain. I listened dreamily to the quiet voices of those I loved as the minutes slipped gently by to measure the happiest hour I had ever spent there; and the promise of other hours, other summers still to come, refreshed my soul like the fragrance of milk-white may blossom, and the haunting notes of cuckoos calling.

'I'll finish the tapestry,' I thought, 'before the Harts come home.'

Bella brought cakes and wine. It would soon be time to go. The girls put on their hats and jackets. As sisters they always dressed alike. Francis set chairs for them at the green-baized table. There would just be time for a game of snap before the carriage came.

The publishers hope that this book has given you enjoyable reading. Large Print Books are especially designed to be as easy to see and hold as possible. If you wish a complete list of our books please ask at your local library or write directly to:

Dales Large Print Books
Magna House, Long Preston,
Skipton, North Yorkshire.
BD23 4ND